File Zero

Jack Mars

Jack Mars is the USA Today bestselling author of the LUKE STONE thriller series, which includes seven books. He is also the author of the new FORGING OF LUKE STONE prequel series, comprising three books (and counting); and of the AGENT ZERO spy thriller series, comprising six books (and counting).

ANY MEANS NECESSARY (book #1), which has over 800 five star reviews, is available as a free download on Amazon!

Jack loves to hear from you, so please feel free to visit www.Jackmarsauthor.com to join the email list, receive a free book, receive free giveaways, connect on Facebook and Twitter, and stay in touch!

Books by Jack Mars

LUKE STONE THRILLER SERIES

ANY MEANS NECESSARY (Book #1)

OATH OF OFFICE (Book #2)

SITUATION ROOM (Book #3)

OPPOSE ANY FOE (Book #4)

PRESIDENT ELECT (Book #5)

OUR SACRED HONOR (Book #6)

HOUSE DIVIDED (Book #7)

FORGING OF LUKE STONE PREQUEL SERIES

PRIMARY TARGET (Book #1)

PRIMARY COMMAND (Book #2)

PRIMARY THREAT (Book #3)

AN AGENT ZERO SPY THRILLER SERIES

AGENT ZERO (Book #1)

TARGET ZERO (Book #2)

HUNTING ZERO (Book #3)

TRAPPING ZERO (Book #4)

FILE ZERO (Book #5)

RECALL ZERO (Book #6)

File Zero

(An Agent Zero Spy Thriller—Book #5)

Jack Mars

Trapping Zero (Book #4) – Summary

A new threat rises to power that threatens to shake the foundation of America to its core. It's up to CIA Agent Kent Steele to pull at the threads and unravel the brilliant but deadly master plan before it is executed—all while staying out of the line of fire of those who want him dead.

Agent Zero: Though he was unable to stop the Brotherhood from destroying the Midtown Tunnel in New York, Agent Zero successfully ended the terrorist organization and helped save thousands of lives. During a clandestine award ceremony at the White House, his lost memories suddenly returned to him all at once—including his knowledge about the war conspiracy.

Maya and Sara Lawson: Now that they know what their father is and does, Zero's daughters understand that they are viable targets for those trying to get to him. However, they refuse to become victims again, displaying intelligence and tenacity far beyond their age.

Agent Maria Johansson: Maria continues to work with the Ukrainians despite Zero's insistence that she break ties. Though stopping the war is crucial to her, she is equally determined to find out if her father, a high-ranking member of the National Security Council, is involved in the government conspiracy—and if not, what might become of him if he doesn't relent.

Agent Todd Strickland: The young CIA agent and former Army Ranger was stunned to learn of the government plot from his friend Agent Zero, but now that he knows, he is as resolute as anyone to help put an end to it and keep innocent people from needlessly dying.

Dr. Guyer: The brilliant Swiss neurologist that initially installed the memory suppressor in Agent Zero's head attempted to bring the memories back with a machine of his own invention. He believed the process had failed, and is unaware that Zero's memories have belatedly returned.

Agent Talia Men-del: The Israeli Mossad agent helped put a stop to the Brotherhood's plot in both Haifa and New York. Though unaware of the conspiracy, Mendel makes no attempt to hide her appreciation for, and attraction to, Agent Zero, willing to help in any capacity she's able.

Fitzpatrick: The leader of the "private security force" known as the Division, Fitzpatrick was sent after Agent Zero by Deputy Director Ashleigh Riker in an effort to stall him in New York. Fitzpatrick was struck by a car driven by Talia Mendel, his fate largely unknown.

Table of Contents

Chapter One

I am *Agent Zero.*

He had already known it, at least for the past few months, ever since the memory suppressor had been violently ripped from his skull by the trio of Iranian terrorists working for Amun. But this... this was different from just knowing. It was an awareness, a sense of being and belonging that had come on as swiftly as a heart attack, and equally pernicious.

"Agent Zero?" said President Eli Pierson. "Do you need to sit?"

Reid Lawson stood in the Oval Office, the President of the United States standing before him with a smile on his lips but puzzlement in his eyes. In his hands, the president held a polished wooden box of dark cherry. The lid was open; nestled in a small pillow of velvet was the Distinguished Intelligence Cross, the highest award the CIA could give.

Only a minute earlier, Reid could not recall ever having visited the White House before. But now he recalled it all. He had been here several times, clandestine meetings just like this one, so the president could commend him on a job well done.

Less than a minute earlier, the president had said, "I'm so sorry. Director Mullen, is this the Intelligence Cross, or the Star? I can't seem to keep them straight."

And that was when it happened. That single word had triggered it all:

Straight.

That word stuck in Reid's mind and lodged there, sending an electric tingle up his spine.

Strait.

And then the floodgates opened suddenly and without warning. It felt as if an intruder had shouldered open the door to his brain, forced his way in, and made it his new home. Quick as a bolt of lightning, he remembered.

He remembered *everything.*

Hunting terrorists in the Gaza Strip. Apprehending bomb makers in Kandahar. Midnight raids on compounds. Briefings, debriefings, weapons training, combat training, flight lessons, languages, interrogation tactics, rapid intervention… In half a second, the dam in Reid Lawson's limbic system broke and Agent Zero surged through. It was too much, far too much to process that quickly. His knees threatened to buckle and his hands trembled. He slumped; Maria's arms caught him before he hit the carpet.

"Kent," she said quietly but urgently. "Are you all right?"

"Yeah," he murmured.

I need to get out of here.

"I'm okay."

I'm not okay.

"It's, uh…" He cleared his throat and forced himself to stand again, albeit shakily. "It's just the pain medication, for my hand. Made me a bit woozy. I'm okay." His right hand was wrapped in layers of metal braces, gauze, and tape, after the terrorist Awad bin Saddam had crushed it with the anchor of a motorboat. Nine of the twenty-seven bones in his hand were broken.

And even though there had been a throbbing pain only a minute ago, he now felt nothing.

President Pierson smiled. "I understand. No one here will be offended if you sit." The president was a charismatic man, young for the office at only forty-six and nearing the end of his first term. He was an excellent orator, praised by the middle class, and he had been a friend to Zero. Now he knew it to be true: his memories told him.

"Really. I'm okay."

"Good." The president nodded and lifted the dark cherry box in his hands. "Agent Zero, it is my great honor and genuine pleasure to give you this Distinguished Intelligence Cross."

Reid nodded, forcing himself to stand straight, to keep himself steady as Pierson presented the gold, three-inch-round medal nestled inside the box. He handed it to Reid gently and Reid took it.

"Thank you. Um, Mr. President."

"No," said Pierson. "Thank *you*, Agent Zero."

Agent Zero.

The room broke out into light applause and Zero looked up quickly, bewildered; he had nearly forgotten there were other people in the Oval Office. Standing to the left of Pierson's desk was Vice President Cole, and beside him were the Secretaries of Defense, Homeland Security, and State. Opposite them were Christopher Poe, head of the FBI, Governor Thompson of New York, and Director of National Intelligence John Hillis.

Beside the DNI was Zero's own boss, CIA Director Mullen, his hands making a show of clapping but hardly emitting any noise. His bald head, ringed with gray hair, gleamed under the lights. Deputy Director Ashleigh Riker was beside him in her usual uniform of a charcoal gray pencil skirt and matching blazer.

He knew about them. These people who were applauding him, he had gathered intelligence on nearly every single one of them that suggested they were involved in the plot. The knowledge came to him as if it had always been there. The Secretary of Defense, retired general Quentin Rigby; Vice President Cole; even DNI Hillis, the only man other than President Pierson that Mullen answered to. Not one among them was innocent. They were not to be trusted. They were all involved.

Two years ago, Zero had discovered the plot, or at least part of it, and he had been building a case. While interrogating a terrorist at the black site H-6 in Morocco, Zero had stumbled upon a conspiracy for the United States to manufacture a war in the Middle East.

The strait—that was the trigger. The intention was for the US to gain control of the Strait of Hormuz, a narrow waterway between the Gulf of Oman and Iran, a global thoroughfare for oil shipping and one of the most strategic maritime chokepoints the world over. It was no secret that the United States had a substantial presence in the Persian Gulf, an entire fleet, and it was all for one reason: to protect their interests. And their interests boiled down to a single resource.

Oil.

That's what this was about. That's what it had always been about. Oil meant money, and money meant that the people in power got to stay in power.

The Brotherhood's attack on New York City was the catalyst. A large-scale terrorist attack was just the provocation the government needed not only to justify a war, but to rally the American people to the side of abject patriotism. They had seen it work before with the attack on September 11, and had been keeping the notion in their back pocket until they needed it again.

Awad bin Saddam, the young leader of the Brotherhood who believed he had orchestrated the attack, had been a pawn. He had unwittingly been led to the conclusions he thought he had drawn himself. The Libyan arms dealer that had supplied the terrorists with submersible drones was undoubtedly a liaison between the US and the Brotherhood. But there was no way to prove that now; the Libyan was dead. Bin Saddam was dead. Anyone who might be able to substantiate Zero's belief was dead.

Now the catalyst had happened. Even though Zero and his small team had thwarted the large-scale loss of life that bin Saddam had hoped for, hundreds had been killed and the Midtown Tunnel was lost. The American people were outraged. Xenophobia and hostility toward Middle Easterners was already running rampant.

Two years ago, he thought he had time to build a case, to gather evidence—but then came Amun, Rais, and the memory suppressor. Now, he was out of time. The men surrounding him, applauding him, these heads of state and government captains, were about to start a war.

But this time around, Zero wasn't alone.

To his left, standing in a line beside him in front of the president's desk, were the people that he counted among friends. Those he could trust; or rather, those he believed he could trust.

John Watson. Todd Strickland. Maria Johansson.

Watson's real name is Oliver Brown. Born and raised in Detroit. Lost his six-year-old son to leukemia three years ago.

Maria's real name is Clara. She told you that after your first night together, during your tryst. After Kate died.

No. After Kate was murdered.

My god. Kate. The memory struck him like a hammer to the head. She had been poisoned with a powerful toxin that caused respiratory and cardiac failure as she walked to her car after work one day. Zero had always believed it was the work of Amun and their top assassin, but Rais's dying words had been but three letters.

C-I-A.

I need to get out of here.

"Agents," said President Pierson, "I thank you once again on behalf of the American people for your service." He flashed a winning smile at the four of them before addressing the entire room. "Now, we have an excellent luncheon prepared in the State Dining Room, if you'll all indulge me. Right this way—"

"Sir," Zero spoke up. Pierson turned to him, the smile still on his lips. "I appreciate the offer, but if it's all the same to you, I, uh, really think I should get some rest." He held up his right hand, wrapped thick as a catcher's mitt. "My head is swimming from the medication."

Pierson nodded deeply. "Of course, Zero. You deserve some rest, some time with your family. Although it feels a bit odd to hold a reception without a guest of honor, I doubt this will be the last time we see each other." The president grinned. "This must be, what, the fourth time we've met like this?"

Zero forced a smile of his own. "Fifth, if I'm not mistaken." He shook the president's hand once more, awkwardly, with his uninjured left. As he left the Oval Office, escorted by two Secret Service agents, he couldn't help but notice in his periphery the expressions on Rigby's and Mullen's faces.

They're suspicious. Do they know I know?

You're being paranoid. You need to get out of here and focus.

It wasn't paranoia. As he followed the two black-suited agents down the corridor, an alarm rang out in his head. He realized what he had just done. *How could you be so careless!* he scolded himself.

He had just admitted, in front of the entire Oval Office of conspirators, that he remembered precisely how many times he'd been commended personally by Pierson.

Maybe they didn't notice. But of course they did. By stopping the Brotherhood, Zero had made it clear that he was the top obstacle that stood in their way. They were aware that Zero knew things, at least partially. And if they suspected even for a moment that his memory had returned, he would be watched even more carefully than he'd been before.

All that meant to him was that he had to move faster than they did. The men he left behind in the Oval Office were already enacting their plan, and Zero was the only person who knew enough to stop them.

Outside it was a beautiful spring day. The weather was finally turning; the sun felt warm on his skin and the dogwood trees on the White House lawn had just begun to sprout small white flowers. But Zero hardly noticed. His head was spinning. He needed to get away from the influx of stimuli so he could process all this sudden information.

"Kent, wait up," Maria called out. She and Strickland hurried after him as he strode toward the gates. He wasn't heading to the parking lot, or back to the car. He wasn't sure where he was going at the moment. He wasn't sure of anything. "You sure you're okay?"

"Yeah," he muttered, not slowing. "Just need some air."

Guyer. I have to contact Dr. Guyer and tell him that the procedure worked belatedly.

No. Can't do that. They might have your phones tapped. Your email too.

Have I always been this paranoid?

"Hey." Maria grabbed him by the shoulder and he spun to face her. "Talk to me. Tell me what's going on."

Zero stared into her gray eyes, noted the way her blonde hair fell around her shoulders in waves, and the memory of them together whirled through his head again. The feel of her skin. The shape of her hips. The taste of her mouth on his.

But there was something else there too. He recognized it as a stabbing pang of guilt. *Kate hadn't been killed yet. Did we… did I…?*

He shook the thought from his head. "Like I said. It's the meds. They're just really messing with my head. I can't think straight."

"Let me drive you home," Strickland offered. Agent Todd Strickland was only twenty-seven, but had an impeccable track record as an Army Ranger and had quickly made the transition to the CIA. He still wore a military-style fade cut over a stocky neck and muscled torso, though he was simultaneously gentle and approachable when the situation called for it. Most importantly, he had been a friend in more than one time of need.

And while Zero recognized that, at the moment he needed to be alone. It felt impossible to think straight with anyone talking to him. "No. I'll be fine. Thanks."

He tried to turn again, but Maria reached for his shoulder once more. "Kent—"

"I said I'm fine!" he snapped.

Maria did not recoil at his outburst, but narrowed her eyes slightly as her gaze bored into his, searching for some understanding.

The memory of their tryst came again, involuntarily, and he felt heat rise in his face. *We were on an op. Holed up in some Greek hotel. Waiting for instructions. She seduced me. I was weak. Kate was still alive. She never knew…*

"I have to go." He took a few steps backward to make sure that neither of his fellow agents would attempt to pursue him again.

"Don't follow me." Then he turned and strode away, leaving them standing there on the White House lawn.

He had very nearly reached the gates before he felt the presence behind him, heard the shifting of footsteps. He spun quickly. "I told you not to—"

A short woman with shoulder-length brunette hair stopped in her tracks. She wore a navy blue blazer and matching slacks with heels, and she raised an eyebrow as she regarded Zero curiously. "Agent Zero? My name is Emilia Sanders," she told him. "Aide to President Pierson." She held out a white business card with her name and number on it. "He wants to know if you've reconsidered his offer."

Zero hesitated. Pierson had previously offered him a spot on the National Security Council, which had made him suspicious of the president's involvement, but it seemed as if the offer was genuine.

Not that he wanted it. But still he took her card.

"If you find you need anything at all, Agent Zero, please don't hesitate to give a call," Sanders told him. "I'm quite resourceful."

"I could use a ride home," he admitted.

"Certainly. I'll get someone for you immediately." She pulled out a cell phone and made a call while Zero stuffed the business card in his pocket. Pierson's offer was the furthest thing from his mind. He had no idea how much time, if any, he had in which to act.

What do I do? He squeezed his eyes shut and shook his head, as if trying to dislodge an answer.

726. The number spun quickly through his mind. It was a safe deposit box at a bank in downtown Arlington where he had been keeping records of his investigations—photos, documents, and transcriptions of phone calls from those leading this secret cabal. He had paid for five years upfront on the deposit box so that it wouldn't go dormant.

"Right this way, Agent." The presidential aide, Emilia Sanders, gestured for him to follow as she led him briskly toward a garage and a waiting car. As they walked, Zero thought again of the suspicious looks from General Rigby, from Director Mullen. It was paranoia, nothing more—at least he tried to tell himself that. But if there was even a chance that they knew he was on to them, they would come after him with everything they had. And not just him.

Zero made himself a mental checklist:

Get girls safe.

Retrieve contents of safe deposit box.

Stop war before it starts.

All Zero had to do was figure out how to stop a group of the most powerful men in the world, with some of the deepest pockets, who had been planning this event for more than two years, had the backing of almost every government agency the United States had to offer, and had everything to lose.

Just another day in the life of Agent Zero, he thought sourly.

Chapter Two

Aboard the USS *Constitution*, Persian Gulf
April 16, 1830 hours

The furthest thing from Lieutenant Thomas Cohen's mind was war.

As he sat at a radar array aboard the USS *Constitution*, watching the small blips as they meandered lazily across the screen, he was thinking about Melanie, his girlfriend back home in Pensacola. It was just under three weeks to go before he would rotate home. He already had the ring; he'd purchased it a week earlier on a day pass to Qatar. Thomas doubted there was anyone on the ship he hadn't proudly shown it to yet.

The sky over the Persian Gulf was clear and sunny, not a single cloud, but Thomas wouldn't get to enjoy it, tucked away in a corner of the bridge as he was, the thick armored port windows obscured by the radar console. He couldn't help but feel mildly jealous of the ensign out on the deck that he communicated with by radio, the younger man holding a line-of-sight visual on the ships that, to Thomas, were just blips on the screen.

Sixty billion dollars, he thought with grim amusement. That's how much the United States spent annually to keep a presence in the Persian Gulf, the Arabian Sea, and the Gulf of Oman. The US Navy's Fifth Fleet called Bahrain its headquarters, and was comprised of several task forces with specific patrol routes along the coasts of North Africa and the Middle East. The *Constitution*, a destroyer-class ship, was part of Combined Task Force 152, which patrolled the Persian Gulf from the northern end all the way to the Strait of Hormuz, between Oman and Iran.

Thomas's friends back home thought it was so cool that he worked on a US Navy destroyer. He let them believe that. But the reality was simply a strange, if not somewhat boring and repetitive, existence. He sat upon a modern marvel of engineering, outfitted with the highest of tech and armed with enough weaponry to devastate half a city, yet their entire purpose basically boiled down to what Thomas was doing at the very moment—watching blips on a radar screen. All that firepower and money and men amounted to a glorified what-if situation.

That wasn't to say there was never any excitement. Thomas and the other guys who had been around for a year or longer got their kicks from watching how nervous the FNGs would get, the newcomers, the first time they heard that the Iranians were going to fire on them. It didn't happen every day, but it was frequent enough. Iran and Iraq were dangerous territories, and they had to at least keep up appearances, Thomas supposed. Every now and then the *Constitution* would get a threat from the Navy of the Islamic Revolutionary Guard Corps, Iran's maritime force in the Persian Gulf. The ships would sail a little close for comfort, and sometimes—on the particularly exciting days—they'd fire off a few rockets. Usually they fired in the complete opposite direction of any US ships. Posturing, Thomas thought. But the FNGs would just about piss themselves over it, and they'd be the butt of the joke for a few weeks after.

The trio of blips on the screen moved ever closer to their location, approaching from the northeast. "Gilbert," said Thomas into the radio, "how are we looking up there?"

"Oh, it's a beautiful afternoon. About seventy-four and sunny," Ensign Gilbert said through the radio, doing his best to keep the laughter out of his voice. "Humidity's low. Wind is maybe five miles an hour. If I close my eyes, it feels like Florida in early spring. How y'all doing in there?"

"Jackass," muttered Lieutenant Davis, the communications officer, seated near Thomas at the radar array. He smirked and said into the radio, "Sorry, *Ensign* Gilbert? Can you repeat that for your lieutenant?"

Thomas chuckled as Gilbert let out a soft groan. "All right, all right," said the young man from the top deck. "I've got visual on three IRGC ships to the northeast, traveling at about fourteen knots or so and looking to be a little more than a half mile out." Then he quickly added, "Sir."

Thomas nodded, impressed. "You're good. They're at point-five-six. Anyone want to take some action on this?"

"I've got a fiver that says they veer off by point-four," said Davis.

"I'll see that and raise," said Petty Officer Miller behind them, swiveling around in his chair. "Ten bucks says they reach point-three. You in, Cohen?"

Thomas shook his head. "Hell no. Last time you guys took me for twenty-five bucks."

"And he's got a wedding to save up for," Davis chided with a nudge.

"Y'all are thinking small," Gilbert said in the radio. "These guys are cowboys, I can feel it. A certain Mr. Jackson says not only do they come within point-two-five, but we get an Iranian dick pic."

"Don't be crass," Davis scolded Gilbert for his lewd metaphor of the IRGC firing off a rocket.

"That'd be a nice change of pace," Miller muttered. "Most exciting thing that's happened around here in two weeks was enchilada day."

It was not at all lost on Lieutenant Cohen that an outside observer might have thought it insane for them to be making small wagers on whether or not a ship fired a missile. But after so many so-called confrontations yielding nothing, it was hardly anything to fret over. Besides, the US rules of engagement were clear; they would not fire unless directly fired upon first, and the Iranians knew that. The *Constitution* was exactly as its class implied: a destroyer. If a rocket fell close enough for them to feel the heat of it, they could obliterate the IRGC ship in seconds.

"Point-four and closing," Thomas announced. "Sorry, Davis. You're out."

He shrugged. "Can't win 'em all."

Thomas frowned at the array. It looked as if the two ships flanking either side of the third were veering, but the central ship continued on a straight path. "Gilbert, check visual."

"Aye aye." There was a moment of silence before the ensign reported back. "Looks like two of the ships are breaking off, south-southeast and south-southwest. But I think that third boat wants to be friends. What did I tell you, Cohen? Cowboys."

Miller sighed. "Where is Captain Warren? We should alert—"

"Captain on the bridge!" a sharp voice bellowed suddenly. Thomas hopped up from his seat and issued a crisp salute, along with the four other officers in the control room.

The XO entered first, a tall and square-jawed man who looked a lot more serious than he usually came off as. He was followed by a hasty Captain Warren, his slight paunch straining the lowest buttons of his tan short-sleeved shirt. On his head he wore a Navy baseball cap, the dark blue looking almost black in the dim lighting of the bridge.

"As you were," Warren said gruffly. Thomas slowly took his seat again, exchanging a concerned glance with Davis. The captain was likely aware of the approaching IRGC ships, but for him to be here with three boats looming so close meant that something was going on. "Listen up and listen good, because I'm going to say this quick." The captain frowned deeply. He normally wore a frown—Thomas couldn't recall ever seeing Warren smile—but this frown seemed particularly dismayed. "Orders have just come down the pipe. There's been a change in ROE. Any ships that fire within a half-mile proximity are to be considered hostile and dealt with using extreme prejudice."

Thomas blinked at the sudden rush of words, failing to comprehend at first.

Petty Officer Miller forgot himself for a moment as he said, "Dealt with? You mean destroyed?"

"That's right, Miller," said Captain Warren as he locked eyes with the young man, "I mean destroyed, demolished, obliterated, devastated, wrecked, and/or ruined."

"Um, sir?" Davis spoke up. "If they fire at all? Or if they fire upon us?"

"The release of a weapon that could result in a loss of life, Lieutenant," Captain Warren told him. "Whether aimed at us or not."

Thomas couldn't believe what he was hearing. The IRGC had fired rockets plenty of times since he had been aboard the *Constitution*, many of those times within a half mile of them. He found it exceedingly bizarre and coincidental that the rules of engagement would be changed so swiftly—and at the precise moment when an Iranian ship was bearing down on them.

"Look," said Warren, "I don't like this any more than you do, but you all know what happened. Frankly, I'm surprised it took the government this long. But here we are."

Thomas knew precisely what the captain was referring to. Mere days earlier, a terrorist organization had attempted to blow up the USS *New York*, an Arleigh-Burke destroyer that was moored at the Port of Haifa in Israel. And only two days ago, the same insurgent cell had taken out an underwater tunnel in New York City. Captain Warren had convened the entire crew in the mess hall to tell them the dire news. The CIA had caught wind of the attack just hours before it was carried out and managed to save a lot of lives, but hundreds had still perished and far too many were yet unaccounted for. The scale of the attack was not nearly that of 9/11, but it was still one of the most substantial attacks on US soil in the last hundred years.

"This is the world we live in now, boys," said Warren, shaking his head in disdain. Clearly he was thinking the same thing as Thomas. They all were.

"It's veering off," said Gilbert through the radio, jarring Thomas out of his thoughts and back to his console. The ensign was right; the third ship was just shy of point-three miles and steering toward the west. "Looks like I'll be out twenty bucks."

Thomas let out a sigh of relief. In another minute the ship would be gone, beyond a half-mile range, and the *Constitution* would continue its easterly patrol route toward the strait. *Please don't do anything stupid,* he thought as he said, "IRGC cruiser is at point-two-eight, veering east. Doesn't look like it's interested in us, sir."

Warren nodded, though if he was as glad as Thomas, he didn't show it. The lieutenant could guess why; the rules of engagement had changed, and quite suddenly at that. How long would it be before they found themselves in another situation like this one?

Lieutenant Davis looked up sharply and suddenly. "They're hailing us, sir."

Captain Warren closed his eyes and sighed. "All right. Relay this, and be quick about it." More than just the communications officer, Davis was fluent in Arabic and Farsi. He translated the captain's message as Warren spoke it, listening and talking at the same time. "This is Captain James Warren of the USS *Constitution.* The US Navy's rules of engagement have changed. Your superiors should be aware of this by now, but if you are not, we are fully sanctioned by the American government for the use of deadly force should any vessel—"

"Rocket out!" Gilbert cried in Thomas's ear.

"Rocket out!" Thomas repeated. Before he even knew what he was doing, he tore the headset from his head and dashed to the port windows. In the distance he saw the IRGC cruiser, as well as the brilliant red streak soaring in a high arc in the sky, a plume of smoke trailing behind it.

As he watched, a second rocket fired off from the deck of the Iranian ship. They were fired on a trajectory parallel to the *Constitution,* far enough off that they would hardly make waves for the destroyer.

Thomas spun to the captain. Warren's face had turned a shade whiter. "Sir—"

"Return to your post, Lieutenant Cohen." Warren's voice was strained.

A knot of dread formed in Thomas's stomach. "But sir, we can't seriously—"

"*Return to your post,* Lieutenant," the captain said again, his jaw flexing. Thomas obliged, lowering himself slowly to his seat but not taking his eyes off of Warren.

"This doesn't come from the admiral," he said, as if trying to explain to them what he knew had to happen. "Not even from the CNO. This is from the Secretary of Defense. Do you understand that? It's a direct order in the interest of national security."

Without another word, Warren plucked up a red phone mounted on the wall. "This is Captain Warren. Fire torpedoes." There was a moment of silence, and the captain said again, forcefully, "Affirmative. *Fire torpedoes.*" He hung up the phone, but his hand lingered upon it. "God help us," he murmured.

Thomas Cohen held his breath. He counted the seconds. He reached twelve before he heard Gilbert's voice, soft and breathy and almost reverent through the radio.

"Jesus almighty."

Thomas stood, not leaving his post but gaining a partial view of the port window. They heard no explosion through the thick armor-plated glass of the bridge, designed to sustain heavy ballistic fire. They felt no shockwave, absorbed as it was by the vast Persian Gulf. But he saw it. He saw the orange fireball rise in the sky as the IRGC ship was, as he had predicted, destroyed in seconds by a wave of torpedoes from the US destroyer.

The green blip vanished from his screen. "Target destroyed," he confirmed quietly. He had no idea how many people they had just killed. Twenty. Maybe fifty. Maybe a hundred.

Davis stood as well, looking out the window as the orange fire dissipated, the ship torn asunder and sinking rapidly into the depths of the Persian Gulf. It might have been the angle, or the reflection of sunlight, but he could have sworn he saw his eyes gloss with the threat of tears.

"Cohen?" he said quietly, his voice almost a whisper. "Did we just start World War Three?"

Five minutes earlier, the furthest thing from Lieutenant Thomas Cohen's mind had been war. But now, he had every reason to suspect he wouldn't be making it home to Pensacola in three weeks.

Chapter Three

"Excuse me," said Zero, "do you think we could drive just a bit faster?" He sat in the back seat of a black town car as a White House chauffeur took him home to Alexandria, less than thirty minutes from Washington, DC. They drove mostly in silence, for which Zero was thankful; it gave him some precious minutes to think. There was no time to sort through the deluge of newfound skills and history that had been unlocked in his head. He needed to focus on the task at hand.

Think, Zero. Who do you know is in on this? The secretary of defense, the vice president, congressmen, a handful of senators, members of the NSA, the National Security Council, even the CIA… Names and faces flashed through his mind like a mental Rolodex. Zero sucked in a breath as a tension headache began to form at the front of his skull. He had investigated many of them, had even found some evidence—the documents he had locked in the safe deposit box in Arlington—but he feared it wouldn't be enough to definitively prove what was happening.

In his pocket, his cell phone rang. He let it go.

Why now? He didn't need his newfound memories for that part. It was an election year. In a little more than six months, Pierson would either be reelected for a second term or ousted by a Democrat. And nothing would drum up more support than a successful campaign against a hostile foe.

He was certain that Pierson was not a part of it. In fact, Zero recalled during Pierson's first year in office when he signed a bill decreasing US military presence in Iraq and Iran. He was opposed to further war in the Middle East without provocation . . . which was why those in the shadows needed the Brotherhood's catalyst.

And while the US decreased their presence, the Russians increased theirs. Maria had mentioned that the Ukrainians were nervous that Russia intended to seize oil-producing assets in the Black Sea. That's why she had made a cautious alliance with them to share information. The US conspirators were in bed with the Russians. The US would get the strait, and the Russians would get the Black Sea. The United States would do nothing to stop Russia from their endeavors, and Russia would respond in kind, possibly even lend support in the Middle East.

Two of the world's superpowers would become richer, more powerful, and nigh unstoppable. And as long as there was peace between them, there would be no one to oppose them.

His phone rang again. The call registered as unknown. He wondered briefly if it could be Deputy Director Cartwright calling. Zero's direct boss in the Special Activities Division of the agency was noticeably absent at the Oval Office meeting with President Pierson. It could have been official business that kept him away, but Zero had his doubts. Still, the caller (or callers) had not left voicemails and Zero did not bother to reach out to the CIA.

As they neared his home on Spruce Street, he made two calls. The first was to Georgetown University. "This is Professor Reid Lawson. I'm afraid I've come down with something. Most likely the flu. I'm going to see a doctor today. Can you see if Dr. Ford is available to take my lectures?"

The second call was to the Third Street Garage.

"Yeah," the man that answered said in a grunt.

"Mitch? It's Zero."

"Mm." The burly mechanic said it as if he had been expecting the call. Mitch was a man of few words, and also a CIA asset who had helped Zero when he needed to rescue his girls from Rais and a ring of human traffickers.

"Something's come up. I may need an extraction for two. Can you be on standby?" The words rolled off his tongue as if they had been well-rehearsed—because they had, he realized, even if he hadn't spoken them in some time. He couldn't risk asking Watson or Strickland; they would likely be watched as carefully as he was. But Mitch operated off the radar.

"Consider it done," Mitch said simply.

"Thank you. I'll be in touch." He hung up. His first instinct was to have his daughters taken to a safe house right away, but any deviation from their normal schedule might instigate suspicion. Mitch's extraction was a failsafe in case he had reason to believe the girls' lives were in imminent danger—and despite the trepidation over this heightened sense of paranoia, he had plenty of reason to believe it was justified.

Home was a two-story house on a corner lot in the suburbs of Alexandria. To the non-street side was a vacant home currently up for sale, having been the former residence of David Thompson, a retired CIA field agent who had been killed in Zero's foyer.

He unlocked the door and quickly punched in the security code for the alarm system. He kept it set that the code needed to be entered every time someone came or went, regardless of who was home at the time. If the code wasn't entered within sixty seconds of the door opening, an alarm would sound and local police would be alerted. In addition to the alarm system, they had security cameras both outside and inside, bolts on the doors and windows, and a panic room with a steel security door in the basement.

Still he feared it wouldn't be enough to keep his daughters safe.

He found Maya lying on her back on the sofa and playing a game on her phone. She was nearly seventeen, and often vacillated between unprompted teenage angst and the foreshadowing of becoming a discerning adult. She had inherited her father's dark hair and sharp facial features, while taking on her mother's fierce intelligence and biting wit.

"Hey," she said without looking away from the screen. "Did the president feed you? Because I could really go for Chinese tonight."

"Where's your sister?" he asked quickly.

"Dining room." Maya frowned and sat up, sensing the urgency in his voice. "Why, what's going on?"

"Nothing yet," he answered cryptically. Zero hurried through the kitchen and found his younger daughter, Sara, doing homework at the table.

She glanced up at the sudden intrusion of her father. "Hi, Dad." Then she too furrowed her brow, seemingly aware that something was amiss. "Are you okay?"

"Yeah, sweetheart, I'm fine. Just wanted to check on you." Without another word, he quickly headed upstairs to his home office. He already knew what he needed and exactly where to find it. The first item was a burner phone that he had picked up, paid in cash with a few hundred prepaid minutes on it. Maya had the number. The second was the safe deposit box key. He knew where it was as if he always had, though earlier that morning he never would have remembered what it was for or why he had it. The key was in an old tackle box in his closet, what he had dubbed his "junk box," filled with all sorts of old things that he couldn't bring himself to get rid of though they hardly seemed worthwhile.

When he returned to the kitchen, he was not all that surprised to find both of his daughters standing there expectantly.

"Dad?" Maya said uncertainly. "What's going on?"

Zero took his cell phone from his pocket and left it on the kitchen counter. "There's something that I have to do," he said vaguely. "And it's …"

Incredibly dangerous. Monumentally stupid to do alone. Puts you directly in harm's way. Again.

"It's something that means people are likely going to be watching us. Carefully. And we need to be prepared for that."

"Are we going to a safe house again?" Sara asked.

It broke Zero's heart that she had to even ask that question. "No," he told her. Then he scolded himself, remembering that he had promised them honesty. "Not yet. That might come later."

"Does this have to do with what happened in New York?" Maya asked candidly.

"Yes," he admitted. "But for now, just listen. There's a man, an agency asset named Mitch. He's a big guy, burly, with a bushy beard and wears a trucker's cap. He runs the Third Street Garage. If I give him the go-ahead, he's going to come here and bring you somewhere safe. Somewhere that not even the CIA knows about."

"Why don't we just go there now?" Sara asked.

"Because," Zero replied honestly, "there's a chance that people might already be watching us. Or at the very least, keeping an eye out for anything strange. If you don't show up for school, or if I do something out of the ordinary, it might ring some alarms. You guys know the drill. You don't let anyone in, you don't go with anyone, and you don't *trust* anyone except for Mitch, Agent Strickland, or Agent Watson."

"And Maria," Sara added. "Right?"

"Yeah," Zero murmured. "And Maria. Of course." He reached for the doorknob. "I won't be long. Lock up behind me. I have the burner; call if you need me." He headed out the door and strode quickly to his car, dismayed to find that the memory of him and Maria together was rattling around his head again.

Kate. You betrayed her.

"No," he muttered to himself as he reached the car. He wouldn't have. He loved Kate more than anything, anyone. As he slid behind the wheel and started the car, he searched his memory for any indication that he was wrong, that he and Maria had not had an affair while Kate was still alive. But there was none. His relationship at home had been a happy one; Kate was none the wiser about his work as a CIA agent. She believed his frequent travels were guest lectures at other colleges, research for a history book, summits, and conventions. She supported him fully while taking care of the two girls. He hid his injuries from her, and when he couldn't, he made excuses. He was clumsy. He fell. At least once he had been jumped. The agency helped with his cover stories and, on more than one occasion, went so far as to create fake police reports to substantiate his claims.

She didn't know.

But Maria did. Maria knew this entire time that they had been together while Kate was still alive, and she had said nothing. As long as Zero's memory was fractured, she could tell him whatever he wanted to hear and withhold anything he didn't know.

He suddenly realized how tightly he was gripping the steering wheel, his knuckles white and his ears burning in anger. *Deal with that later. There are more important things to do right now,* he told himself as he headed to the bank to retrieve the evidence that he could only hope was enough to put a stop to this.

Chapter Four

There was little traffic in the early afternoon as Zero drove quickly to the Arlington bank. Twice he blew stop signs and even slammed the accelerator through a yellow light, each time reminding himself that avoiding scrutiny would be a good idea, and that a traffic violation would no doubt get flagged in the CIA system, alerting the agency-oriented conspirators to his whereabouts.

But his mind was hardly on the rules of the road. He had taken the precautionary measures to keep the girls safe, at least for now; next he would retrieve his files from the deposit box. That much was easy. But then would come the difficult part. *Who do I take it to? The press?* No, he realized, that would be too messy. Despite any muck and mire he might drag names through, the process of dismissing any of the figureheads from their posts would be lengthy and involve trials.

The United Nations? NATO? Once again the political and judicial process would hinder real progress. He needed something rapid; to bring what he knew to someone with the power to do something immediate and irreversible.

He already had the answer. *Pierson.* If the president was truly unaware of the plot, Zero could appeal to him. He would have to get the president alone somehow, bring him everything he had and knew. The president could stop all of this and could dismiss those responsible for it. Pierson seemed to hold Agent Zero in high regard; he trusted him and treated him like a friend. Although those traits had caused Zero to cast doubt and aspersions on Pierson in the past, he was now armed with his memory, his real memory, and he saw the president for what he was: a pawn in this game. Those in power wanted four more years so that they could manipulate things to their liking, in a manner that meant longevity regardless of who was in office.

He parallel-parked two blocks from the bank, no simple task with only one good hand. Before getting out of the car he reached over, popped the glove box, and rooted around until he found the small black tactical folding knife that he had stowed there.

Then he hurried down the street to the bank.

Zero tried to look patient as he waited for the three customers in front of him to finish their business, and then presented his photo ID to the teller, a middle-aged woman with a kind smile and too much lipstick.

"Let me get the branch manager," she told him politely.

Two minutes later a man in a suit led him through a vault door to the deposit boxes. He unlocked the narrow rectangular door to 726, slid the box out, and set it on an otherwise empty steel table, bolted to the floor in the center of the room.

"Take your time, sir." The manager nodded to him and gave him some privacy.

As soon as the man was gone, Zero lifted the lid to the box.

"No," he murmured. He took one step backward and looked over his shoulder instinctively, as if someone might be there.

The box was empty.

"No, no." He pounded a fist on the table with a dull thud. "No!" All of his documents, everything he had dug up on those that he knew were involved in the plot, were gone. Every piece of illegally obtained evidence that could potentially force the dismissal of heads of state was gone. Photos, transcriptions, emails… all of it, vanished.

Zero put his hands on his head and paced the room back and forth rapidly. His first thought was the most likely solution: someone else knew about the documents and took them. *Who else knew about this box?* No one. He was sure of it. *You definitely didn't give the information to someone and forgot about it?* No. He wouldn't have done that. He almost laughed at himself, at how insane the notion was that he might forget something that he didn't know he knew only hours ago.

But then Zero remembered something else, not an unlocked memory, but one that he had experienced only days earlier, in the office of a Swiss neurosurgeon.

I should forewarn you, Dr. Guyer had told him before performing the procedure to bring Zero's memories back. *If this works, some of the things that you recall may be subconscious: fantasies, wishes, suspicions from your past life. All of those non-memory aspects were removed with your actual memories.*

Zero had frowned at that. *So you're saying that if I remember things, some of the things I remember may not actually be real?*

The doctor's reply had been simple, yet harrowing. *They'll be real to you.*

If that was the case, he reasoned, couldn't it be possible that he had done something with the documents himself? Could he have imagined that they were here, in this safe deposit box, when really they were elsewhere?

I'm losing my mind.

Focus, Zero.

He pulled the lockback knife out of his pocket, unfolded it, and carefully wedged the razor-sharp tip into the edge of the bottom of the box. He worked it back and forth gently, careful not to scratch it, until the bottom panel came loose.

He breathed a small sigh of relief. Whoever had taken his documents didn't know about the false bottom he had installed in the box, less than an inch above the real bottom. Nestled beneath it was a single object—a USB stick.

At least they didn't find the recordings. But is it enough? He wasn't sure, but it was all he had. He snatched it up, pocketed the knife and the USB drive, and then carefully replaced the false bottom. Then he slid the box back into its narrow vault and closed the door.

When he finished, Zero headed back to the lipsticked teller.

"Excuse me," he said, "can you tell me if anyone else accessed my safe deposit box in the past two years?"

The woman blinked at him. "Two years?"

"Yes. Please. You keep a log, right?"

"Um... certainly. One moment." Fingernails clacked against the keyboard for a long minute. "Here we are. There has only been one access to your deposit box in the past two years, and it was only a couple of months ago, in February."

"It wasn't me," Zero said impatiently. "So who was it?"

She blinked at him again, this time in confusion. "Well, sir, it was the only other person authorized to access the box. It was your wife. Katherine Lawson."

Zero stared at the teller for longer than the woman found comfortable.

"No," he said slowly. "That's impossible. My wife passed away two years ago."

She frowned deeply, the lipsticked corners of her mouth drooping as if they'd been tugged. "I am very sorry to hear that, sir. And that is certainly strange. But... we require photo ID, and the person that accessed the box obviously had it. Your wife's name wasn't taken from the box's lease when she passed."

Zero remembered putting her name on the lease. Kate hadn't known about it at the time; he had forged her signature as a joint lease so that someone would know about it in the event of his death.

And only two months prior, someone had pretended to be her, had even gone so far as to create identification that could pass as valid to a bank, and taken the contents of his box.

"I assure you," the teller told him, "we will look further into this matter. The branch manager just left for the day, but I can have him reach out to you tomorrow. Would you like to report a theft?"

"No, no." Zero waved a hand dismissively. He didn't want to get any legal authorities involved and have the safe deposit box flagged in any system that the CIA might see. "Nothing was taken," he lied. "Let's just forget it. Thanks."

"Sir?" she called after him, but he was already at the door.

Someone came here posing as Kate. He knew there was little he could do about it now; the bank might still have the security footage from that day, but they wouldn't allow him access unless there was an investigation and a warrant.

But who? The agency was the most obvious culprit. With the vast CIA resources, they could have created a passable ID and sent a female agent in under the guise of Kate. But Zero hadn't accessed the box in years. If they knew about it back then, why would they wait until only two months ago to get into it?

Because I came back. They thought I was dead, and when I wasn't, they needed to know what I knew.

Another thought flashed through his mind: Maria. *Are you sure you never told her about it? Not even in case of an emergency?* She was one of the best covert agents he had ever known; she could have found a way. But still he came back to the question of why she would do that now, why wait if she knew about the safe deposit box.

He suddenly felt tired and overwhelmed. He had lost so much of what he had uncovered before, the smallest shred of potential evidence sitting on a USB stick in his pocket. He had no idea how much time he had to get Pierson alone, try to convince him of what was happening, and somehow persuade him to look further into those responsible with almost nothing to go on.

It felt insurmountable. He realized grimly that if he had still been Reid Lawson, trapped in the hell of his partial memories as Agent Zero, he might have given up. He might have scooped up his daughters and whatever they could carry and fled somewhere. The Midwest, maybe. He might have stuck his head in the sand and let things happen as they would. Reid Lawson's highest priority was his girls.

But Agent Zero had a responsibility. This was not just his job. It was his life. This was who he truly was, and there was no way in hell he was going to sit idly by and watch a war unfold, watch innocent people die, watch American servicemen and Middle Eastern civilians be forced into a conflict that was manufactured for the benefit of a handful of megalomaniacal men to maintain their power.

He heard the footsteps like an echo of his own and resisted the urge to turn around. As he neared his car, parked two blocks from the bank, the heavy footfalls of boots kept pace with his almost stride for stride.

About ten feet behind you. Keeping their distance. They're walking heavy; definitely a man, probably close to six foot, two-ten to two-twenty.

Zero didn't stop at his car. He walked right past it to the next corner and turned right onto a side street. As he walked past a flower shop, the same one that he had once bought bouquets for his girls before picking them up from a safe house six blocks to the west, he checked his periphery. It was something that he had instinctually done as Reid Lawson, but with his memories also came back his skills. It was as easy as glancing in a mirror; without averting his gaze from the sidewalk ahead, he focused on the outermost borders of his field of vision.

A man in a black T-shirt was crossing the street toward him. He was large, easily two-fifty, with a neck as thick as his head and heavily muscled arms testing the limits of his shirtsleeves.

So this is how it's going to be. The hairs on Zero's arms stood on end, but his heartbeat remained steady. His breathing normal. No sweat prickled on his brow.

He wasn't being paranoid. They were after him. They knew. And he was more than ready to meet the challenge.

Chapter Five

Without breaking his stride, Zero turned right again, slipping down a narrow thoroughfare between two buildings. It was barely six feet across, not even wide enough to be called an alley. About halfway down its length he stopped and turned.

At the mouth of the throughway stood one of his two pursuers. The man was around his age, a few inches taller, with a wiry frame and a few days' worth of coarse dark hair on his chin. He wore black boots and jeans and a black leather jacket.

"Baker," Zero said instinctively. This man was a member of the Division, a private security group that the CIA occasionally contracted to assist with international affairs. They were veritable mercenaries, the same group that had made a bid for his life not a week ago at the Brotherhood's compound outside of Al-Baghdadi. The same group that had attempted to jump Agent Watson and kidnap his daughters in Switzerland.

But this man in particular was familiar to him. As soon as Zero saw his face, he remembered: back in 2013, the Division had been called in to help out with a hostage situation between a faction of Al Qaeda and a dozen US soldiers. Baker had been among them.

The mercenary raised an eyebrow. "You know me?"

Shit. Zero scolded himself for blurting out the man's name. He had shown his hand. He shrugged and tried to play it off. "Some things come back. In pieces."

Baker smirked. "Sure, Zero. What was in the bank?"

"Money. I made a withdrawal."

The merc shook his head. "I don't think so. See, I called it in. You don't have an account there. But techs noticed a safe deposit box in you and your dead wife's name."

Zero saw red for a moment at the offhanded comment about Kate and nearly lost his cool, but he forced himself to remain calm.

"I'm guessing you made a withdrawal," Baker said, "but not money. What was in the box, Zero?"

Guessing? Either Baker was bluffing, or the agency really didn't know about the safe deposit box before now. Which meant that the CIA was not responsible for the missing documents. *But he could be lying.*

Zero heard footsteps behind him and glanced quickly over his shoulder to see the big man from the street corner stepping into view at the opposite end of the narrow causeway. His head was shaved bald but his chin was obscured in a thick brown beard, the bottom lip jutting in a scowl. He looked like he could have been a linebacker or a professional wrestler.

I don't know him. Must be new, Zero thought wryly.

When he turned back to Baker, the wiry mercenary had one hand inside his jacket. It came back out slowly, and Zero wasn't the least bit surprised to see it gripping a black Sig Sauer.

"What's that for? You going to shoot me in broad daylight?" Zero held up his damaged right hand. "I'm unarmed and one-handed."

"I've seen what you can do with one hand," Baker said nonchalantly as he screwed a suppressor to the barrel of the pistol. "This is for self-defense. What was in the box, Zero?"

Zero shrugged a shoulder. "You're going to have to shoot me first." *How the hell am I going to get out of this?* He wasn't taunting when he said he was one-handed. He was at a huge disadvantage against one of them, let alone two.

"Our orders are nonlethal force," Baker remarked. He looked past Zero to his burly cohort. "What do you think, Stevens? A shot to a kneecap isn't lethal, right?"

The big man, Stevens, didn't respond—at least not in words. He merely grunted.

Nonlethal force. These two weren't sent to kill him; they were sent to take whatever he had retrieved from the bank, and likely determine whether or not they should bring him in. *It's too late to kill me now.* The powers-that-be needed to know what he knew, and who else he had told. It might not be too suspicious to those not involved in the plot if Agent Zero suddenly ended up dead, but if they had to take out others—Strickland, Watson, Maria—people would start asking the wrong sort of questions and poking around where their dirty laundry might be found.

I need a distraction. "Say, how's Fitzpatrick?" he asked as casually as he could. He knew he would be goading them, but he needed to buy some time. "Last I saw him he was kind of... smeared, for lack of a better term."

Baker's lip curled slightly. The leader of the Division, Fitzpatrick, had been hit by a car in a New York parking deck by Mossad Agent Talia Mendel. As far as Zero knew, Fitzpatrick was still alive, but he didn't know the extent of his wounds.

"He's alive," Baker replied evenly, "despite your friends' best efforts. Seventeen broken bones, a punctured lung, loss of vision in his right eye."

Zero clucked his tongue in dismay. "I should really send him some flowers—"

Baker snapped the pistol up in both hands. "That's enough. It's been real nice catching up, but if you don't tell me what was in the box, I am going to shoot you. And then I'm going to have Stevens here drag your bleeding body by the ankle to a nice quiet place where we can hook you up to a car battery until you tell us exactly how much you remember."

Zero wrinkled his nose. "That sounds unpleasant."

Baker fired a shot. The gun made a *thwip!* and a small chunk of the brick façade to Zero's right exploded, sending small pieces of stone smacking against his face.

His hands were up in an instant. "Whoa! All right. Jesus. I'll tell you." Still his pulse hardly quickened.

I have what they want. I am in control here.

"It's a USB stick. It has information on it."

"Give it here," Baker ordered.

"Can I reach into my pocket for it?"

"Slowly," Baker growled, the Sig Sauer trained at Zero's forehead.

"Okay." Zero showed his empty left hand, wiggling the fingers, and then slowly snaked the hand down to his pants pocket. *Baker is about five yards away.* With his hand in his pocket, he gripped the USB stick with two fingers, pinching it between the index and middle. *Stevens is about seven yards away.* He palmed the lockback knife with his pinky and ring fingers, securing it with his thumb. *Just like the Tueller Drill.*

That morning, he would have sworn he had never heard the name Dennis Tueller, but anyone who had ever been trained to bring a knife to a gun fight would know it. In 1983, Sergeant Tueller ran a series of tests to determine how quickly an attacker with a knife could cover a distance of approximately twenty-one feet—and if a defender with a holstered gun could react in time.

Less than two seconds. That was the average time it took an attacker to sprint twenty-one feet—seven yards—to a target. The problem was that Baker's gun wasn't holstered.

But Stevens hadn't drawn yet.

"See?" Zero raised the USB stick, pinched between two fingers, keeping the back of his hand facing Baker.

"Toss it," Baker demanded. Over the mercenary's shoulder, a few passersby talked and laughed as they walked by the mouth of the narrow alley. A young man among them glanced down the causeway, but with Baker's back to them he didn't see the Sig Sauer. Instead the man just flashed a brief frown and kept right on walking.

I could really use a distraction. But Zero wasn't willing to call out to anyone, to put anyone else in harm's way.

Baker shifted the grip on his pistol to one hand and held the other out, palm up, waiting for Zero to toss the USB stick.

So he did. He curled his arm back and tossed the USB drive toward Baker in an underhand motion, flicking it into a high arc.

As he released the stick, he slid the lockback knife from his palm to his fingers.

Then he catapulted himself from his mark like a shot, snapping open the knife as he did.

As Baker's gaze rose from his target to the skinny black drive soaring in an arc through the air, Zero sprinted from his position—but not toward Baker. He hurtled toward the larger man like a shot.

One-point-four seconds. He had performed the Tueller Drill a thousand times, had trained for this exact scenario, even remembered it as clearly as if it had happened yesterday. A high-precision radar gun in a CIA training field had clocked him at an average of one-point-four seconds to reach a target approximately seven yards away.

The amount of minute math that crossed his mind in an instant was staggering. It had always been there, ingrained through insane amounts of repetition and study, locked away in the recesses of his limbic system, waiting for the opportunity to burst out again. Average human reaction speed was a half second to three-quarters of a second. Even a professional like Baker required at least a quarter of a second between shots on a semi-auto pistol like the Sig Sauer. And Zero was a moving target.

The big man, Stevens, was not quick. He barely had the pistol free of his holster, his eyes involuntarily widening in surprise at Zero's speed as he vaulted toward him. The blade was already snapped open. Zero launched himself the last six feet, leaping toward Stevens and sliding the tip of the knife, in and out, one motion, into his throat.

With his wrapped right hand he reached out for Stevens's big shoulder and, as the knife tip slid out again, Zero slingshot himself around the large man's body. Two shots rang out behind him—*thwip-thwip* from the suppressed pistol—and struck Stevens in the chest as Zero landed behind him. Sharp, astounding pain burned in his injured hand, but the adrenaline was there now, coursing through him as he dropped the knife and reached around for Stevens's pistol before the big man could fall. He snapped it out of the beefy fist and, safe behind his broad human shield, fired two shots at Baker.

He was a good shot with his left hand, though not quite as good as his right. One of the shots missed. Glass shattered somewhere beyond the alley. The second thunderclap of a shot—Stevens's Beretta wasn't outfitted with a suppressor—struck Baker in the forehead.

The mercenary's head snapped back. His body followed.

Zero didn't wait around or stop to catch his breath. He sprinted ahead again, grabbed up the USB stick that was still lying on the cement, and then ran the opposite way down the alley. He stuffed it in his pocket, along with the bloodied knife, and then took Stevens's Beretta with him. It had his fingerprints on it.

Somewhere a car alarm whooped loudly. The shattered glass he'd heard must have been a car window. He hoped no one had been hit.

The large man's chest heaved up and down. He was still alive. But Zero didn't have the luxury of finishing him off or waiting around; besides, with the knife wound to the throat and two shots to the chest, he'd be dead in seconds.

People shouted in alarm from somewhere nearby as Zero sprinted to the end of the alley, stuffing the gun in the back of his pants as he did. He turned the corner and looked all around in bewilderment, hoping that he looked as much the shocked passerby as anyone else.

As he hurried to the end of the block, he heard the shriek of a woman—no doubt discovering the two bodies in the narrow alley—and then a male shout, "Someone call nine-one-one!"

They had to die. There was no way around it. He had known it as soon as he had accidentally tipped his hand and said Baker's name. He knew it when he showed them the USB drive he had retrieved from the bank.

Oddly, there was no remorse. There was no "what if?" of whether or not he could have talked them out of trying to take the drive or seeing them from his perspective. It was a situation of him or them, and he decided it wasn't going to be him. They made their choice, and they chose wrong.

The entire ordeal, from tossing the USB stick to fleeing from the alley, had unfolded in a matter of seconds. But he could see every moment clearly like a slow-motion instant replay in his head. The strange thing was that when Baker had fired the gun mere feet from his head, hitting the brick wall, Zero's thoughts were not of how close the bullet had come, or that Baker could have easily killed him if he wanted to. It wasn't of the girls. Instead he was keenly aware of the dichotomous nature of his scholarly mind against his rediscovered memories. Zero was cool, calm, and believed, perhaps due to some hubris or experience or a combination thereof, that he was still in control of this situation.

It was a bizarre sensation. Worse still was how much it frightened and thrilled him at the same time. *Is this who I am? Was Reid Lawson a lie? Or have I been living my life for two years with only the weakest parts of my psyche?*

Zero strode to the end of the block, looped back around toward the flower shop, and went straight to his car. He could see that a sizable crowd of onlookers was gathering around the corner, many in shock or even crying at the sight of two dead bodies.

No one was paying any attention to him.

He drove casually, maintaining the speed limit and careful not to blow any stop signs or lights. There was no doubt that police were en route, and the CIA would know in moments that shots had been fired and two men had been killed a mere three blocks from the bank that the Division had reported Zero to have been at.

The question was what they would do about it. There was nothing at the scene that could definitively link him to it, and whoever sent the Division mercs after him—Riker, he presumed—wouldn't be able to admit it openly. Still, he needed help, and more than he could ask of his fellow agents. They would be watched as well. If this was the type of open season it was going to be on Agent Zero, then he needed allies. Powerful ones.

But first, he needed to get his girls to safety.

As soon as he felt he'd made a safe distance from the grisly scene in the alley, he pulled into a gas station and around to the back. He buried the gun, the knife, and the safe deposit key in the dumpster under offensively awful-smelling trash. Then he got back into the car and made the call. It rang only twice before Mitch answered with a grunt.

"Need extraction right away, Mitch. I'll meet you somewhere."

"Meadow Field," the mechanic said immediately. "You know it?"

"I do." Meadow Field was an abandoned airstrip about twenty miles south. "I'll be there."

Chapter Six

Maya parted the blinds of the window near the front door for what must have been the twentieth time since their father had left. The street outside was clear. An occasional car drove by, but they didn't slow or stop.

It scared the hell out of her to think what her dad might be caught in the middle of this time.

Just for good measure, she crossed the foyer to the kitchen and checked her dad's phone again. He had left his personal cell behind, on silent, but his screen showed that he had missed three calls since Maya had last talked to him.

Maria apparently was desperate to get in touch with him. Maya wanted to call her, to tell her that something was going on, but she refrained. If her dad wanted Maria to know, he would contact her directly.

She found Sara in the same position she had been in for the last half hour, seated on the sofa in the living room with her legs drawn up beneath her. There was a sitcom on TV, but the volume was so low she could barely hear it, and she wasn't looking directly at it anyway.

Maya could tell that her sister had been suffering in silence ever since they had been taken by Rais and the Slavic traffickers. But Sara wouldn't open up, wouldn't talk about it.

"Hey, Squeak, how about something to eat?" Maya prodded. "I could make grilled cheese? With tomato. And bacon..." She smacked her lips, hoping to amuse her little sister.

But Sara merely shook her head. "Not hungry."

"Okay. Do you want to talk about anything?"

"No."

A wave of frustration rolled over her, but Maya swallowed it. She had to be patient. She too was affected by the events they had experienced, but her reaction had been anger and a desire for retribution. She had told her dad that her plan was to become a CIA agent herself, and it wasn't simply teenage angst talking. She was very serious about it.

"I'm here," she told her sister. "If you ever feel like talking. You know that, right?"

Sara glanced over at her. A smile very nearly passed her lips—but then her eyes widened and she sat up suddenly. "Do you hear that?"

Maya listened intently. She did hear it; the sound of a powerful engine rumbling nearby. Then it stopped abruptly.

"Stay here." She hurried back to the foyer and once again parted the blinds. A silver SUV had pulled into their driveway. Her pulse quickened as four men got out. Two of them wore suits; the other two wore all black, with tactical vests and combat boots.

Even from this distance Maya could see the insignia emblazoned on their sleeves. The two black-clad men were from the same organization that had attempted to kidnap them in Switzerland. Watson had called them the Division.

Maya rushed to the kitchen, sliding in her socks, and pulled a steak knife from the bamboo block on the counter. Sara had risen from the couch and hurried to join her.

"Go downstairs." Maya held the knife out, handle first, to her sister. "Get in the panic room. I'll be right behind you."

The doorbell rang.

"Don't answer it," Sara pleaded. "Just come with me."

"I'm not going to open the door," Maya promised. "I'm just going to see what they want. Go. Close the door. Don't wait for me."

Sara took the knife and hurried down the basement steps. Maya crept carefully to the front door and peeked through the peephole. The two men in suits stood right outside.

Where did the other two go? she wondered. *Back door, most likely.*

Maya jumped a little as one of the two men knocked briskly on the door. Then he spoke, his voice loud enough to hear from outside. "Maya Lawson?" He held up a badge in a leather ID holder as she peered through the peephole. "Agent Coulter, FBI. We need to ask you some questions about your father."

Her mind raced. She was certain that she was not going to answer the door for them. But would they try to force their way in? Should she say something, or pretend they weren't home?

"Ms. Lawson?" the agent said again. "We would really prefer to do this the easy way."

Long shadows danced against the floor of the foyer in the setting sun. She glanced up quickly to see two shapes passing by the rear entrance, a sliding glass door that led to a small deck and patio. It was the other two men, the ones from the Division, stalking around behind the house.

"Ms. Lawson," the man called out again. "This is your last warning. Please open the door."

Maya took a deep breath. "My father isn't here," she called out. "And I'm a minor. You're going to have to come back."

She peered through the peephole again to see the FBI agent grinning. "Ms. Lawson, I think you're misunderstanding the situation." He turned to his partner, a taller and burlier man. "Kick it in."

Maya sucked in a breath and backpedaled several steps. The doorjamb cracked, splinters of wood hurtling through the air, and the front door flew open.

The two agents took one step into the foyer. Maya felt frozen to the spot. She wondered if she could make a run for the basement and get to the panic room in time. But if Sara had done as Maya had told her and closed the door, they'd never get it shut again before the agents caught up to her.

Her gaze must have flitted toward the basement door, because the closer of the two agents smirked. "How about you stay right there, little lady?" The agent that had spoken through the door had sandy hair and a face that might have been friendly and boyish if they hadn't just kicked their way in. He put his empty hands up. "We're not armed. We don't want to hurt you or your sister."

"I don't believe you," Maya said. She glanced over her shoulder quickly, just for a half second, to see the shadows of the two black-clad men still stalking outside on the deck.

WHOOP! WHOOP! WHOOP! A siren suddenly blared out through the house, an earsplitting klaxon that had all three of them looking around in bewilderment. It took Maya a moment to realize that it was their alarm system, activated when the door was kicked in and set to go off in sixty seconds if the code wasn't punched in.

The police, she thought hopefully. *The police will come.*

"Shut it off!" the agent shouted at her. But she didn't move.

Then—glass shattered behind her. Maya jumped and spun instinctively at the sound as the sliding patio door exploded inward. One of the black-clad men stepped through.

She didn't stop to think, but a memory flashed through her mind in an instant: the hotel in Engelberg, Switzerland. The Division man posing as CIA, forcing his way in, attacking her.

Maya spun again quickly to face the FBI agents. One of them was near the panel, but he was facing her as the alarm continued to blare wildly. The eyes of the other agent, the boyish one, were wide and his hands were slightly in the air. His mouth was moving, but his words were drowned out by the screaming alarm.

Strong arms grabbed her from behind and she yelped. She struggled against her assailant, but he was strong. She smelled sour breath as the man wrapped her tightly, immobilizing her.

He hauled her off her feet and held her there, legs kicking and arm forced upward at a painful angle. She wasn't strong enough to fight him off.

Relax, her brain instructed. *Don't struggle.* She had taken self-defense classes at the university with a former Marine who had put her in this exact scenario—a larger, heavier assailant grabbing her from behind.

Maya tucked her chin down, almost touching her clavicle.

Then she slammed her head backward as hard as she could.

The Division man holding her cried out in pain as the back of her skull connected with his nose. His grip fell slack, and her feet touched the floor again. As soon as they did, she twisted her body, ducked her head low to get out of his arms, and then dropped her weight in a crouch.

She was all of a hundred and five pounds. But as she dropped, the man's arm still looped in her elbow, he was suddenly a hundred and five pounds heavier, and his balance was thrown by the sharp blow to his face.

He teetered and sprawled onto the tile of the foyer. Maya jumped backward, away from him, as he fell. She glanced over her shoulder to see the second Division man standing in the broken doorway, seemingly hesitant to make a swift move now that she'd dropped his pal.

She was only a few feet from the basement door. She could make a run for it, get to the panic room until the police arrived…

The mercenary in the doorway reached behind him, and he pulled out a black pistol. Maya's breath caught in her throat at the sight of it.

CRACK! Even over the blaring alarm they both heard the sharp sound. Maya and the mercenary both spun again.

The FBI agent who had kicked in the door, the one closest to the alarm panel, had his head stuck in the drywall of the foyer. His body was limp.

A figure lumbered forward and swung the tire iron again, landing a solid smack across the second agent's jaw. The sound of it set Maya's teeth on edge, and the agent slumped like a limp noodle.

As the Division merc lifted his gun at the new threat, the burly man reared back and hurled the tire iron through the air. It flipped end over end, passing by Maya by less than a foot, and smacked solidly into the merc's forehead. He barely made a sound as his body fell backward through the broken doorway.

The large man wore a trucker's cap over a bushy beard. His eyes twinkled blue. He nodded to her once and gestured toward the alarm panel.

Maya's legs felt like jelly as she rushed over to it and punched in the code. The alarm finally fell silent.

"Mitch?" she said breathlessly.

"Mm," the man grunted. On the floor of the foyer, the Division member that Maya had dropped attempted to get to his feet, holding his bloody nose. "I'll take care of him. Call nine-one-one. Tell them there's no problem."

Maya did as he instructed. She hurried to the kitchen, snatched up her dad's cell phone, and dialed 911. She watched as Mitch the mechanic stepped over to the Division merc and lifted one heavy brown boot.

She looked away before he dropped it on the man's face.

"Nine-one-one, what's your emergency?"

"My name is Maya Lawson. I live at 814 Spruce Street in Alexandria. Our alarm system went off by accident. I left the door open. There's no emergency."

"Please hold one moment, Ms. Lawson." She heard the clacking of a keyboard for a moment, and then the dispatcher told her, "We have a patrol car on the way, about three minutes out. Even if you say there's no emergency, we'd still like to have someone stop by. It's protocol."

"Really, everything's fine." She glanced over at Mitch desperately. They couldn't have a cop come by with four bodies in the house. She wasn't even sure if any of them were dead or just unconscious.

"Even so, Ms. Lawson, we'll have an officer at least check in. If there's no emergency, then there's no problem."

Mitch reached into a pocket of his oil-stained jeans and pulled out a flip phone that must have been fifteen years old. He dialed a number and then grunted something quietly into it.

"Um ..." The dispatcher hesitated. "Ms. Lawson, are you certain there's no emergency?"

"I'm certain, yes."

"All right. You have a nice day." The dispatcher abruptly ended the call. From beyond the shattered glass door, Maya heard sirens suddenly erupt in the distance—fading quickly.

"What did you do?" she asked Mitch.

"Called in a bigger emergency."

"Are they … alive?"

Mitch glanced around and then shrugged one shoulder. "He's not," he grunted, gesturing toward the agent with his head in the wall. Maya's stomach churned as she noticed a thin rivulet of blood running down the drywall where the agent's head was jammed in it.

How many people are going to die in this house? she couldn't help but wonder.

"Get your sister. And your phones. We're leaving." Mitch stepped over the Division merc's body and over to his friend. He grabbed the man by the ankles and dragged him into the house, and then scooped up the black pistol.

Maya hurried down the stairs to the basement. She stood in front of the camera that was mounted over the door to the panic room. "It's just me, Sara. You can open the door."

The thick steel security door pushed open from the inside, and her sister's timid face appeared. "Are we okay?"

"For now. Come on. We're leaving."

Back upstairs, Sara noted the carnage with wide eyes, but said nothing. Mitch was rummaging in the kitchen. "You got a first-aid kit?"

"Yeah. Here." Maya slid open a drawer and pulled out a small white metal box with a hinged lid and a red cross on the top.

"Thanks." Mitch pulled out an antiseptic wipe and then snapped open a razor-tipped knife. Maya took a step back at the sight of it. "I'm real sorry," the mechanic said, "but this next part is going to be a little unpleasant. You both got trackers in your right arm. They gotta come out. It's subcutaneous; under the skin and above the muscle. That means it's gonna sting like hell for a minute, but I promise it won't be too bad."

Maya chewed her lip nervously. She had nearly forgotten about the tracking implant. But then, much to her surprise, Sara stepped forward and tugged up her right sleeve. She reached for Maya's hand and held it tightly. "Do it."

⚜ ⚜ ⚜

There was a lot of blood, but not much pain as Mitch made quick work of the two trackers. The implant was hardly the size of a grain of rice; Maya marveled at it as Mitch dabbed the half-inch long cut and pressed a bandage over it.

"Now we can go." Mitch took the first-aid kit, the mercenary's gun, both of the girls' phones, and the two tiny implants. They followed him outside and watched as he put the phones and the implants in the agents' SUV. Then he made another call on his flip phone.

"I need a cleanup," he grunted. "Zero's house on Spruce Street. Four. One car. Take it west and then vanish it." He hung up.

The three of them climbed into the cab of an old pickup that had "Third Street Garage" emblazoned on the side. It rumbled to life and pulled away from the curb.

Neither of the girls looked back.

Maya, seated in the center between Mitch and Sara, noted the mechanic's thick knuckles, his fingertips stained in both grease and blood. "So where are we going?" she asked.

Mitch grunted without taking his eyes off the road. "Nebraska."

Chapter Seven

Zero parked the car right on the abandoned airstrip of Meadow Field. He had taken a slightly circuitous route there, sticking to back roads and avoiding the highways for fear that the CIA might have flagged his car—which he was certain they had.

Meadow Field was comprised of just a single runway, the building and hangar long since torn down in the fifteen years of disuse. Weeds and flowers sprouted up through cracks in the tarmac and the ignored grass on either side of the runway grew tall with disregard.

But despite its appearance, it was a gratifying and welcome sight for Zero. About thirty yards away was an old pickup truck, the side of it painted with stenciled letters that read "Third Street Garage." The burly mechanic leaned against the driver's side door, his trucker's cap pulled low over his brow.

As Zero hurried over to the truck, his daughters climbed out of the cab and ran to him. He grabbed one of them in each arm, ignoring the pain in his broken hand as he squeezed them both tight.

"You okay?" he asked.

"There was some trouble," Maya admitted as she hugged him back. "But we had help."

Zero nodded and released them, but stayed down on his knee so that he was just about eye level with Sara. "All right, listen to me. I'm going to be straight with you." He had been thinking about it the whole ride here, what he would say to them, and he'd decided to just lay it out. Their lives were already in danger as it was, and they deserved to know why. "There are some powerful people who want to start a war. They've been planning it for a long time, and it's all for their personal gain. If they're allowed to get away with this, it will mean a lot of innocent people dying. I'm going to talk to the president directly and alert him to what's going on, but I can't trust that he won't put his faith in the wrong hands. This could very well lead to a new world war."

"And you can't let that happen," Sara said quietly.

Maya nodded solemnly.

"That's right. And ..." Zero breathed a heavy sigh. "And it means that things are probably going to be bad for a little while. They know that the two of you are the easiest way to get to me, so you need to disappear and hide out until this is all over. I don't know when that will be. I don't know..." He stopped himself again. He wanted to tell them, *I don't know that I'll survive this*, but he couldn't bring himself to say the words.

He didn't have to. They knew what he meant. Tears welled in Maya's eyes and she looked away. Sara hugged him again, and he squeezed her tightly.

"You're going to go with Mitch, and you're going to have to do whatever he says, okay?" Zero heard tremors in his own voice. He was keenly aware, now more so than ever, that this might be the last time he ever saw his girls. "He'll keep you safe. And you watch each other's back."

"We will," Sara whispered in his ear.

"Good. Now you stay put for a minute while I go talk to Mitch. I'll be right back." He let go of Sara and strode over to the pickup truck where the mechanic was waiting idly.

"Thank you," Zero told him. "You don't owe me anything. I appreciate all of this, and when it's done I'll pay you back in whatever way I'm able."

"No need," the mechanic grunted. His trucker's cap was still pulled low, obscuring his eyes while his thick beard covered the rest of his face.

"Where will you take them?"

"There's an old WITSEC house in rural Nebraska," Mitch said. "Small cabin just outside a small town, practically middle of nowhere. Hasn't been used in years but it's still a government listing. I'll take 'em there. They'll be safe."

"Thank you," Zero said again. He didn't know what else to say. He wasn't even sure why he was so easily able to trust this man with the two most important people in his life; it was a feeling, an instinct that transcended logic. But he had learned long ago—and relearned only hours ago—to trust his instincts.

"So," Mitch grunted. "It's finally happening, isn't it?"

Zero blinked at him in surprise. "Yes," he said cautiously. "You know about all this?"

"I do."

He almost scoffed. "Who are you really?"

"A friend." Mitch checked his wristwatch. "Chopper should be here any moment. It'll take us to a private airfield, where we'll hop a plane out west."

Zero deflated. It didn't seem like he was getting any more answers out of the mysterious mechanic. "Thanks," he murmured once more. Then he turned back to say goodbye to his girls.

"You're back," said the mechanic behind him. "Aren't you?"

Zero turned. "Yeah. I'm back."

"When?"

He chuckled. "Today, if you can believe it. It's been a very strange afternoon."

"Well," Mitch said. "I wouldn't want to disappoint you."

Zero froze. An electric tingle ran up his spine. Mitch's voice had changed suddenly, no longer the grunting basso from just seconds prior. It was smooth and even, and so oddly familiar that Zero forgot about the Division and his situation and even his waiting daughters for a moment.

Mitch reached up beneath the brim of his trucker's cap and rubbed his eyes. At least that's what it looked like he was doing, but when his hand came away there were two tiny concave discs on his fingertips, crystalline blue.

Contacts. He was wearing colored contacts.

Then Mitch took off the trucker's cap, smoothed his hair, and looked up at Zero. His brown eyes looked forlorn, almost ashamed, and in an instant Zero knew exactly why.

"Jesus." His voice came out in a hoarse whisper as he looked at his eyes.

He knew those eyes. He'd know them anywhere. But it couldn't be. It wasn't possible. "Christ. You ... you were dead."

"So were you for a couple years there," the mechanic said in his smooth, almost lilting tone.

"I saw your body," Zero choked out. *This can't be real.*

"You saw a body that looked like mine." The burly man shrugged one shoulder. "Let's not pretend I wasn't always smarter than you, Zero."

"Good god." Zero looked him up and down. He'd put on about thirty pounds, maybe more. Grown out the beard. Wore the trucker's cap and colored lenses. Changed his voice.

But it was him. He was alive.

"I don't believe it." He took two steps and hugged Alan tightly.

His best friend, the one who had his back on so many ops, the one who had helped him have the memory suppressor installed instead of killing him on the Hohenzollern Bridge, the one that Zero thought he had found dead, stabbed to death in an apartment in Zurich ... he was here. He was alive.

He thought back to the discovery in Zurich. The dead man's face had been puffy and bloated, and his mind had immediately linked the doppelganger to Reidigger. *Your mind fills in the blanks,* Maria had once told him.

Reidigger had faked his own death, just like he had helped Kent Steele fake his. And he had been living under the guise of a well-connected mechanic only twenty minutes away.

"All this time?" Zero asked. His voice was hoarse, and his vision blurred slightly as a well of emotions bubbled to the surface. "You've been keeping an eye on us?"

"As best I could. Watson helped."

That's right. Watson knows. It was John Watson who had first introduced Reid Lawson to Mitch the mechanic—but he had only done so when Reid's daughters were taken, when the stakes were too high and the CIA was of little help.

"Does anyone else know?" Zero asked.

Alan shook his head. "No. And they can't. If the agency catches on, I'm a dead man."

"You could have told me sooner."

"No, I couldn't have." Alan smiled. "Without your memory intact, would you have recognized me? Would you have believed me if I simply told you?"

Zero had to admit he had a point.

"Was it Dr. Guyer? Did you go to see him?"

"I did," Zero said. "It didn't work at the time. It happened later, with a trigger word. And now…" He shook his head. "Now I know. I remember. I have to stop it, Alan."

"I know you do. And you know that there's nothing I'd like more than to be by your side while you do."

"But you can't be." Zero understood completely. Besides, Alan had a task that was, in Zero's eyes, just as significant to stopping a war. "I need you to keep them safe."

"I will. I promise I will." Alan's eyes lit up suddenly. "That reminds me, I have something for you." He reached through the open window of his truck and pulled out a Sig Sauer pistol. "Here. Compliments of the Division merc that assaulted your house."

Zero took the pistol incredulously. "The Division was at my house? What happened?"

"Nothing we couldn't handle. Those two are definitely your kids." Alan grinned, but it faded quickly. "You need help too, you know. Call Watson. Or your new pal, the Ranger."

"No," Zero said adamantly. He refused to compromise Watson or Strickland any further than he already had. "I'm better on my own."

Alan sighed. "Just as bullheaded as ever." In the distance, the telltale rotors of a helicopter drew nearer. "That's our ride. You take care of yourself, Zero."

"I will." He hugged Reidigger once more. "Thank you for doing this. When all this is over, you and I are going to sit down and have a very long conversation over several beers."

"You got it," Reidigger agreed. But there was a melancholic dip in his tone, one that suggested he was thinking the same as Zero was at the moment—that one or both of them might not survive this ordeal. "Until then—don't trust them."

He frowned. "Who?"

"Anyone in the agency," Alan said. "They were ready to kill you before, and they were happy to have me as the triggerman. They're not going to make that same mistake again. This time around they'll send someone who won't lose a minute of sleep putting a bullet in the back of your head."

"I know." Zero shook his head. "I was thinking of at least getting in touch with Cartwright. I don't think he's in on it—"

"Christ, what did I just say? No one, you understand?" Alan's gaze bored into his. "Especially not Cartwright. Zero … two years ago, Cartwright was the one that sent me and Morris after you on the bridge."

"What?" A shiver ran up Zero's spine.

"Yes. He didn't send the Division. He didn't send any killer asset. The order came down the chain for your assassination and Cartwright didn't argue it. He sent us."

A wave of fury rose like heat in his chest. Shawn Cartwright had pretended to be a friend, an ally, and had even warned Zero against trusting others like Riker.

The pounding of the chopper's rotors roared overhead as it hovered over Meadow Field. Alan leaned in and said in his ear, "Goodbye, Zero." He clapped his friend on the shoulder and strode away to meet the helicopter as it descended to the tall grass.

Zero hurried over to his waiting girls and hugged them both tightly once more. "I love you both," he said in their ears. "Be good and take care of each other."

"Love you too," Sara told him with a squeeze.

"We will," Maya promised as she wiped her eyes.

"Now go." He let them go, and they hurried over to the black helicopter. They both glanced back at him once more before climbing into the cabin with Alan's help. Then the door slid closed, and the chopper lifted off again. Zero stood there for a long moment, watching it as it got smaller and smaller in the sky. His head was still spinning from the knowledge that Alan Reidigger was somehow alive, but knowing that his daughters were in Alan's hands gave him hope—and all the more determination to survive this.

Finally he tore his gaze from what was now a mere speck on the horizon and headed back to the car. For a few brief moments he sat there behind the wheel, wondering if that was the last time he would ever see his daughters. The sound of blood rushing in his ears was deafening.

He reached over and turned on the radio just for some noise. A male broadcaster's voice immediately filled the cab.

"Our top story today continues to be the unfolding situation in the Persian Gulf," the host said somberly. "Only hours ago an Iranian battleship fired rockets at the USS *Constitution*, an American destroyer on patrol with the Navy's Fifth Fleet. In response, the *Constitution* returned fire, destroying the Iranian vessel and claiming the lives of all seventy-six crew members aboard."

They're moving fast. A pit formed in Zero's stomach. He hadn't expected this to unfold so quickly. *That just means I have to move faster.*

"The Iranian government has already issued a public statement," the broadcaster continued, "in which they expressed their outrage over the destruction of their ship and proclaimed, and I quote, that 'this event has been a clear and blatant act of war.' Though there has not been a formal declaration, it appears that Iran is intent on igniting a new conflict with the US. White House Press Secretary Christine Cleary issued a very brief statement in response, stating only that President Pierson is fully aware of the situation and his cabinet is working quickly to convene the joint chiefs. He is expected to address the nation this evening."

So that was their next play. The Brotherhood's attack on American soil would stir the people into a state of xenophobia against Iranians, and the "attack" on the USS *Constitution* was a timely follow-up to incite a war. The president would meet with his advisors, and they would convince him that a renewed conflict in the Middle East was their only course of action.

Unless, he thought suddenly, *he had a new advisor.*

He pulled a card out of his pocket and dialed the number on it.

"Sanders," answered the female aide who had approached him on the White House lawn.

"This is Agent Kent Steele," he told her. "We met earlier today—"

"I recall," she said abruptly. There was a tension in her voice, undoubtedly due to the recent events. "What can I do for you, Agent?"

"I need to speak with President Pierson."

"I'm afraid he's in a meeting," said Sanders. "I'm sure you're aware of what's happening—"

"I am." This time Zero cut her off. "And that's why I'm calling. This is matter of national security, Ms. Sanders. So you can either get me a meeting with President Pierson, or you can explain to him later that you stood between him and everything that's about to happen."

CHAPTER EIGHT

Less than a half hour later, Zero found himself once again in the White House, being ushered down a hall toward the Oval Office. He tried to smooth the wrinkles from his shirt, though it hardly mattered under the circumstances.

He was admitted to the president's inner sanctum, where he was surprised to find Pierson alone. Zero had expected a flurry of activity, a coterie of aides and cabinet members making calls, setting up laptop networks and communicating with a dozen different agencies and foreign powers.

Yet there was none. President Pierson rose from his desk when Zero entered, looking as if he'd aged a decade since only a few hours earlier. His tie was loosened around his neck and the top two buttons of his pressed white shirt were undone.

"Agent Steele." Pierson stuck out his right hand, and then scoffed at himself and shook Zero's left. "Sorry. Forgot about the hand. Jesus, this is a mess."

"I've heard." Zero glanced about the office. "I have to admit, I was expecting more of a reception."

"The joint chiefs are gathering currently in the Situation Room." Pierson sighed and leaned against his desk with both hands. "I'm expected there any minute. While I'm glad you're here, Zero, I'm afraid this meeting is going to have to be postponed."

"Mr. President," Zero pressed, "I have information." The fingers of his left hand lingered near his pocket, inside of which was the USB stick. "Before you convene with the joint chiefs, there's really something I need you to—"

"Sir." The door to the Oval Office opened just a few inches, and the face of Emilia Sanders peered in. Her gaze flitted from the president to Zero and back. "They're ready for you."

"Thank you, Emilia." Pierson tightened his tie to his throat and ran his palms down the front of his shirt. "I'm sorry, Zero, but my attention is required elsewhere."

"Sir." He took a step forward and lowered his voice to a conspiratorial level. He had to throw a Hail Mary; there was no way he could let Pierson enter the Situation Room uninformed. "I have very strong reason to believe that you cannot trust the men that are advising you."

The president's brow furrowed. "What reason? What do you know?"

"I have ..." Zero started, but he threw a glance over his shoulder to find a Secret Service agent standing in the doorway to the Oval Office, waiting to escort the president to the Situation Room. "I can't explain it right now. All I need is five minutes. Alone."

Pierson rubbed his chin. He looked tired. "Come with me."

"Sir?"

"Sit in on this meeting. Afterwards, I'll give you your five minutes." Pierson started toward the door, and Zero followed. It was all he could; he couldn't dissuade the president from attending a meeting regarding a crisis of national security. And if it would get him five minutes alone with Pierson, then he would follow him into the lion's den.

The John F. Kennedy Conference Room, located in the West Wing basement and known to most as the Situation Room, was the intelligence management center of the White House, more than five thousand square feet of communications equipment that allowed some of the most powerful men in the world to maintain security from a single place.

And Zero, it seemed, had just been awarded earned a seat at the table.

President Pierson swept into the room on the heels of two Secret Service members, who immediately positioned themselves on either side of the double doors that granted them access. Zero followed behind him. Now this was the flurry of activity that he had expected upon arrival; there were fourteen people occupying the long rectangular table that ran the length of the room, and every one of them stood when the president entered.

Zero glanced around quickly, scanning the faces. He recognized nearly all of them; the National Security Advisor was present, the Homeland Security Advisor, the White House Chief of Staff, Secretary of Defense Quentin Rigby, DNI John Hillis, and Press Secretary Christine Cleary, among others. He couldn't help but note wryly that besides himself, Pierson, and Cleary, every other person in the room was a man over fifty-five.

He was mildly relieved to see that the CIA did not have a presence there. He'd half-expected to find Director Mullen or possibly even Deputy Director Riker rearing their heads. But this was a matter for heads of state, and the CIA was represented by DNI Hillis, who would be the one to relay any orders to Mullen.

"Please, take your seats." Pierson lowered himself into the black chair at the head of the table, closest to the doors. He gestured toward the empty seat to his right and Zero took it.

Several pairs of eyes were on him as he did, but only the Secretary of Defense spoke up. Retired four-star general Quentin Rigby carried a stiffness in his neck and shoulders and wore deep worry lines in his face that suggested he had seen the worst sides of humanity, and though discerning, he was not afraid to speak his mind.

"Mr. President." Rigby remained standing as he addressed Pierson. "I don't think I need to remind you that what we're about to discuss is highly discretionary—"

"Noted, General Rigby, thank you." Pierson cut off the general with a wave of his hand. "Agent Steele is here acting as a security advisor. He's been vetted by the CIA and has proven his capacity for discretion time and time again. Not to mention that he's the only one in this room with any recent experience with the type of situation we're dealing with."

"Even so," Rigby pressed, "it is highly unorthodox, sir."

"I don't think I need to remind *you*, General, that I am the only person that gets to decide who is in this room." Pierson stared Rigby down.

Zero almost smirked. He had never heard Pierson speak to anyone like that; usually his approach was diplomacy and charm. On the one hand, Zero could tell that the president was bedraggled by the events. On the other, it was nice to see him showing some real backbone.

Rigby nodded and lowered himself back into his seat. "Yes sir."

"Mr. Holmes." President Pierson nodded to his Chief of Staff, a short balding man with owlish glasses. "If you would."

"Of course, sir." Peter Holmes rose and cleared his throat. "At approximately seventeen hundred hours local time, an Iranian battleship fired two rockets at the destroyer USS *Constitution* during a routine patrol in the Persian Gulf. Due to the recent change in ROE, with which I believe we're all familiar, the *Constitution* was authorized to—"

"Excuse me." Zero raised his hand as if he was in a classroom, cutting off the Chief of Staff. "What change in ROE?"

"The rules of engagement, Agent," said Holmes.

"I know the acronym," Zero said shortly. "What was the change?"

"In light of the recent attack on American soil," Rigby cut in, "the president signed an executive order just this morning which dictates that any foreign force that fires within a specific proximity to American military personnel are to be considered hostile and dealt with using extreme prejudice."

Zero didn't let himself show any reaction, but his mind churned. *What a coincidence*, he thought. "And what is the specific proximity, General?"

"We're not here to outline the details of an executive order," Rigby shot back. "We're here to discuss an extremely pressing and volatile situation."

Rigby was dodging the question. "What was the trajectory of the rockets?" Zero asked.

"Sorry?" Holmes pushed his glasses up the bridge of his nose.

"The trajectory," Zero repeated. "Angle of ascent, descent, type of rocket, proximity, anything. How much of a threat was this ship to the *Constitution*?"

"Enough of a threat for a captain in the United States Navy to make a judgment call," said Rigby forcefully. "Are you questioning the captain's judgment, Agent Steele?"

I'm questioning his motivations, he nearly said. But he held his tongue. He couldn't afford to tip his hand again like he had twice already. "Not at all. I'm merely suggesting that there are three sides to this story. The captain's, the Iranians', and the truth. What about cameras?"

"Cameras," Rigby repeated flatly. He flashed a patronizing smirk. "Do you know a lot about destroyer-class ships, Agent?"

"Can't say I have a lot of experience." This time Zero flashed a smirk of his own. "All I know is that the USS *Constitution* is an Arleigh-Burke class destroyer, built in 1988 and first commissioned in 1991. They were the only US destroyer class used from 2005 to 2016, until the Zumwalt class was commissioned. The *Constitution* would be outfitted with an Aegis integrated weapons system, anti-submarine rockets, a passive electronically scanned radar array, and Tomahawk missiles—the latter of which I'm assuming was used to destroy the Iranian vessel and claim seventy-six lives. Considering it is one of the most technologically advanced machines on the entire ocean, and that it's carrying enough firepower to conquer any number of banana republics, I would assume that cameras weren't out of the question."

Rigby stared him down for a long moment. "No cameras picked up the angle of attack," he said finally. "But you're welcome to read the captain's report if you'd like." The general slid a folder Zero's way.

He opened it; the first page was a very brief report, only a few paragraphs, from a Captain Warren. The details were sparse.

Warren claimed simply that an IRGC ship fired two rockets at the *Constitution.* Neither hit, but the attempt was deemed enough of a threat for Warren to make the judgment call to return fire—with, as Zero had predicted, eight Tomahawk missiles. The enemy ship had been obliterated.

Not only was it overkill, but that was the only part of the report that Zero actually believed. Anything else would have been easy to falsify. The Persian Gulf, and Captain Warren, was thousands of miles away. Far from anyone being able to question him meaningfully.

"Brass tacks," said Rigby, "are that Iran is publicly considering this an act of war. They say we fired first. We say they fired first. There's been no formal declaration of war from them, but the American people are going to expect a definitive answer. We cannot abide another attack—"

"Another attack?" Zero interjected again.

Rigby blinked at him. "Were you not in the Midtown Tunnel at the time of the bombing, Agent? When hundreds of American lives were lost?"

Zero shook his head. "That was the work of a radical terrorist faction that consisted of less than twenty men. Not an entire nation or region."

"Tell that to the American people," Rigby argued.

Zero said nothing in response, but he knew in that moment that his assumption was right. The conspirators wanted to use the recent attack as a way to rally the people to the cause of war.

"All right," Pierson cut in, holding up a hand. "Let's take a step back here. Roland, what sort of global responses are we seeing?"

The Secretary of State, Roland Kemmerer, quickly scanned his notes as he spoke. "Bad news first, I suppose. Intelligence and satellite recon suggests that Iran is already seeking allies in Iraq and Oman, as well as some Syrian nationalist groups. If they banded together, they would have the ability to close the Strait of Hormuz."

There was a moment of reverential silence to allow the comment to sink in before Rigby said, "You know how detrimental that could be, Mr. President."

"Not only would that eliminate a strategic advantage for the Fifth Fleet," Holmes added, "but we could be facing a major economic downturn."

"A recession, to say the least. Possibly worse." Kemmerer shook his head.

Zero bit his tongue to keep from reacting. *Sons of bitches.* This was as rehearsed as a play. They'd been waiting for years for this exact moment. He never would have imagined that he would be present for it, yet here he was, sitting in the Situation Room as these warmongers attempted to sway a president.

Pierson rubbed his chin pensively. His face was ashen; not only was he the sole person responsible for whether or not America would go to war, but a recession was clearly not something he had considered previously. "Is there any good news?"

The Secretary of State sighed. "Eventually. The UN wants to investigate the incident. The European Union, China, Japan, and most other allies are already issuing proclamations of neutrality in any future conflict that might arise. Except for one."

Zero knew it well before Kemmerer even said it.

"Russia." The Secretary of State fidgeted slightly in his seat. "It seems their own trade agreements with Iran have been deteriorating. They're ready to lend their support if we need it."

"President Ivanov has already pledged resources to our cause if we decided that it was in our best interests," said Holmes.

"War," the president murmured. "Might as well call it what it is. If war is in our best interests."

Zero glanced over at Pierson. The president's complexion had taken on a sallow aspect, and he stared blankly at the shiny mahogany tabletop. Despite how adept Zero was at reading expressions and tells, he couldn't say whether or not Pierson was buying the load of bullshit that his cabinet was selling. But if he had to guess, he would say that Pierson was caving.

"General Rigby," the president asked, "what's your position?"

Here it comes. The blatant advice that the US go to war in the Middle East.

"It is my position that we mobilize the Fifth Fleet," said Rigby, "and show them our full potential in the Persian Gulf. We can call in additional assets from the Gulf of Oman. But…" The general paused and shook his head. "I cannot advise that we initiate a war over this."

Zero balked. He couldn't hide his reaction this time; his mouth fell open slightly at the general's remark. Rigby was playing a part, he was certain, but it was still a curveball.

"I believe that we should hold our position in the Gulf and let the Iranians know that we want to avoid conflict in any way possible," he continued. "If they act, we react, but until then, we stay the course."

"With all due respect, General," said Holmes, "I'm not sure that perspective will sit well with the American people in the wake of recent events."

"No," Pierson agreed, "but the general is right. We can't allow this situation to get blown out of proportion, and I don't believe the Iranians are going to declare war without further provocation. Mr. Holmes," he addressed his Chief of Staff, "let's begin immediately on an address to the nation. We'll explain that the attack in the Persian Gulf did not result in any loss of American life, and that we will not be goaded into any hostilities."

"Yes sir, Mr. President."

Zero's mind was working a mile a minute. He had fully expected this to be the meeting in which the US declared war on Iran and took swift action to control the Strait of Hormuz…

Oh. The realization struck him like a brick to the head. To declare war now would make their intentions too obvious. He, Agent Zero, had figured it out, and while he knew he was fiercely intelligent—there was that hubris again—others were too. Someone else could assume the same as him. No, these people had years to plan this. They weren't in any rush.

He had thought, had assumed that this entire meeting was the play. But this was just the rehearsal. Which meant… *There is going to be something else. Not an attack. Not a fight.*

They already know that Iran is going to close the strait.

Pierson would have no choice but to take action then. They had introduced the concept. Now they had to only bide their time. From there, the escalation would be quick and ruthless—and it would end with the US controlling the strait, since Iran and Oman would no longer be trustworthy or stable.

Pierson stood. "All right, thank you, everyone. I want to be kept fully updated. Until then, dismissed." As the assembly stood from their seats, Pierson glanced down at his wrinkled shirt and muttered, "I should probably change before the address."

"Sir." Zero kept his voice low over the sound of wheels scraping against the floor and papers rustling. "Our meeting?" He still had a chance to stop this. The war hadn't been declared yet, and the USB stick was still burning a hole in his pocket. "There's something I need to share with you."

Pierson scrutinized him for a moment. He opened his mouth to respond, but another voice cut in before he could.

"Agent Steele." The Director of National Intelligence, John Hillis, was in his mid-sixties. The skin beneath his chin hung in jowls but his eyes were as sharp and observant as a bird of prey. "Director Mullen didn't tell me you would be here. You're not thinking of leaving the agency for a cushy security job, are you?" Hillis chuckled lightly.

Director Mullen doesn't know I'm here. But he will now. Zero's cover would be blown. He had no doubt that Hillis would report this to Mullen, and the CIA would soon know that Agent Zero was dodging their calls while rubbing shoulders with the president.

"What is it you need to share with me, Zero?" Pierson asked.

He definitely noticed the tiny, almost imperceptible raise in Hillis's eyebrow. "Whatever it is, protocol would dictate that you bring it to your superiors, would it not?" Hillis smiled, though his eyes did not. "Allow them to decide whether or not it should go up the chain?"

"Ordinarily, yes." Zero locked eyes with Hillis and returned the joyless smile. "But you know how these sensitive reports can be. Sometimes it requires a firsthand account, sir."

Pierson glanced between the two men. He seemed to at least understand that something was going on, some mutual understanding was passing between them, though he didn't know what.

"You have five minutes, Zero." Pierson nodded to the two Secret Service men posted at the door. "Oval Office."

"Sir," said Hillis, stepping forward, "perhaps I should join you. Anything the CIA might have to share is of particular interest to me."

A knot formed in Zero's stomach. This wasn't a situation that he could fight or shoot his way out of. If he denied the DNI, they would certainly know something was up and that Zero had information—which many of them would likely already be assuming by virtue of his presence in the Situation Room. He couldn't allow John Hillis to be present when he presented what was on the USB drive to the president.

But he didn't have to. As he stood there trying to think of some excuse to keep Hillis out of the way, a female voice piped up from the now-open double doors of the Situation Room.

"Director Hillis?" It was Emilia Sanders, the brunette aide. "You're needed right away on line three."

Hillis frowned. "It's going to have to wait—"

"It's your wife," Sanders pressed. "She said it's urgent."

The DNI gritted his teeth. Then he whisked past them without another word.

Zero was keenly away of how fortuitous—and how equally unlikely—it was that Hillis would be called away in the moment he needed to be rid of him.

Stranger still was that as the director left the Situation Room, Zero could have sworn that the woman, Sanders, gave a tiny nod in his direction.

Definitely strange, he thought. It was just one more thing to figure out, right behind who had posed as his wife and stolen his documents, who had sent the Division members after him, and how to stop an international crisis from unfolding.

Chapter Nine

"Five minutes, Zero." President Pierson closed the doors to the Oval Office with the two of them once again alone inside it. "That's all I can afford under the circumstances. You understand."

"Of course, sir." He reached into his pocket and pulled out the USB stick. Then he gestured to the laptop on the president's desk. "May I use that?"

Pierson nodded. Zero rounded the desk and powered up the computer. He wondered if it was being monitored. *Doesn't matter much now,* he thought. What was important was that Pierson heard what he had stowed on the small black drive.

"I haven't had a drink in six months," the president mused quietly.

"That so?" Zero pushed the drive into the USB port.

"Mm-hmm. Had some problems with the stuff in my youth. I learned moderation, then cut it out altogether. But I'll be damned if I'm not having one tonight."

There was a knock at the door of the Oval Office. Emilia Sanders appeared once again, holding a coat hanger on which hung a dark suit jacket and a fresh red tie. "Sir," was all she said as she draped the outfit over an armchair.

Despite Zero's attempt to make eye contact with her, she was gone just as quickly as she'd appeared, and then the door was closed again.

He looked down at the screen. The laptop was fairly new and the USB drive was two years old. The computer had to download the drivers before it could open any files. He resisted the urge to curse aloud and instead bit his lip.

Pierson tugged off his tie and plucked up the new one. He gestured toward a portrait hanging on the wall to the right of the desk and beside the wide window with golden curtains. "What do you think he'd make of all this?"

Zero looked up at the portrait. "Nothing good." The drivers were still downloading. *Hurry up.* "George Washington was an isolationist. Did you know that?"

Pierson smirked a little and furrowed his brow. "I didn't."

"He was. After the Revolution, he disbanded the Continental Army. Didn't think the country needed one. He was quite vocal about never going through that again—a war like that. An expenditure of American lives, let alone resources." He felt like he was in a lecture hall again, speaking casually to a group of grad students. It felt so natural that he doubted his earlier thought, about Reid Lawson being his alter ego and Zero being his reality. This felt just as real. "He wanted nothing to do with foreign affairs, world wars, any of that. The whole Second Amendment thing that gets everyone all fired up? That was pretty much to avoid ever needing an army, you know."

Pierson chuckled. "You're talking to a Republican president. Try explaining that to my voters."

Zero grinned. "My point is that Washington wouldn't be very pleased with what we've done with his country for the last two hundred years or so."

Finally. A popup window appeared and told him that the device was ready to be used. He double-clicked the drive and opened it. There were only a handful of files on it, audio clips, and each was only thirty seconds long.

Before opening the first file, he said, "Washington dreamed of an America that was self-sustaining. That relied only on itself." He paused for a moment. "You know what the opposite of an isolationist is, right?"

"It's been a while since ninth grade history," Pierson admitted, "but I believe that would be an imperialist."

Zero met the president's gaze. "That's right. One who wants to build an empire. America is an empire, Mr. President. Make no mistake about it. And there are people who want to expand that definition and what it encompasses, whether you're aware of it or not. Would you join me over here for a moment, please?"

Pierson frowned at Zero's sudden change in demeanor, from conversational to somber, and rounded the desk. "What am I looking at?"

"You're not looking at anything. You're listening." He opened the first audio file and played it.

There was a hiss of static, and then a familiar male voice spoke, the audio file picking up mid-sentence. "...Sent the Division to rendezvous with Ivanov." The voice was unmistakable, at least to Zero's ears. It belonged to CIA Director James Mullen. "He's in Afghanistan with an attaché of Russian politicians under the guise of a goodwill mission. You'll be there to meet him?"

"I'm en route now." The second voice was gruff, with a slight rasp, and one they had both heard only minutes earlier. It was the Secretary of Defense, General Quentin Rigby. "What about the other thing?"

"I believe we've found someone," said Mullen on the recording. "There's a Libyan at our Moroccan site, H-6, that could do the job when the time comes. He's certainly not going anywhere in the meantime."

"Good," said Rigby. "And the scapegoats?"

"Nothing definitive yet. We've located a potential cell, a group of former Hamas members that have been hiding out in a compound in Iraq. They're inactive—for now. Intelligence shows they're led by an old man called bin Mohammad. It wouldn't be difficult to create a situation—" The recording cut off there, after thirty seconds.

Just over two years earlier, Zero had managed to slip a piece of tech from Bixby's lab that he used to tap Mullen's cell phone and record the call. However, the device could only be active for thirty seconds at a time; any longer than that and CIA security would be aware that there was a track on it.

He had logged hours and hours of conversation, at thirty seconds a clip, waiting for something pertinent to his case to be revealed. It had taken a long time, and yielded very few results—only two, in fact.

Pierson shook his head slightly. "I don't understand."

"You know those voices," Zero said. "That was CIA Director Mullen speaking to General Rigby." He looked Pierson right in the eye and kept his tone low. "Mr. President, I'm going to lay it right out for you. Two years ago, I discovered the makings of a plot created by people in your administration. Their plan was to manufacture a war between the United States and the Middle East, with the goal of gaining control of the Strait of Hormuz and, from there, other key oil-producing regions. Their intention is to make America into a larger empire. To solidify our standing as the world's premier superpower. To keep those in power in their seats, and for the rich to get richer. This is not about patriotism. This is not about showing strength or saving lives. This is about control. Two years ago, I thought I had time to investigate, to find evidence. But that time is up. What we're seeing now is the beginning. And they are expecting you to bend."

Pierson let out a ragged sigh. "Zero," he said quietly, "this is an extremely grave and sensitive accusation you're making."

"I'm aware, sir, but I'm making it nonetheless. The Brotherhood attack was orchestrated; bin Mohammad's death was somehow arranged, and Awad bin Saddam was goaded into believing that the plan was his own. But it wasn't. The Libyan arms dealer that supplied them with the submarine drones was from the CIA black site, H-6. The drones themselves were CIA tech. Given time, I could confirm all of this—"

"But you don't have time," Pierson concluded. "Is this all you have? Audio clips of vague conversation?"

Zero gritted his teeth. "I had documents. I was building a case. But they were stolen from me."

"So you have nothing more to go on…"

"Except the truth," he said forcefully. "Do you really believe that an Iranian ship fired on our own within hours of the change of

ROE? Do you think it's a coincidence that this came in the direct wake of an attack on American soil, while the media is shoehorning Muslims everywhere, vilifying them?"

Pierson rubbed his forehead. "Your superiors don't know that you're here, do they?"

Zero shook his head. "They didn't. They probably do now." *Thanks to Hillis.* He had little doubt that the DNI would be reporting to Mullen that Zero had been present in the Situation Room and had requested to see the president alone. "I hope you understand how dangerous this is for me. For my family. But it's important. This could save hundreds of thousands of lives."

"All right. Let's just say, for a moment, that you're right. You bring this to me now, when it's almost too late? What do you want me to do about it?"

"It's not too late. You're the only person who could take swift and immediate action." Zero paused for a moment. "Dismiss them. Fire them. Get rid of them."

Pierson scoffed. "You're asking me to fire my Secretary of Defense while we're actively dealing with an international crisis?"

"No, Mr. President. I'm asking you to fire your entire cabinet."

Pierson paled. He turned away from Zero and paced slowly. "Zero, I really want to trust you. But you're out of your mind if you think I can do that and survive the American public, let alone the next election."

"That's what they're counting on, sir."

"Maybe it doesn't have to be so drastic. We could open an investigation—"

"You can't," Zero argued. "We have no idea how deep this goes. It's not just Rigby, Holmes, Hillis, Mullen. It would require more than that. FBI, NSA, congressmen, senators... possibly even the VP."

Pierson spun to face him, a flash of anger crossing his face. "There's a line, Zero—"

"And crossing it means war." Zero wasn't backing down from this and he wasn't about to apologize. It was his only chance.

"I've known Cole for decades. There's no way he would keep something like this from me."

Zero shook his head sadly. "Believing that makes him the perfect person to do it."

Both of their heads turned abruptly at the sound of a sharp knock at the door to the Oval Office. "One moment!" Pierson called out.

Zero had run out of time. He tugged the USB stick from the laptop and pushed it into Pierson's hand. "Keep this. Keep it safe. Listen to the other files when you're able. They'll sound vague, possibly coded, but if you put them in the context of what I've told you, I think you'll see that I'm right."

Pierson nodded. "It's my military. I won't let them start a war."

"They've been planning this for a long time. They'll find a way. Don't trust anyone, Mr. President. You can't afford to."

There was a second knock, and then the office door swung open. On the other side were DNI Hillis and Chief of Staff Peter Holmes.

"Sir," said Holmes. "We have a statement prepared whenever you're ready."

"Agent Zero." Hillis smiled pleasantly. "Director Mullen would like to see you as soon as possible."

"Of course," said Zero. He had no intention of visiting Mullen or going anywhere near Langley.

"Thank you, Zero." Pierson shook his left hand. As he did, Zero leaned in and said, in practically a whisper, "The strait. Iran will close the strait, and that will force your hand. They're counting on it. Don't let them." Then louder he said, "Thank you, Mr. President."

He headed for the door, passing Peter Holmes as the Chief of Staff entered the office. He had a bad feeling that he hadn't been as persuasive as he could have been, or could have said more. Pierson was putting his trust in the wrong people, and those people would still be around him when the cards came tumbling down. They'd be the ones whispering in the president's ear, while Zero—well, the

CIA knew now that he had come here, that he had spoken to the president alone.

They've already come after me. Now they have nothing to lose.

Did I roll the dice and fail?

As he strode past Hillis, the director turned on a heel and followed. "There's a car waiting outside to take you to Langley."

Zero did not pause, though the DNI kept pace. "I drove myself here. I'll drive myself there."

Hillis's fake smile did not leave his face. "I don't think you understand, Agent Zero. I'll be escorting you there personally." As he said it, two Secret Service agents fell in stride with them. "Now."

Chapter Ten

Zero's throat ran dry. He was in the White House with a hundred people and a thousand cameras. He couldn't run. He couldn't fight his way out of this. The pair of Secret Service agents flanked him on either side, almost shoulder to shoulder.

"Let's keep those hands where we can see them," Hillis said casually.

Outside, the two Secret Service agents led him toward a waiting black SUV. The DNI got in the passenger-side back seat and motioned for Zero to get in on the other. As soon as the doors were closed again, the Secret Service men retreated back into the White House.

Behind the wheel was a man clad all in black wearing aviator sunglasses. Beside him was another, similarly dressed and wearing a black ball cap backward on his head. Zero recognized the insignia on the hat: it was a coiled silver snake set in an upside-down triangle.

They were from the Division.

Hillis sighed. "This is all just a real shame. You were our top guy. You could have played ball. You could have stayed dead."

Zero said nothing, though neither of those were options for him.

"You think we're the enemy, but we're not. This is for the greater good, Zero. The good of the American people. The good of the country. Everyone."

Not the innocents who will be slaughtered. Not the people whose homes will be bombed, whose families and neighbors will be killed all for the sake of a resource. But still he said nothing.

"It will be better for all of us if you don't try anything," Hillis continued. "These two gentlemen are pretty disgruntled at the moment, considering their two friends that were found dead in Arlington."

Zero didn't recognize either of them the way he had with Baker. Neither of them looked particularly pleasant. The man in the passenger seat held a pistol in his lap.

"You're no good to anyone dead," said the DNI. "Least of all your little girls."

"Threaten them again," he said quietly, "and I'll kill all of you."

Hillis sighed. "You've been in the field too long, my friend. This sort of situation can't be shot at. This is politics. This is the game. Are you really going to make death threats to the Director of National Intelligence? Because we don't have to go to Langley. We can go straight to Dulles and I can put you on a military plane to H-6."

Zero had been to Hell-Six, the nickname for the CIA black site in Morocco, several times. On some occasions he had personally escorted known terrorists there; other times it had been for interrogations of the prisoners held there. But calling it a prison wasn't accurate. It was an arrangement of holes in the ground where people were thrown and forgotten, left to die, rot, and eventually become the hole.

Hillis nodded to the driver. "Let's go."

The mercenary turned the key and the engine rumbled to life.

Before he could shift into drive, white smoke jetted out of the air conditioning vents.

"What the he—" The shout of the merc in the passenger seat was cut short by a racking spasm of a cough. The white smoke poured out of the vents, filling the SUV in just a few seconds.

Zero's eyes burned suddenly and he found himself caught in the paroxysm of a violent cough. He could hear the others, the driver and Hillis, doing the same. His throat burned fiercely; his eyes felt scorched even as he squeezed them shut.

He tried to pull the collar of his shirt up over his mouth and nose, but the gas had come so quickly and unexpectedly that there was no time. He hacked uncontrollably, unable to breathe, while the roiling nausea in his stomach threatened to make him vomit.

Then he heard a sound—the click of a car door. There was an arm on his, tugging. He didn't fight it. He went with it, clambering out of the car and falling to the pavement. The door slammed shut again. The arms hefted him up; they weren't strong enough to lift him, but he rose to his feet, still choking and rasping, his eyes burning so fiercely that he couldn't see a thing through the tears.

The arms guided him a short distance away, Zero stumbling and staggering and still coughing. A car door opened and he was shoved inside. The driver's side door opened. The engine started.

"Here." A female voice. A damp cloth in his hand. He pressed it over his face and wiped his eyes, even as he continued to cough and wheeze into it.

"Thank—" He tried to speak, but coughed again. "Thanks." The car jolted forward, the tires screeching slightly. "Thanks, Sanders."

As his vision began to clear, he saw her hazy figure beside him, staring straight ahead, focusing as she guided the car out to the street and around a corner. Emilia Sanders, the supposed president's aide, looked different now. She wore an expression of grim determination as she told him, "That was extremely foolish."

"Sorry?" he rasped.

"Why did you get in the car with them?" she demanded.

"What was I—" He coughed once more. "What was I supposed to do? Punch the Director of National Intelligence?"

"Considering what you know is at stake? Yes. You should have punched the Director of National Intelligence."

He wiped his face once more with the damp cloth and then balled it up and tossed it to the floor of the car. "Who are you?"

She said nothing in response.

"If you think I won't jump out of a moving car, you've got another think coming." He reached for the door handle.

"I'm not going to tell you my name." She said it quickly—and not in English, though he understood it nonetheless.

"You're Ukrainian." He scoffed. This was the last thing he wanted, getting mixed up with them again. "Are you FIS?" The Foreign Intelligence Service was Ukraine's version of the CIA.

"I was, when I went undercover two and a half years ago," she admitted. "But now… I don't know what I am. The FIS is compromised. Russian spies have infiltrated their ranks. Many of my superiors have been bought."

"So now you're just a freedom fighter?" he mused.

"I suppose."

"So how much do you know?"

"I know that my cover is likely blown," Sanders said bitingly. "Because you made a stupid decision and got in the car. Did you at least give the president what you had?"

"How in the hell do you know about…?" He trailed off, examining her. Her height. Her build. Even her facial features. *Son of a bitch.* "It was you. You posed as my wife to get into my safe deposit box. Where are my documents?"

"Safe."

"Not good enough." He reached over with his left hand and buckled his seatbelt.

"What are you—" Sanders started to ask, but before she could finish Zero grabbed the steering wheel and jerked it to the side.

The car skidded wildly into oncoming traffic. Brakes squealed and car horns blared as the sedan turned sharply, threatening to slam into the brick façade of a bank. Sanders slammed her foot on the brake, and the car screeched to a stop less than two feet from impact.

"Are you insane?!" she shrieked at him. "I am trying to help you!"

"Then answer me!" he hissed back.

"Let go of the wheel!"

He did so, and she put the car in reverse. More car horns honked angrily as she pulled back onto the road, letting loose a fusillade of muttered curses in Ukrainian.

"We've been following you for a long time," she said at last. "We knew about the case you were building because of your friend,

Johansson. It wasn't difficult to tail you to the bank. We hacked their system and found your deposit box. When you went dark for those two years, we let it lie. But when you were activated again, we took the documents for safekeeping. We weren't sure if you could be trusted with them, considering your lapsed memory. Or who else might know about them."

"Where are they?"

"My handler has them."

"That's not an answer."

"Richmond. He's hiding out in Richmond and he has the documents. He's been reviewing them. We're afraid your case is thin, Zero."

"I have evidence of the conspiracy," he argued. "Those documents would provide just cause for the dismissal of those involved."

"You would be extremely naïve to believe that would work. They'll fight it."

"You're not much of a people person, are you, Sanders?" He scoffed lightly. "Where are we going?"

"To a rendezvous," Sanders answered cryptically. "What did you give the president?"

"Audio files," he told her. "I had them hidden."

"And you think this will be enough?"

"We'll see," Zero answered quietly. "The ball is in Pierson's court, for now. There's no way I'm going to get close to him again. They won't let me. Besides, they're going to be looking for me."

"The CIA?" Sanders asked.

Zero looked out the window as Washington, DC, passed by. "Everyone."

Chapter Eleven

"Add just a little more color under the eyes." White House Chief of Staff Peter Holmes watched as a makeup artist carefully applied small amounts of foundation to President Pierson's cheeks, adding some color to his pallor. "No offense, Mr. President, but you've looked better."

"No kidding," Pierson murmured.

Holmes had his suspicions about what the CIA agent, Steele, had said to him when they were alone. But he hadn't asked, hadn't said anything at all about it. "Are you ready to address the nation, sir?"

"No," Pierson said flatly. "I'm not." To the makeup artist he said, "Please excuse us."

The woman nodded and abruptly left the office.

As soon as she was gone, Pierson rose from his chair and tugged the white cloth that had been draped over his neck to protect his clothes. He paced anxiously.

"Are you all right, sir?" Holmes asked cautiously.

"You've been with me since the beginning, Pete."

Here it comes, Holmes thought. They had prepared for this.

"You've never given me any reason to suspect you of lying or withholding information."

"Of course not, sir." It was true; Holmes had been the Chief of Staff since Pierson's inauguration. Their relationship went back even before then; Holmes had previously served in the House of Representatives for Pierson's home state of New York. The president had appealed to him on behalf of his business dealings to assist with legislation that would aid in aggressive expansion.

Not more than fifty years ago his position would have been known as Assistant to the President, and though he was glad for the change in title the former might have been more apt. As the Chief of Staff, he managed the president's schedule, arranged meetings, and controlled the flow of information in and out of the White House.

In essence, Holmes's involvement in the upcoming war effort was instrumental.

"I need the truth now more than ever." Pierson faced him, locking eyes, imploring him. "I trust you, Pete. I need you to tell me what's real."

Holmes sighed heavily. "I am so sorry, Eli," he said dramatically, using the president's first name for effect. "I didn't want you to have to hear this from me, and I wanted to wait until after your address to tell you."

"Tell me what?" Pierson raised his eyebrow.

Holmes paused for a long moment. "We have received confirmation from the CIA, straight from Director Mullen himself, that Agent Steele has gone rogue."

Pierson frowned in confusion. "I'm sorry?"

"I understand this might be difficult to hear," Holmes continued, speaking with conviction the words he had already been instructed to say. "He is, after all, the most decorated agent the CIA has ever known, and he's done more for this country than we can say about almost any man alive. But it's no secret that he's been having issues with his memory. Director Mullen has informed me that Steele has been having delusional episodes. Just last week he sent his two daughters to a safe house because he believed his fellow agents were trying to kill them."

"He thought the CIA was going after his children?" Pierson sat again heavily in the chair. "That doesn't make any sense."

"I know. I'm sorry, sir. I know that you two are—were—friendly."

Pierson's gaze flitted from the carpeted floor to his desk, just for a second, but long enough for Holmes to make a realization. *Zero gave him something.* He would have to report that.

"It was so convincing." Pierson had a faraway look in his eye. "He truly believes it."

"Mr. President, if you trust me, then you'll listen to me now." Holmes positioned himself in front of Pierson so that the president had to look at him, to see the sincerity that he had practiced so carefully. "No one wants war. It's an economic burden. It's a loss of American life. It's an expenditure of resources. Not even General Rigby wants it to come to that. You heard him in the meeting today. We should avoid it at all costs. However... I don't think it's wise to have someone that's potentially unstable whispering in your ear. You built this administration. You built this cabinet. Let us do our jobs. And let the CIA bring Agent Steele in."

"I want to speak to him again," said Pierson. "You get Mullen on the phone and you tell him that Zero isn't to be harmed. When he's brought in, I want to talk to him."

"Of course, sir." Holmes was afraid of that wrench in the gears. But then serendipity reared its beautiful head.

There was a brisk knock at the door and it opened quickly. A black-suited Secret Service agent swept in, a man named Raulsen. Holmes knew him as a former Navy SEAL and particularly discreet ever since both his sons' tuitions had been paid in full.

"I apologize for the intrusion, Mr. President," Raulsen said hastily. "Director Hillis was just attacked in his vehicle, along with both of his bodyguards."

Pierson was on his feet in an instant. "What? By whom?"

"Agent Kent Steele, sir."

Even with the makeup on his face, the president blanched.

"He used some sort of biological agent, a gas. All three are on their way to the hospital. But there's more, sir. Our camera feed picked up an accomplice. The driver of his getaway car... it was Emilia Sanders."

"What?" Pierson looked as if he might fall over.

Even Holmes was shocked at that news, but he also recognized opportunity when he saw it. "My god," he murmured. "Steele had someone on the inside? On *my* staff?" Holmes put a hand over his mouth. "Mr. President, I think it's time to acknowledge that you might not be safe here. Raulsen, what do you suggest?"

"My recommendation would be immediate relocation. Camp David, perhaps."

Holmes nodded. "You can address the nation from there while we work to vet every person working in this building." But Pierson said nothing. He hardly moved. "Sir?"

"Pete. This is too much." The president appeared shell-shocked. "Sanders was just an aide. She never ... She wouldn't have ..."

Holmes turned to Raulsen. "I'm making a judgment call here. Tell them to get Marine One prepped. You don't leave his side, do you understand?"

"Yes sir."

"Good. Get him out of here. Discreetly, Raulsen."

The Secret Service agent took Pierson gently by the arm. "Please come with me, Mr. President."

At last Pierson rose, and Raulsen ushered him out of the Oval Office.

"Thank you, Agent Steele," Holmes murmured to himself as soon as he was alone. The CIA agent had made it much easier now that he had assaulted the DNI. But Emilia Sanders was a curious angle, and Holmes did not like it at all.

He pulled out his phone and made a call.

"Rigby," the general answered gruffly.

"It's Holmes. Zero got to Pierson, just as we expected. But he's gone and attacked—"

"The DNI. I've already heard."

"Then you know that we have to move quickly," Holmes said quietly. "He's out there, and he has help. I've already discredited him; now we need to get rid of him."

"We've discussed this," said Rigby. "We can't just kill him. We don't know who he's told or what evidence he might have gathered."

"I think we're beyond that, General. Zero is no longer just an annoyance; he is a very real threat to our plan. Even with the attack on the DNI, I could see doubt in Pierson's eyes. Whatever Zero said to him was enough to make him think twice. We need to..." He trailed off as a new notion struck him. "We might need to kill two birds with one stone."

Rigby was silent for a long moment. "That is an absolute last resort, Holmes."

"I'm aware. But we might be at that point, General." Holmes rounded the desk and quickly rifled through the drawers, looking for whatever it was that Steele might have given the president. "Let's keep it between us and in our pocket, for now."

"In the meantime, I'll get the CIA on the line and see what they plan to do about Zero."

"Good." Holmes hung up as he reached for the bottommost desk drawer. He tugged on it, but it was locked tight. And he was certain that whatever Zero had given Pierson was inside.

It doesn't matter, he thought. The president would be en route to Camp David in minutes. Whatever was in the drawer could wait.

And if they had to use their absolute last resort, Pierson wouldn't be alive long enough to retrieve it anyway.

Chapter Twelve

Emilia Sanders, or whatever her real name was, pulled the car into the parking lot of a convenience store and cut the engine.

"What are we doing here?" Zero asked.

"Switching cars. There's a good chance the White House was able to get an angle on this one. They'll be looking for us." She left the keys in the ignition as she pushed open the door. "Come on."

Zero scoffed lightly, but he got out without further question. Despite Sanders rescuing him from Hillis and the Division, he didn't know enough about her motivations to know whether or not she could be trusted. Still he followed her as they strode across the lot toward the gas pumps. There was a black sedan parked there, clean, late-model, nondescript. And standing beside it pumping gas was an athletic woman in a red T-shirt, her blonde hair pulled into a casual ponytail, sunglasses over eyes that Zero knew were slate gray.

"Maria." He breathed a sigh of relief and concern in equal measure. "What are you doing here?"

She looked up sharply, and her own expression mirrored his—relieved but worried. "Kent." She gave him a quick but tight embrace. "My Ukrainian contact called me. He told me you'd be here…" Maria threw a glance at Emilia Sanders. "Who's she?"

"I'm Emilia Sanders, aide to the president."

"She's FIS," Zero cut in. He had already guessed that Maria's Ukrainian contact was the same person that Sanders had holding his documents in Richmond.

Maria scoffed. "I can't get rid of you people, can I?"

"You shouldn't be here," Zero told her. Even as he said it, the memory of their tryst spun through his head once again. *In a hotel room, amidst an op, before Kate's death…* He pushed it out. "There's a reason I didn't call you."

Maria frowned deeply. "I'm sorry, it seemed like you could use some help, considering you're at the very top of the CIA's most-wanted list."

Zero blinked at her. "What? Why?"

"The buzz about town says you threatened the president's life…"

"No I didn't," Zero protested.

"And that you attacked DNI Hillis…"

"That wasn't me!" Zero exclaimed.

"And that you killed two Division men in downtown Arlington."

"I never—actually, that was me." He sighed. "Who are they sending after me? Anyone we know?"

"No such luck," Maria said as she finished pumping gas into the black sedan. "It's not Watson or Strickland, though both are ready and willing to help you out at a moment's notice. I've been keeping in touch with Cartwright, too. He's on the outside looking in on this one."

"Great. You have his number?"

"Yeah. Right here." Maria passed him her burner.

Zero reared back and hurled it as far as he could, beyond the parking lot and into a narrow field of tall grass.

Maria stared at him blankly. "Why'd you just throw my phone?"

"Can't trust Cartwright," he said simply. He hadn't forgotten Reidigger's stern warning about the deputy director. "What about the Iran situation? Any developments?"

"No," Maria replied. "Pierson hasn't even made a public address yet. The media is buzzing about some sort of turmoil in the White House, but they don't know what. All they know is that the president was moved. With the attack on New York, there are all sorts of theories flying around. But I know that Holmes, the White House Chief of Staff, contacted the CIA and put them on alert that Agent Zero had threatened his life."

"Yeah. That snake Holmes is in on it," Zero muttered. "This is what they wanted. I played right into their hands."

"How so?"

"I took a risk trying to convince Pierson of the truth. Not only were they able to make me persona non grata, but they got the president out of the White House. He'll be easier to manipulate from a distance." He turned to Sanders. "I need those documents. Can you have your guy in Richmond meet us?"

"I'll reach out." Sanders pulled out her phone and climbed into the back seat of the black sedan to make the call.

Maria replaced the gas pump before turning to him somberly. "We're three people with a couple of pistols between us and every law enforcement agency in the country looking for you. We're not going to be able to get within a mile of the president, while conspirators whisper in his ear. What the hell are we supposed to do about this?"

Zero stared at the ground. "I'm not sure yet." Even if he recovered the documents from the Ukrainians, he wasn't sure what he could do with them. It might be time, he thought, to consider going higher. To the United Nations or Interpol. He could make a call to his friend Vicente Baraf. But any avenue he considered would end in lengthy investigations, and they didn't have that sort of time.

"Hey." She put her hand on his arm. "We'll figure it out. Together."

The memory ran through his mind anew at her touch—the two of them together. Before Kate had died. He closed his eyes, but it didn't stop. He knew it was a ridiculous thing to concern himself with, considering everything else that was going on. But the memory was there, lodged in his head like a kernel in a tooth, and he couldn't get it out.

"I know you don't like it," she continued, "but we should get in touch with Cartwright."

"No," Zero said immediately. "I told you. Can't trust him."

"Why not? We both know he's not in on this. He should know about it. He has connections that we don't—"

"He's done things, Maria."

"We all have," she argued. "You and I, we've done things too. And we don't lose sleep over it. Cartwright came to me right away and told me what he knew. We should tell him what we know—"

"I remember, Maria." He blurted out the words before he could think twice about it.

She stared at him for a long moment. "What do you mean? What do you remember?"

"All of it. Everything. Today, in the Oval Office, when I almost collapsed? It came back. My full memory came back."

"Wow." Maria ran a hand through her hair, considering the gravity of what he'd just told her. "That's... good. That's great news, Kent. Isn't it?"

"You tell me," he said quietly. He was trying to gauge her reaction, to see if she was at all worried that he could remember. But she seemed only to be concerned with how morose he was over the revelation.

"What are you getting at, Kent?"

"You told me that you and I were only together once, after Kate died, when you came to me in Rome. But that isn't true, is it?" He wanted to summon some anger, but he couldn't bring himself to. Maybe she had lied to him, and been part of the betrayal, but so had he. He had been weak too. In fact, he was the one who had been married at the time.

He expected some amount of anger or possibly even remorse from her, but Maria's face was a mask of confusion. "That *is* the truth, Kent. Jesus, *that's* what you want to talk about right now? The time we slept together?"

"Yes. Because it keeps coming back to me, and I'm not sure I can keep going with you knowing what we did to her."

Maria shook her head. "Kent, I'm telling you. That's the truth. It was one time, and it was after she died." She tried to take his hand in hers, but he pulled it away. "Look. We don't have time to process all this right now, okay? But I need you to know, and trust, that whatever you're remembering about us didn't happen.

It didn't, Kent. I can't prove it to you. But whatever's in your head, it's not real."

"But I..."

If this works, some of the things that you recall may be subconscious. Dr. Guyer had told him that in Zurich.

He remembered it so vividly. The feel of the sheets. The view out the hotel window.

Fantasies, wishes, suspicions from your past life. All of those non-memory aspects were removed with your actual memories.

Zero breathed into his fist. It felt so real, even now, thinking back on it.

They'll be real to you.

How could he act on anything he thought he had known before if he couldn't be sure whether or not it was real? What good was having his memory restored if he couldn't trust what was in his own head?

"Tell me what you're thinking," Maria prodded.

"I'm thinking..." He drew a long, even breath. "I'm thinking that I don't know what's real anymore."

"Then let me help you," she implored. "We'll sort all of this out together."

He nodded. He needed her there, he realized suddenly, needed someone there who could help him separate fact from fiction. "Okay," he agreed quietly.

"Excuse me." Emilia Sanders had rolled down her window and stuck her head partially out at them. "Not to intrude on whatever's happening here, but how long have those cops been sitting there?"

Chapter Thirteen

Zero looked over sharply, past the gas pumps, to the pair of state police cruisers sitting in the parking lot of the convenience store.

Idiot, he scolded himself. He'd been so overly concerned with the Maria ordeal that he had hardly been paying attention to his surroundings.

Maria frowned deeply, apparently thinking the same. "They're probably just getting a coffee or something. They're not here for us."

"Even so," said Sanders, "I'd prefer to not linger."

"Agreed. I'll drive." Zero held his left hand out for the keys.

"You have one hand," Maria noted.

"I'm good with one hand," he replied. Though his real motivation was that if the cops gave chase, he might have to ditch Maria and Sanders fast. It would do them no good for all three to be caught at once.

Maria reluctantly handed over the keys and got in the passenger seat. Zero slid in behind the wheel, adjusted the seat and mirror, and then guided the black sedan slowly away from the gas pump. He pulled back onto the road casually, without drawing any attention to them.

"We're fine," he said aloud, more for his own benefit than theirs. A glance in the rearview showed him that the cruisers hadn't moved from the lot. "This car is clean, right?"

"Of course," Maria said. "Watson passed it off to me from his asset. The mechanic."

"Mitch," Zero murmured. He thought again of Reidigger and his girls, most likely on a plane by now heading west. The weight of the secret sat heavy inside him, begging to come out. Maria deserved to know; she had been part of the team, back then. Zero, Reidigger, Johansson, and Morris.

But it wasn't Zero's secret to tell.

He took the ramp back to the highway and maintained the speed limit to avoid any suspicion. "We need a safe place to hole up for at least a little while," he said. "Until we can meet with Sanders's liaison and get my documents back."

"How did she get them in the first place?" Maria asked.

"I posed as his deceased wife and stole them," Sanders said candidly.

"Seriously?" Maria twisted in her seat and shot Sanders a look of disgust. "What are they?"

"All of the evidence I was digging up two years ago," Zero told her. "I don't know if it'll be enough to prove the conspiracy, but if we can get them into Pierson's hands it might be enough to sway him. I have some bank records for offshore accounts that show hush money funneled to people in the NSA and FBI. There are a few transcripts of phone calls between congressmen. It's vague at best, but coupled with what we know, it could be—"

"It won't be enough," Sanders interjected. "You know it."

"Well, I don't have a better idea," Zero shot back. "We get the documents, and then ... we'll figure out what to do with them."

"Agent Zero," Sanders said suddenly from the back seat. "You should see this." She passed her phone to him. The screen was open to a browser window, a news website—and staring back at him was his own face.

"I don't believe it," he muttered. He didn't think they would go so far to smear his name across the headlines, but there he was—Professor Reid Lawson of Alexandria, Virginia, a wanted man. The photograph was taken from the university's faculty website. The brief article said nothing about the CIA or the attack on Hillis; rather it claimed that he was being sought for treason and terroristic threats against the president. He was considered armed and dangerous. Anyone with leads should immediately call emergency services.

"Looks like I've been disavowed. Again." He passed the phone back to Sanders. "They can't track you on that thing, can they?"

"Of course not. It's not in my name and the GPS has been disabled."

"Good." Zero tried to come off as aloof, but internally he was panicked. The CIA, the White House, whoever was in league behind the plot, had just made an extremely heavy accusation against him—the real him, Reid Lawson. He was keenly aware that even if he managed to come out of this alive, there was now a good chance he could never go back to his ordinary life. And the girls… they would always be associated with him. What would they do? They'd have to move. Change their names. Possibly even his appearance, like Alan had done.

Whoop-whoop! A warning siren blared, jarring Zero from his thoughts. In the same instant red and blue flashers lit up behind them.

"Shit," he hissed. There were two pairs of lights in the rearview, both state cruisers. *Likely not the ones from the gas station.* The cops at the convenience store must have recognized him—his injured hand was a dead giveaway, he realized—and they must have called it in. *I bet the CIA told them not to engage until we were on the road again.*

Sanders glanced casually over her shoulder. "Police."

"No kidding. Thanks." He turned to Maria. "You said this car came from Mitch?"

"I did."

"Good." *Thank god it's an automatic.* He wouldn't be able to shift gears with his right hand.

Zero slammed the gas and the car lurched forward, jumping to eighty in a few seconds. He'd driven cars from Mitch—or rather, Alan—before, and he knew that they were tailored for performance.

Behind him, Sanders fastened her seat belt. "This is not exactly how I thought this day would go," she mused.

Both cruisers behind him turned on their sirens, startlingly loud even with the windows closed and the engine roaring. Even with Mitch's modifications, Zero knew he couldn't outrun the cops on the highway. Virginia State Interceptors were built with turbo-charged engines capable of top speeds in excess of a hundred and fifty. And they were proving it quickly as they came up behind him, less than a car length from their front bumper to his rear.

"We're going to run out of road," Maria said, gripping the handle over her window. "They waited to see where we'd go. You know there's going to be a roadblock before the next exit."

"I know," Zero grunted. To their left was a concrete median dividing the two sets of lanes; to the right were metal guardrails. Neither side was an option. He was boxed into a corridor with cops behind him and, judging by the shining red brake lights he saw in the distance, Maria was right about a roadblock.

He swerved onto the shoulder to veer around a car in the slow lane and then careened back to the asphalt. The cops stayed on pace, side by side, barely more than a few feet between them. Zero kept the rearview in his periphery as he veered left and right; each time he did, the headlights of the cruisers moved in sync with him.

"Damn it," he muttered. He was hoping to separate them, drive a wedge wide enough to get between the two cars, but they weren't going to let him. They were going to run out of road in less than a mile.

"Give me a gun," Sanders offered.

"Fat chance." Maria pulled a Glock 17 from a handbag at her feet.

"Wait," said Zero. "Grab the wheel. And hold onto something."

Maria reached over and took the steering wheel in one hand, the other firmly gripping the handle over the door. Behind them, Sanders braced herself. Zero reached for the Sig Sauer he had tucked in his pants.

Then he slammed the brake.

The tires screamed and the brakes screeched as the car skidded. The acrid smell of burning rubber filled the cab almost immediately, and the two cruisers behind them, close as they were to each other, both slammed into the back of the black sedan.

The trunk crumpled and the impact jostled Zero forward. He put his arms up as he bounced against the steering wheel. He shook it off as the force of the two cruisers continued to push their car forward, and then he leaned out the window and fired several shots at the two cars behind him.

The gunshots cracked the night air. Oncoming cars swerved wildly at the sound, unsure of where the shooting was coming from but knowing what it meant. He avoided the windshields, and the cars were too close for him to shoot the tires. Instead he shot at the hoods in a rough approximation of the engine, hoping to hit a vital organ of the cruisers.

Then he slung himself back into the car and slammed the gas again. The car lurched forward as he spun the wheel, fishtailing in a tight arc, and was off like a shot, going the wrong direction down the highway. He flicked off the headlights and rode the line between the lane and the shoulder to avoid oncoming traffic.

A glance in the rearview told him that the cruisers were not disabled, but slow to resume the chase. He also caught a glimpse of Sanders. Her eyes were wide and her face had paled. "You all right back there?"

"Surviving," she murmured.

"Zero, look out!" Maria grabbed onto the steering wheel and jerked it to the right as two cars ahead of them swerved sideways, forming a barricade.

He clenched his jaw as the right side of the car scraped against the concrete median, throwing a shower of sparks behind them. He pressed the pedal to the floor; the engine roared and the car jumped forward. They slammed into the rear bumper of one of the perpendicular cars and pushed it out of their way.

Shots rang out and smacked the driver's side door. Zero instinctively put an arm up. *As if that would somehow protect me against bullets,* he noted wryly.

"Suits and unmarked cars," Maria reported, craning her neck for a look at the cars quickly getting smaller behind them. "Looks like Feds."

"Great," Zero grunted. He weaved in and out from lane to shoulder to avoid the headlights ahead of him. "We have to get off this road before more come." He saw only one way to do that. "What's back there?" He pointed off the side of the highway, beyond the metal guardrail and the trees.

"Um ... on this stretch, that would be the Potomac," Maria told him. Then she did a double-take as she realized why he was asking. "No. Don't even think about it."

"Just hang on." The red and blue flashers in the rearview were gaining again. The FBI cars were somewhere back there too, headlights going in the wrong direction to pursue them. And up ahead, less than a half mile away, were more oncoming police.

They think I've only got two ways to go—forward or back. So let's make a new way.

"I knew I shouldn't have let you drive." Maria braced an arm against the dashboard. Sanders put both arms up to cover her head.

Zero yanked the wheel to the left and angled the car directly toward the guardrail at seventy miles an hour.

This type of guardrail, he knew, was designed to slow a vehicle down if it was veering off the road. They were specifically tested for a dispersion of energy. They were not, contrary to popular belief, made to sustain a direct impact. In fact, most modern guardrails were mounted on wooden posts for that precise reason—to break if a car hit one head-on.

The black sedan smashed into the guardrail and a twenty-foot section of it broke, like driving through a fence. The car rolled over it, bouncing its passengers violently. Zero's head smacked the roof of the car. A horrible grinding noise told him that the steel rail had torn something out of the undercarriage.

But the momentum of the car carried it forward, down a slight embankment and into the trees. He steered as best he could over stones and ruts in the grass, directing the car between tall, thin-trunked firs. They were eighty feet from the highway before he finally stopped.

"Go," he told them breathlessly. "Get out and get lost. Both of you."

"What?" Maria exclaimed. "No, we're not leaving you—"

"There's no time. They'll see the brake lights from the highway. Go with Sanders. Get the documents. I'll find you."

Sanders unclipped her seat belt and pushed the door open, but Maria didn't move. "What are you going to do?"

"I'm going to lose them." He tried to have some conviction in the words, but the truth was that he wasn't certain he'd make it out of this. But if he could at least distract their pursuers, Maria could get away. She could retrieve the documents, and he knew she would stop at nothing to get them into the right hands.

"Didn't we just have this conversation?" Maria argued. "It's not you against the world."

"I know that." He reached over his body and squeezed her arm with his good hand. "But I need you out there. If anything happens to me someone else needs to keep this going. We're of no use to anyone if we're both caught." He saw in the rearview that the red and blue flashers had come to a stop at the top of the embankment, where the sedan had burst through the guardrail. Several pairs of headlights were clustered close together, and he could see figures passing in front of them. "There's no time to argue. Just—"

Maria grabbed the back of his neck and pulled him close, pressing her mouth against his. It took him by surprise; he didn't even get the chance to return the kiss before she pulled away. "See you soon." She grabbed up her black handbag, pushed the door open, and hurried out into the night after Sanders.

Not two seconds after she'd left a spotlight swept over the sedan from the embankment behind him, half blinding Zero as he glanced in the rearview.

They'll have to pursue me on foot. He reached for the door handle when something jumped in the side mirror—headlights, bouncing and then angling downward.

"Oh, shit." A black Jeep with powerful halogen high beams and thick-treaded tires rumbled down the embankment toward him.

Chapter Fourteen

The headlights in the rearview mirror leveled out as the Jeep reached the bottom of the embankment, the chassis bouncing on powerful shocks. Zero could hear voices over its engine, shouts of people following the vehicle on foot, likely cops and Feds alike.

"All right," he murmured to the car, "just need you to go a little further. Please don't die on me." He eased his foot off the brake and the black sedan rolled forward. Bright red warning lights blared on the dashboard—the engine was getting hot, he was leaking oil, tire pressure was low, and he'd lost power steering—but he ignored them and pressed his foot gently on the gas.

The car's engine groaned, but it held. He drove forward deeper into the trees, navigating carefully and with some difficulty. It was no easy task to steer one-handed without power steering, and with the headlights off the trees appeared quickly. Still he gave it a little more gas and dared to speed up to twenty-five.

The Jeep behind him roared closer, but the people on foot wouldn't be able to catch up to him at this pace. Then he heard another sound, over the Jeep's engine; it was the rotors of a helicopter. No sooner did he recognize the sound than a powerful spotlight shone down from above, bathing a section of the forest in fragmented blue light filtering down from between the canopies of the fir trees. The spotlight swept left and right, and then finally caught his car.

"Great," he groaned as he wrenched the wheel to swerve around a thin tree just ahead. It was a tight fit; the trunk of the tree swiped off the passenger-side mirror. "Even better."

He glanced in the rearview for the Jeep and saw its bouncing headlights in pursuit of him. Gaining steadily. Who was in it, he didn't know—and didn't much want to find out.

Shots rang out. The rear windshield exploded, scattering bits of glass throughout the cab. Zero winced and shielded his face, but did not slow. Instead he pushed the pedal harder, daring to jump to thirty-five. The helicopter's spotlight still had the car engulfed, so he flicked on the headlights. There was no hiding from them.

More shots pierced the night, sharp and jarring even over the sounds of the helicopter and the approaching Jeep. He heard metal smack against metal. *They're shooting indiscriminately. So much for taking me alive.*

The gears ground horribly under the hood as he tried to speed up again. The car refused; in fact, the engine sputtered and clanked. "Hold out," he begged it. "Just hold out a little longer."

There was no such luck. The engine clanked twice more and died. The car rolled another twenty feet or so and then slowed to a stop.

"Dammit!" He awkwardly reached over himself and twisted the key in the ignition to the off position, and then tried to turn the engine over again. It chugged once, but failed. "Come on!"

Wait a second. Zero paused and looked around quickly. He heard voices shouting out there in the dark woods, but he did not hear the roar of the Jeep's engine. *There's no way I lost it. They must be out there somewhere…*

As soon as he thought it, powerful floodlights kicked on to his left, nearly blinding him. The waiting Jeep roared and rumbled rapidly toward him.

All he could do was cover his head as it slammed into the side of the sedan. The entire left side of the car lifted from the ground and then came crashing back down with a stupendous bounce that sent Zero's head once again smacking into the roof.

He groaned as the Jeep backed up several feet. The engine revved, seemingly ready for a second ramming. Instead it idled, and he heard the sound of a car door opening and closing.

Zero reached down past his hip for the seat lever and pulled it. The driver's seat fell backward, the headrest hitting the bench seat in the rear as several pistol shots cracked. The bullets whistled over him and blew out the passenger-side window, passing through the space where his head had been only a second earlier.

He lay back like that for a moment, though it felt like an eternity, just listening. The Jeep's engine rumbled in park. The helicopter hovered over the trees, illuminating the sedan from above. Voices shouted in the distance as people on foot caught up to them.

Then a twig snapped. Footfalls, getting closer. A male voice called out, singsong: "Zero? You dead yet?"

I know that voice. Where do I know that voice from?

He didn't move, didn't make a sound. The footfalls stopped, and the voice called out again. But this time, it wasn't to him. It was to someone with him in the Jeep. "Hey. Give me that SAW. I want to make good and sure."

Zero's heart raced. SAW, he knew, stood for "squad automatic weapon." *An M249 light machine gun. It'll shred this car in seconds—and me with it.*

He had to take a risk. Gripping the Sig Sauer in his left, he popped up, took a half second to aim, and fired off three shots. Sparks flew as he hit the Jeep's hood. One of the headlights blew out. In the suddenly dim light, he saw a figure crouch instinctively, hitting the deck.

He squinted in the darkness as the figure slowly looked up at him. They locked eyes for the briefest of moments.

The man was tall, lean, with angular features and sandy hair. Zero *did* know him; he had last seen that face when it was trying to kill him in the freight train depot of Marseille-Saint Charles, France.

Carver. Watson's former partner. A man who had fled for his life from Zero and, allegedly, the CIA was going to track down and bring in.

Agent Carver sneered and scrambled to his feet. "The SAW! Give me the SAW!"

More shots rippled from the darkness of the trees. Zero ducked back again and covered his head, unsure of where they were coming from. Bullets slapped the grille of the Jeep and blew out its other headlight as Carver once again flopped to the dirt.

Maria. It must have been her, unless the cops and agents were firing blindly in the dark. He was glad for the assist, but wished she would just get herself clear.

He reached over himself again and awkwardly twisted the key in the ignition. "Come on," he grunted. "I need help here." The engine chugged a couple of times, but choked and died. "Just a little further. Come on!" He twisted the key anew, so hard he thought it might break off in the ignition column.

The engine wheezed and kicked over, sending a strong burning odor through the air vents. It sounded like a wounded animal, but it stayed on.

"Thank you," he sighed. He pulled the selector into drive and pressed the gas. The car lurched, threatened to stall out for a moment, and then rolled forward. He pulled the wheel to the right with his one good hand, edging closer to a thick stand of trees.

A salvo of automatic gunfire slammed into the back of the car. Taillights burst and Zero winced, keenly aware that a single bullet to the gas tank would be the end of him. He gritted his teeth and took a chance, slamming the pedal down. The car lurched between two trees. Branches bent and snapped; the trunks on either side scraped and groaned against the panels, but the car squeezed through. The front driver's side tire bounced against a large stone and sent Zero smacking against the steering column. His injured hand throbbed with pain, but he did his best to ignore it and pushed forward.

The Jeep's rumbling faded. *It's too big to get through.* At least he hoped. But he had another problem: voices. They were getting closer. The stall and brief altercation with Carver had allowed the cops and agents on foot to gain some ground, and they weren't far.

He leaned out the window with the Sig Sauer, doing his best to keep the car on a straight path with his knees, and fired three shots into the darkness. He had no idea where the voices were coming from, but as the echoes of the blasts dissipated he heard panicked cries fleeing away from him.

Where is it? he thought desperately. *Where is the river?* The Potomac was supposed to be on the other side of this stretch of woods. He didn't have a plan once he reached it; well, he did, but it was simply to drive the car straight into it, jump out, and let the current carry him downstream until he was able to climb out on the other side. *The Potomac runs parallel to the stretch of I-95 where I jumped the barrier; it shouldn't be this far—*

"Shit!" He pressed his entire weight on the brake pedal. The car was slow to respond, brakes squealing horribly, white smoke pouring out from under the hood. Zero groaned as he yanked the wheel to one side. The car slid with it, coming to a stop at the edge of a cliff.

He panted. Glancing out his window showed him that he'd brought the car to a stop less than two feet from the sheer drop of about sixty feet to rushing water below.

"Great," he muttered breathlessly. "That's great." His getaway plan had been soured by a sheer drop into the river.

Otets. He remembered the Russian mobster, not from his life before but from only a few months prior, before he had truly known who he was. He had driven a car right off of a cliff with his prisoner, and they'd both jumped before the car hit the water.

The rotors of the helicopter roared closer as it sought him again, the sweeping spotlight making him squint in the sudden blue light.

I could do it again now. It would, perhaps, be his best option. Take the plunge, literally, and drive into the river. The helicopter would catch it all. Would it be enough for them to assume he was dead? A man presumed dead could get a lot farther than one being pursued by every law enforcement agency in the nation.

"Okay," he told himself. "Let's do it." He unbuckled his seatbelt and then shifted the car into reverse, hoping it had just enough life left in it to go over the edge.

With the headlights out, he didn't see the Jeep coming. By the time he heard the roaring engine, he had just enough time to look to the right, through the shattered passenger-side window, before he saw the black shape of it barreling toward him.

The cow-catcher on the front of the Jeep slammed into the side of the sedan and sent it hurtling sideways over the cliff. The last thing Zero remembered was putting his hands over his head, bracing his arms against the roof of the car as it flipped, over and over, plummeting sixty feet. The car struck the river's surface. Then everything was black.

Agent Carver stood on the edge of the cliff, looking down at the dark water of the Potomac River rushing by below. The helicopter hovered overhead, its powerful spotlight illuminating the exposed underside of the battered sedan as it sank.

Just for good measure, Carver aimed the submachine gun and fired a volley of powerful rounds, emptying the remainder of the magazine. Then he spat over the side and made a call.

The call was answered mid-ring. "It's done," he said immediately.

"Already?" Riker sounded either impressed or sarcastic. He couldn't tell which. "Good. Bring me the body."

"Body's in the Potomac."

"Find it," she ordered. "We need confirmation."

Carver scoffed. "I just sent him over the side of a cliff, in a car, and into the river—"

"You sent Agent Zero over the side of a cliff," she corrected. "If there's no body, he's not dead."

Carver groaned. He was glad to be back stateside; after failing to kill Zero in France, Riker had ordered him dark and sent him to slum it with the Division until her recent call. But he wasn't exactly keen on going night-fishing for a dead agent.

"Wait," Riker said suddenly. She was pensively silent for a moment and then added, "This might present us with an opportunity. Stand down. Call off the troopers. I'll put a call in at the FBI and tell them we got him."

Carver frowned. He was fairly certain that Zero *was* actually dead, but still it was a strange change of heart to have so suddenly. "Now you want to confirm him dead?"

"Yes," she said simply. "Because no one but you is going to be looking for a dead man."

Chapter Fifteen

To the general public, Camp David was a country retreat for the President of the United States, located in Maryland approximately sixty miles northwest of Washington, DC. Its location was the wooded hills of Catoctin National Park, a pleasant and tranquil place for the highest office in America to host foreign dignitaries or simply enjoy a modicum of solitude. The home on the property was large and elegant, though it lacked the pomp and pageantry of the White House.

There was even a swimming pool.

To those in the know, Camp David was a military installation. The retreat was staffed by the US Navy and Marine Corps. Despite its peaceful air, the camp was carefully monitored by radar and F-15 flyovers. No fewer than two dozen Marines scouted its perimeter, and half as many Secret Service agents stuck close to the house.

In short, there was little about the mountain retreat that Eli Pierson found tranquil.

He sat in an armchair in the home office of the main house, twirling the small device in his fingers like a fidget spinner. His jacket was draped over the chair's back; his tie, still knotted, lay in a heap on the floor.

In his fingers was the small black USB drive that Zero had given him.

"Ridiculous," he muttered to himself. In less than twenty-four hours, he had gone from giving commendations to Agent Zero to hiding out at the retreat, fearing for his life, unsure of who he could trust on his staff. Zero had seemed so confident in his accusations. But then there was Sanders, the aide, and the attack on Hillis…

He pushed himself out of the armchair, rounded the desk, and opened his laptop. As he was about to push the drive into the USB port, there was a knock on the office door.

"Come in."

Agent Raulsen opened the door gently, his black suit perfectly pressed and hair combed neatly. He held a cell phone in his hand. "Sir. It's Mr. Holmes."

"Good. Thank you, Raulsen." Pierson hid the drive in his fist as he strode over to take the phone. "Have you contacted my wife?" Melissa Pierson was attending a charity event for veterans in California at the time the president was moved, and he didn't want to take any chances.

"Yes sir. The First Lady is secured at Miramar. We'll move her here as soon as possible—"

"No." Pierson waved a hand. "Don't bother. I don't plan on being here long myself. Thank you, Raulsen."

The Secret Service agent nodded. "I'll be right outside if you need me, sir."

Raulsen left, leaving the door ajar only slightly as Pierson put the phone to his ear. "Pete. Tell me good news."

Holmes sighed gently through the phone. "I'm afraid I don't have much, sir. Satellite shows that IRGC ships are moving towards the strait. It appears their intention is to blockade it."

"Christ." Pierson shook his head. "But they haven't closed it?"

"No sir. Not yet."

That was at least some measure of a good sign. He thought back to Zero's bizarre prophecy, the one he had made in the Oval Office. *Iran will close the strait. That will force your hand. They're counting on it.*

"Let them blockade," Pierson said. "And let's make sure there's nothing there for them to get agitated over."

"Well…that's just it, sir," Holmes said hesitantly through the phone. "The Fifth Fleet is en route to the strait."

Pierson's throat ran dry. "I didn't order that."

"You did, sir. Earlier today, in the Situation Room, General Rigby suggested mobilizing the Fifth Fleet as a show of force in an effort to dissuade Iran from escalating. You agreed. You gave verbal consent with all of us present as witness." Holmes paused for a moment. "Do you not recall that? Are you all right, sir?"

Pierson rubbed his forehead. *No,* he thought, *I don't recall. And I'm not all right.* He remembered the general suggesting mobilization, as well as calling in additional assets from the Gulf of Oman. A blockade on the strait would hinder that. All they needed was a single IRGC ship to get fidgety over the sight of the convening Fifth Fleet, and all hell could break loose.

"Call them off," he ordered. "Have our ships fall back to Bahrain. I want to address this situation myself. I want to arrange a meeting with President Sarif." If he could speak with the Iranian president, they could come to an amiable conclusion to all of this, he was certain. Reparations could be made for the incident in the Persian Gulf. Whatever it would take to avoid war.

"Yes sir. I'll try. Though Sarif's administration has so far been refusing our attempts to communicate."

"Keep trying!" Pierson demanded. He spun the drive in his fingers anxiously. "And what about the other thing? Has Agent Zero been apprehended?"

"In a manner of speaking, sir." Holmes cleared his throat. "Mr. President, Agent Zero has been killed."

The drive slipped from Pierson's fingers and bounced across the carpet. "What?"

"He's dead, sir. The CIA confirmed it only minutes ago."

Anger swelled in Pierson's chest. "I ordered him taken alive. I wanted to speak to him myself—"

"I understand, sir," Holmes said hastily, "but Zero was discovered heading north on I-95. We believe he was intent on returning to the White House. He initiated a chase with state troopers. He shot at federal agents. He drove a car off of the highway and … and right off a cliff, into the Potomac."

"My god." Pierson absentmindedly stooped and picked up the USB drive. He set it on the edge of the desk. *He drove off a cliff?* Holmes was right. Zero had not been in the right state of mind.

"I'm sorry, sir. At least he's at peace now. We're doing our best to keep it quiet. There's no reason to publicly drag his name through more mud."

Pierson sighed. He couldn't just forget what Zero had told him, but at the same time he couldn't discount the fact that a conspiracy that involved nearly his entire administration sounded insane. Zero had asked him to dismiss his entire cabinet in the wake of a major terrorist attack and on the brink of a major conflict in the Middle East.

That does not sound like a man who was in control of his mental faculties, Pierson admitted internally.

The president pushed open a side door in the office and stepped out onto a small terrace. The night air was cool and smelled of pine trees. "What about Sanders? Was she with him?"

"No, sir. She's MIA. In fact, the troopers who initially spotted him claimed there were two women with him. One was confirmed to be Sanders. We don't know where they went, but there is a full-scale manhunt currently ongoing. We'll find her."

The president looked out over the lawn, to the darkness of the trees beyond. A slight shiver ran up his spine. Someone could be out there right now, watching. Waiting. He was surrounded by Marines and Secret Service agents, yet still hardly felt safe at the country retreat. "I want to come back."

"Sir, that is highly inadvisable—"

"The White House is the safest place for me to be," Pierson argued.

"We can't say that for certain until we've cleared every staff member. Someone beyond Sanders could be compromised. Please, sir," Holmes implored. "Just let us do our jobs. It won't take long. We'll have our analysts running all night. Get some sleep, and return tomorrow."

Pierson rubbed his chin. He needed to shave. He needed to address the American people. He needed to get this situation under control. He needed to be in a position that didn't feel like hiding out.

"All right, Pete. I'll give you one night. But I want you to put everyone on alert—Rigby, Kemmerer, the joint chiefs. We'll be convening as soon as I return, and we're going to get this situation under full control. And get that meeting with Sarif."

"Yes sir. Good night, sir." Holmes hung up.

Pierson's arm and the phone fell limply by his side as he stared out again at the darkness beyond the lawn. How quickly everything could fall apart. He'd certainly had his fair share of issues in the last three years, but nothing like this. Nothing close to this.

He couldn't help but think of how former President George Bush must have felt on September 11, 2001. One moment, reading a story to a classroom of children and the next, having it whispered in his ear that the largest terrorist attack in American history had occurred. He had handled it decisively and with poise. He had heeded the advice of his administration, while he, Pierson, hid out at Camp David and argued with those he had appointed to be his advisors.

He briefly considered calling the former president. He could use a friendly voice, a mentor at the moment. But it was after nine o'clock. It could wait until tomorrow.

Pierson headed back into the office and shut the door behind him. He set the cell phone on the desk and then frowned. He patted his pockets and looked around in confusion.

The USB drive was gone.

Where did I put it? He remembered having it in his hand. He remembered dropping it to the floor at the news of Zero's death. He got down on his hands and knees and searched the carpet, looked under the desk. It wasn't there. *Did I have it when I went outside?* He checked the small terrace, the desk drawers, the cushion of his armchair.

The door to the office was shut tight. He hadn't heard it open or seen anyone come in.

But it was gone. The drive was gone.

⚜ ⚜ ⚜

Chief of Staff Peter Holmes ended the call with President Pierson before turning to the other three occupants of the conference room at Langley. "It's done," he said simply. "The president will return to DC tomorrow. We have until then."

"I'll keep Sarif's people under the radar," said Secretary of State Roland Kemmerer. "NSA is working to block out any communications from Iran."

"Good. Have them do the same with any incoming transmissions from the Fifth Fleet. Everything goes through Rigby. We can't rely on luck for this; we'll have to sow some confusion out there." Holmes turned to CIA Director Mullen and the woman at his side, Deputy Director Riker. "The president believes Zero is dead. You're certain this will work?"

Mullen looked to Riker, who nodded confidently. "Zero is crafty, but he's also predictable. He'll always do what he believes is the right thing, even if it's not in his best interest. He will try to get to Pierson again and convince him of what he knows."

"You'd better hope you're right," Holmes warned. "Three years of planning and billions of dollars are riding on this."

Riker's eyes narrowed at him. "You don't have to remind me. There's only one man in the field looking for him currently. If my guy finds him first, we'll go with the original contingency. But if he doesn't, Zero will go to the president."

"Good. I'll be in touch." Holmes nodded briefly to them and left the conference room, striding swiftly down the corridor.

He hadn't lied to the president about everything. There were actually background checks currently ongoing to confirm the identity of every White House staffer, but only for them to ensure that there were no further moles like Sanders.

Zero had forced their hand by going to the president and attacking Hillis. The plan had to change—but they had anticipated a possible event like this.

There would be no calling off the Fifth Fleet. American battleships would soon be facing off against an Iranian blockade, with miscommunications abounding and both sides anxious, fingers on proverbial triggers.

By the time Pierson discovered that his orders had been ignored, it would be too late. Agent Zero would rise from the dead and assassinate the President of the United States.

Chapter Sixteen

Zero grabbed onto a half-submerged rock with his good hand and clung there, gasping for breath and trying to stand against the rushing river. The water near the shore was shallow, only a couple of feet deep, but the pull of the current was strong and, at the moment, he was not.

He had survived the plummet over the cliff only by virtue of the shot-out window. The car had struck the river's surface angled toward the driver's side and the force of it shoved him out through the opening. His limbs had smacked painfully against the door frame, but fortunately he hadn't hit his head or lost consciousness.

I should be dead.

Even under the darkness of the water he could see the powerful blue spotlight of the helicopter, so he held his breath and swam, straining against the pain in his hand and limbs and neck and spine, clawing at the water with all his might while his lungs burned and begged for air.

When he dared break the surface, it was only to take a liberal gulp of oxygen, and then he plunged back down and swam some more. When his arms grew too tired to continue, he let the current carry him along. His three-minute swim felt like an hour. He came up for air four times before his feet touched the riverbed and he reached out, clinging to a mossy rock and struggling to stand.

He dragged himself out of the river. His clothes were heavy and dripping; his injured hand burned with pain. Every limb throbbed. His neck and spine ached with the whiplash of the impact. He would definitely need to see a good chiropractor when all this was over.

As soon as he regained control of his ragged breathing, Zero scanned the skies. He heard no rotors and saw no spotlights sweeping the river. *I couldn't have gone that far in just a few minutes.* The helicopter seemed to have simply vanished.

Do they think I'm dead? He doubted he was that lucky.

One thing was certain: Riker had sent Carver after him, and Zero was guessing that the other guys in the black Jeep were the Division. He wasn't afraid of Carver, but he wasn't happy that the seemingly renegade agent would have access to all of the resources of the CIA and the Division while he, Zero, had none.

He didn't even have a working phone, thanks to his plunge in the Potomac. He tossed the useless device into the river.

He staggered up onto the shore and collapsed to his knees, feeling nauseous from swallowed river water and hurting all over. *Think. You're Agent Zero, and you need help.* He ran through a mental Rolodex of the people he could reach out to. He couldn't risk getting in touch with any of his CIA contacts from two years prior; he wasn't even sure who was still active, let alone alive, and if they were they might not be on the same side anymore.

Maria was out there somewhere with Sanders, hopefully hiding out and eluding authorities. Alan was on a plane to Nebraska with Zero's daughters. He didn't have a secure number to reach Watson, who was undoubtedly being monitored by the agency for helping Zero in the past.

That left only one person, and as much as he didn't like to further implicate a friend, he needed to. After resting for a few minutes in the silence of the shore, certain that no one had followed him down from the cliff, Zero hauled himself to his feet and started walking as quickly as he could inland.

He was only vaguely aware of where he was. He couldn't recall the exact point where he'd left the highway, let alone how far he'd driven through the woods or drifted down the Potomac. It seemed to be mostly wilderness on this side of the river, but after a short stretch of about a half mile the woods broke and he happened upon a narrow road and a few homes, spaced far apart with wide front yards and trees dotting the landscape.

He didn't like it, but he didn't see much choice. *You're already a wanted criminal. Might as well add breaking and entering to the list.*

The Sig Sauer was still tucked in the back of his pants. The clip was empty and the gun was so waterlogged that it wouldn't have worked anyway. But whoever he pointed it at wouldn't know that.

He strode up the driveway of the nearest house. There was a single light on in one window, and the flickering blue of a television screen in another. He drew the Sig, took a deep breath, and knocked twice briskly on the door.

A deadbolt clicked and the door opened about five inches. An older man, possibly mid-sixties, frowned out at him. He wore a white tank top and shorts, a belly spilling over the waistline, and looked pretty disgruntled about being disturbed at this hour.

"Yeah?"

Zero said nothing. Instead he shouldered the door in. The man grunted and stumbled back, nearly falling over. His eyes widened in shock as Zero leveled the Sig Sauer at his face.

"Don't move. Don't shout. Don't make a sound, or I will shoot you," he said quickly and quietly. "Nod if you understand."

The man nodded emphatically, his mouth hanging open slightly.

"Is there anyone else in the house?"

The man seemed too stunned for words. A slight whimper escaped his lips as he shook his head, no.

"I need a cell phone. Where is it?"

The man pointed through the doorway to the living room, where the television set flickered.

Zero tucked the gun back into his jeans, and then plucked up the man's iPhone from the coffee table in the adjacent room. It was a few years old with a small crack in the upper right corner. "Is there a screen lock on this?"

The man shook his head again, not daring to move from his spot on the floor.

"Good. I'm taking this." He glanced over his shoulder and saw that the old man had been watching a rerun of *Cheers*. "Here's what I want you to do. You're going to sit there, on the sofa, and not make a move until this episode is over, got it? Then you can get up. Call the police. Whatever you feel you need to do. But if I hear sirens in the next few minutes, I'm going to come back here and shoot you. Do you understand?"

The man's head bobbed up and down quickly.

"Good. Stay put." Zero backed out of the living room, ran out the open front door, and crossed the front yard back to the road. He almost didn't see the car coming until he was awash in its headlights, and for a moment he froze there, his one good hand clutching the stolen phone and a useless gun in his pants.

But the car didn't stop or even slow. It passed him by and curved with the road.

He breathed a sigh of relief and hurried across the road, back into the woods, striding as quickly as he could while still being careful of ruts and stones. He swiped at the iPhone screen and dialed a number he had memorized.

The call was answered in the middle of the third ring, but the person on the other end of the line didn't speak.

"Todd?" Zero said cautiously.

"Jeez." Strickland half-scoffed and half-laughed. "I didn't know who this was. Only three people have this number." Strickland had given him the number of a burner he'd picked up after learning about the conspiracy, just in case Zero or his girls needed help.

"Where are you right now?"

"I'm at home. What do you need?" Home, for Strickland, was a second-floor apartment in Bethesda, with a doorman, a front desk guard, and (most likely) a CIA wiretap.

"Go outside."

"I'll call you right back." Strickland hung up without questioning it. He knew as well as Zero did that his place was likely bugged. In fact, Strickland had discovered only a few days earlier that he had been injected with a tracking chip, much like Zero's daughters had, which he had to cut out of his own bicep.

Zero continued on through the woods, trekking parallel to the road. After a minute and a half, the silence was suddenly shattered by the chorus to "Who Let the Dogs Out," the ringtone of the iPhone.

"Good god," Zero muttered, startled by the sudden cacophony. He answered it quickly. "Strickland?"

"I'm outside. Walking down the block. You're dead, by the way."

Zero paused abruptly. "Come again?"

"Yeah. A voice memo went out just a few minutes before you called. They sent it to the whole Special Activities Division, agents and bosses. They're saying you were killed in a car crash."

Zero scoffed. "Well, you know what Twain said."

"I actually don't," Strickland admitted.

"Never mind." *There's no way the CIA truly believes I'm dead.* Without a body, Riker and the others behind the plot would never simply assume. This was a ploy—but to what end, he wasn't sure. *Maybe in the hopes I let my guard down?* "I need help, Todd."

"Tell me where to meet and I'm there."

"No," Zero said quickly. "I just need some resources. I've got to do this alone—"

"The Lone Ranger act gets old fast, Zero. Let me help you."

Zero pinched the bridge of his nose. "I'm sure you saw the reports. You know what they're saying I did. They used my real name. Now they're claiming I'm dead. If I'm spotted, I will be. If you're spotted with me, you'll be dead too. Besides, I've got some help." Maria was out there somewhere, hopefully not in the hands of the Feds or the Division. But he had ditched her phone for fear of Cartwright following them. He had no way to get in touch with her.

He would have to find her the old-fashioned way, and hopefully by then she and Sanders had secured his documents.

"So what do you want me to do?" Strickland asked.

"I need a car. I need a gun. I need a burner. And I need a secure way to get in touch with someone in the IRGC hierarchy."

Strickland was silent for a long moment. "How do you feel about three out of four?"

"There must be a way," Zero insisted.

"You want to put a call in to a commanding officer in Iran without the NSA, FBI, or CIA knowing about it? There's not a way, Zero. You of all people should know that."

"You're a former Ranger. You were able to get in touch with Sergeant Flagg in Morocco without being tracked."

"He's an American soldier," Strickland argued. "They're a little easier to get hold of than a foreign power that has us on their shit list."

Zero snapped his fingers. "You're right. What about someone in the Fifth Fleet?"

"I don't know. Maybe? I'd have to look into it."

"Please do," Zero implored. "And carefully. You've seen the news. It's happening now, and I think the people behind this have something else up their sleeve, something big enough to spark the powder keg that the Persian Gulf is about to become. We need to get in touch with someone over there and make them aware of what's happening." His ideal situation would be to contact the IRGC directly, attempt to explain what was happening, plead with them to stand down and give him time to resolve the US front. But if they could contact someone high enough in the Fifth Fleet, it might be enough.

"First things first," Strickland said. "Where are you?"

"Hang on." Zero brought up the GPS app on the iPhone and read Strickland his coordinates. "That's where I am right now, but I'm not staying. I need to get clear of the area fast. Division and FBI might be still be poking around."

"You're on foot?"

"Yeah. And I'd like to stay that way." The last thing he needed was a report of a stolen vehicle, another chase, another opportunity for Carver to actually kill him.

"There's a place about fifteen miles north by northeast of you. It's a ridge called Indian Head Point. You know it?"

Zero found it on the GPS. "I do now."

"Head there. By the time you reach it, I'll have a car and some gear waiting for you."

"And you won't be," Zero said forcefully. "Right? Todd?"

"Right," Strickland murmured. "I won't be. But the second you find yourself in over your head, you call me. Got that?"

"I got that. Thanks." He grimaced with the pain in his injured hand. "And maybe throw a few aspirin in the glove box."

"I will. Be safe." Strickland hung up.

Zero checked the location of Indian Head Point again on the phone. It looked like a small park, with a ridge overlooking the Potomac. As long as he stuck close to the shore and followed its northerly direction, he would reach it.

"Fifteen miles," he grumbled as he started off. His legs already ached. As he walked, he pried the back off the iPhone, pulled out the battery, and hurled it into the trees. Then he slipped the SIM card out of it, snapped it in half, and tossed the two pieces aside.

In the distance, he heard sirens wailing. The old couple had called the police. He picked up his pace, picking his way through the trees. They would report a soaking wet man with a gun and one hand bandaged. But he knew just as well that the CIA would bury the report immediately if they wanted Zero to stay dead.

But why? Declaring him KIA would mean that the Feds and police would call off the search. Carver would still be on the trail, likely with the Division. Maybe they didn't want the fallout of any dead cops or agents.

Or maybe they're trying to draw you out. Trying to lull you into a false sense of security.

Suddenly it dawned on him: *They think you'll try to get to Pierson again.* They didn't know what he had, what evidence of the plot. If that was their plan, it wouldn't work. There was no way that Zero would get within a thousand yards of Pierson after what they had accused him of, and he knew it.

Besides, it wasn't Pierson he needed to get close to. Maria and Sanders would get the documents, as they had planned. That's where he would be next, to rendezvous with them and form a new plan.

And while I'm at it, try to persuade a Fifth Fleet commander to mutiny against the United States government at the behest of a rogue CIA agent.

Chapter Seventeen

Lieutenant Thomas Cohen hadn't slept much in the brief span since the USS *Constitution* had demolished the IRGC ship. He'd been given a four-hour shift rotation, which was usually a welcome reprieve for him to stretch his legs, nap, enjoy some sunshine, or send a few emails back home. But all he could see in his mind's eye was the explosion, seventy-six lives extinguished as quickly as the small green blip had vanished from radar.

He spent the four hours in his bunk, staring up at white-painted metal of the ceiling, and wondering about everything.

That was the worst part, the not knowing. The crew of the *Constitution* was only aware of what they were told, and they weren't being told much. Mere minutes after the destruction of the IRGC vessel, the crew's Wi-Fi went dark. They could not access any American news sites; they couldn't ask family back home what was happening. They didn't know what the media was reporting, what the Iranian government was saying, or what the White House's stance was.

Cohen understood the brass's position. The last thing they needed was some careless ensign to send a message back home that mentioned something about their ship's position or where they were headed. Or worse, post on social media. Even so, it was infuriating being told so little and knowing even less.

He wasn't the only one who thought so.

"I wish they'd tell us what was happening out there," Lieutenant Davis muttered from his station only a few feet from Cohen's array. The air on the bridge felt stuffy, wrought with the tension of a mostly oblivious crew. "What do you think we're going to find when we get there?"

"I don't know, Lieutenant." Cohen couldn't begin to guess. He knew only that the USS *Constitution* had been ordered to head directly toward the Strait of Hormuz. As they drew nearer, blips appeared on the radar that, with coordinated effort from Davis and visual confirmation from Gilbert out on the deck, turned out to be other Fifth Fleet ships. They too were heading toward the strait, the first dozen or so that would arrive due to proximity with the remainder of the fleet coming in from either Bahrain or the Gulf of Oman on the other side of the strait.

That too was strange. A convening of the fleet's divisions without synchronization could only mean that they had all been given the same orders, but independently and from someone higher than the admiral.

And *that* could only mean that the mobilization of the Fifth Fleet was being ordered and monitored by someone back home—very likely a particularly powerful someone seated at a desk in the White House. Cohen could not say with any certainty, but it felt very much like President Pierson was preparing for war.

Perhaps stranger still was that Cohen had been ordered only to utilize the average marine radar, an apparatus that was roughly the equivalent of the type of radar one might find on a commercial fishing boat. His surface search range was limited to about fifteen nautical miles, though the destroyer's full radar capabilities could allow them to paint targets from three hundred nautical miles and to an altitude up to thirty-five thousand feet if they desired.

There was only one reason for that. Radar was a "see and be seen" technology. Limiting their range meant limiting the ability of others to see them. In short, the one-hundred-fifty-five-meter-long American destroyer-class warship was attempting to sneak up on the Strait of Hormuz.

"Captain on the bridge!" a voice bellowed sharply.

"As you were." Captain Warren strode onto the bridge and quickly ordered them down before Cohen could rise from his seat. "Miller, what's our ETA?"

Petty Officer Miller spoke up from behind Cohen, at a console facing in the opposite direction. "We're about sixteen miles out from the strait, sir. Maintaining our current speed of approximately twenty-eight knots, we should arrive in about thirty minutes."

Warren nodded. "Cohen, how are we looking?"

"Nothing on the horizon on short-range surface search, sir."

"Good. Davis, any transmissions?"

"Only our own, sir," Lieutenant Davis reported. "The rest of Combined Task Force 152 is trailing us by about three miles, and 158 is incoming from the northwest."

Warren nodded. "Let's keep those lines open." The captain paced to the observation windows of the bridge and peered out at the sunny, cloudless morning, his hands clasped behind his back.

No one spoke for several minutes. Cohen studied Captain Warren, with his back to him, and tried to determine what might be going through the captain's mind. He didn't seem troubled as much as he did pensive, but Warren was hardly a man who wore his emotions on his sleeve.

"Sir," Cohen said suddenly before he could stop himself. "I'd like to inquire about the current state of relations between us and Iran. If I may."

Petty Officer Miller swiveled in his seat and gawked at Cohen's audacity. But Davis had his back. "We all would, sir," he added quickly. "We believe we have a right to know what we may be sailing into."

Warren looked down at his boots. "You're not wrong, Lieutenants. You do have a right to know." He turned to face them. "We're not at war, if that's what you're asking. Not yet. The Iranians are being somewhat perfunctory with their declarations. I wish I had something more to tell you, but the truth is that I can't say because I don't know. I do know that wars don't unfold in a day. Sometimes it can be months, even years, before tensions escalate to that point. We're already in a tense situation. If the dam breaks, we're on the front line. But our government will do whatever is in their power to avoid it coming to that, rest assured."

"Yes sir," Cohen murmured. It seemed to him that Warren had said a lot of words without saying much at all. The captain was normally a succinct man who gave more direct orders and information.

None of this felt right, but Cohen didn't have time to question it further.

The radar array beeped a warning as a pair of green blips appeared on the short-range surface scan. "Sir..." he started to say, and then two more appeared. "Captain, we've got four—no, six unidentified vessels on radar, about fifteen miles out. Make that eight, and rising."

The radar was picking up a growing number of targets, arranged in a line to the southeast with a span of approximately a quarter mile between them.

He got on the radio immediately. "Gilbert, do you have visual? Over."

"Negative," Gilbert announced. "Horizon is about twelve miles out. It'll be a few minutes before I can confirm visual. Over."

Captain Warren rounded the array and peered over Cohen's shoulder. "IRGC ships?" he asked.

"Can't confirm yet," Cohen replied. "But if they are..." He trailed off. "Jesus. Twenty-three of them. It looks like they're—"

"Blockading the strait," Captain Warren finished his thought. "Cutting off the Fifth Fleet in the Gulf of Oman from us. Miller, slow us to twenty knots. Davis, get on the horn to the rest of 152 and see if anyone else has confirmation."

"Should I hail them, sir?" Davis asked.

"No," Warren said adamantly. "We stay the course and do what we came here to do."

But what did we come here to do? Cohen wanted to ask. But he already realized the answer. Mobilizing the Fifth Fleet was an intimidation tactic, and the IRGC was responding in kind. In minutes, there would be American warships facing Iranian warships, within firing range of each other.

God help us if they make a move.

"Sir," Cohen said as he studied the array, "it looks like three of them are breaking off from the blockade."

"Headed where?" Warren asked quickly.

"Right for us, sir."

Gilbert's voice crackled in the radio. "Got visual on three boats, heading north by northwest... Are they coming straight at *us*?"

Lieutenant Davis snapped to attention. "Captain, one of them is hailing us." His eyes unfocused for a moment as he listened to whatever message was coming through his headset in one of the three foreign languages he spoke. "They... oh, god."

"Davis," Warren said sternly.

"I'm sorry, sir." He cleared his throat and announced, "They're asking us to identify ourselves. They want to know if we're the ship that fired on theirs yesterday."

Warren clenched his jaw, deliberating for a moment. "No point in lying or trying to hide. Tell them that Captain Warren of the USS *Constitution* confirms that we returned fire on a ship that fired upon us first. Tell them to stand down and allow our assets from the Gulf of Oman to pass through the strait, or the consequences will be swift and severe."

Davis shot Cohen a panicked look. "Sir..."

"That's an order, Lieutenant," Warren said sternly.

"Yes sir." Lieutenant Davis closed his eyes for a moment and then repeated the message in Farsi to the IRGC ship.

On the radar screen, Cohen could see that the trio of Iranian ships was not slowing their approach. Behind the *Constitution*, six other ships from Combined Task Force 152 were gaining fast. Three were destroyers, and one was the USS *Pennsylvania*, a dreadnought-class battleship more than twice the size of theirs. The ships fell into a line formation as they made their approach toward the strait and the three IRGC vessels.

"Sir," said Davis, "they're demanding that we stand down and return to Bahrain."

Warren scoffed. "You can tell them we don't take orders from terrorists."

Jesus. Cohen's heartbeat doubled its pace. *Has the captain lost his mind?* Moreover, what did the Iranians have to threaten them with?

If they fired, they'd be lucky to get a single direct hit before the *Constitution* blew them out of the water. All three ships were within range of Tomahawk missiles, and were quickly entering torpedo range.

Davis relayed the message in Farsi, though Cohen doubted that he used the same terminology as Warren. The captain stared out the observation window, his jaw set in grim determination or, as Cohen saw it, mulish obstinance.

"Tell them to stand down, Davis."

"Sir, that's the same thing they're telling us," Davis said, desperation measured in his voice.

"Four miles," Cohen announced as the gap between them closed.

"Our job is to protect the strait," Captain Warren declared.

"Sir," Davis pleaded, "don't you see that's what they think they're doing?"

"We have orders, Davis, from the highest office in the world," Warren growled. "We don't stand down because a few ramshackle boats get in our way and tell us to. Miller, stay on course!"

Don't fire at us, Cohen thought. *Don't be stupid. Just let us pass.* But he already knew that wasn't an option.

"Cohen," Warren said, his voice low, "I want to know the instant they fire on us."

"Yes sir," he murmured. His gaze was glued to the radar console, waiting for the tiny blip or Gilbert's voice in his ear to confirm visual confirmation that the Iranians had fired rockets. One day earlier, it had been a joke, something to laugh about while the new guys pissed themselves over rockets that were three hundred meters or more from target.

Today it would mean the unyielding demolition of these three ships.

A blip appeared on the screen and Cohen's breath caught in his throat.

But it wasn't from the IRGC ships.

"Missiles out!" Gilbert shouted through the radio.

"Sir!" Cohen couldn't believe his eyes. The missiles were fired from behind the *Constitution*, six of them in all, and on the two-dimensional radar screen it appeared that they were coming straight at the destroyer.

Before Cohen could relay the message, a half dozen tactical ballistic Scud missiles, thirty-seven feet long and carrying a payload of approximately fifty kilotons each, soared over the *Constitution*. Even behind the thick protective glass of the bridge, the roar was deafening. The seat quaked under Cohen. He tore off his headset and stood, looking over the array and out the observation window, as the Mach-5 missiles struck the three IRGC ships from less than four miles out.

To call the damage immediate and devastating would have been an understatement. Where the ships had once been was instantly a conflagration, a swirling maelstrom of fire and smoke visible from more than twenty miles in any direction.

Davis put one hand over his mouth. Miller sat at his console with his head bowed and eyes closed. Warren watched, unblinking, as the three IRGC ships were utterly and completely destroyed.

The Scud missiles had come from the USS *Pennsylvania*, there was no doubt about that. The dreadnought was the only ship in the vicinity carrying that sort of payload.

And they had just broken the rules of engagement.

At long last, Warren turned from the window. He took a measured breath before addressing Davis. "Get on the horn to the *Pennsylvania*. Confirm targets destroyed."

Cohen looked over at him and saw a shadow of anger flash across his face. Davis held his chin high as he said, "With all due respect sir, if I get back on this radio it's going to be to report this incident to the admiral."

"I see." Warren appeared disappointed. "They fired first, Davis."

He frowned in confusion. "What?"

Warren looked from him to Cohen to Miller. "They fired first. We refused to stand down, and the IRGC fired a rocket. The *Pennsylvania* returned fire with long-range missiles to ensure destruction." He let that sink in for a moment before continuing. "That's what the report is going to say. That's what the report from the *Pennsylvania* is going to say. If you have a different version of the account, speak up now. You'll have plenty of time to get your facts straight in the brig before the inevitable court-martial."

He glanced about again. Davis stared back in stunned silence. Cohen could not meet the captain's eyes. Miller kept his head bowed.

"Good," Warren said quietly. "I'd hate to lose any of you. Miller—continue on course to the strait. Cohen, keep an eye on those blockade ships."

Lieutenant Cohen slowly sank back into his chair, staring ahead at the radar screen but hardly noticing it. The captain's words from only moments earlier ran through his head: *No point in lying or trying to hide.* He was right. The United States wanted a war, and they were going to get it.

Chapter Eighteen

"Make a right up here," Carver instructed, studying the map open on the tablet in his hands. Two red dots, so close they nearly overlapped into one, showed a position about a mile down the dirt road cutting between two vast Virginia orchards.

The driver, a Division man named Denham, eased the black sports car to the right. "I still don't get it," he muttered. "Why'd the CIA declare Zero dead if they think he survived that fall?"

Carver held back his sigh of irritation. Like most of the Division's ranks, Denham—and his compatriot, Barrett, seated in the back seat—was thick-necked, handy with knife and gun, and unaccustomed to thinking on his own. It was a trait that made them apt soldiers, but made Carver prone to repeating himself.

"Because Agent Zero is smart," Carver said evenly, "and clearly has help. But he is also predictable. By now he knows that he's supposedly dead. The first thing he'll do is get his daughters to safety. Slow it down a bit. Cut the headlights."

Denham did as he was told. After sending Zero's car plunging into the Potomac, Carver and his Division pals traded in the shot-up Jeep for the sports car and immediately went in pursuit of Zero's girls, at the order of Deputy Director Riker. The four Division men who had been sent to Zero's house earlier—two of them posing as FBI agents in an attempt to lend credibility to their little visit—had gone dark and, if Carver had to guess, were likely dead.

Their SUV's GPS signature, however, was still active. And according to CIA techs, it just happened to be in the exact same place as both of the Lawson girls' tracker implants, as well as their personal cell phones. According to the tracking app that Carver was currently monitoring, they were sitting on the very same dirt road, about fifty miles west of I-95 where Zero had met his ersatz demise.

Carver had had his doubts that Zero was still alive after the tumble over the cliff, but then a police report had cropped up mere minutes after; a man with a gun and an injured right hand had broken into a home and stolen a cell phone.

The CIA had stifled the report quickly, and their techs confirmed that the stolen phone was now inactive. But Carver was sure of what it meant: Zero must have contacted his daughters.

There was no way he could have gotten to the farm faster than Carver and his two cronies, which meant that this was their rendezvous point, and they were waiting for their father to arrive. With a little luck, Carver would get both of the girls and whoever was helping Zero. Then all they had to do was wait for him to get there.

"Can't see a damn thing," Denham muttered as the car bounced over tractor ruts in the dirt road. With the headlights off, the road was little more than a swath of shadow with silhouettes of trees on either side.

"Stop here," Carver instructed. "We don't want them to hear us coming. They're a little less than a quarter mile ahead, as the crow flies." He set the tablet in the center console and hefted the SAW, checking to make sure the magazine was full.

The three of them hiked for about a hundred and fifty yards before Carver held up a fist to stop them. "Denham, flank left through the trees," he whispered. "Barrett, head right. Keep your eyes and ears open. They might be hiding. No flashlights. No shots fired unless absolutely necessary. Meet at the SUV. Got it?"

"Got it." Barrett picked his way into the carefully planted rows to the right, and Denham headed in the opposite direction, both with pistols drawn. Carver held the SAW barrel down and, keeping his posture in a slight crouch, continued straight onward down the dark dirt road.

He might be expecting us, Carver told himself. *Someone like Zero doesn't just forget about tracker implants. But he's desperate. He knows we're on him.*

It felt like it took a long time to reach his destination, and it did; in the darkness and at his slow pace, it was a full five minutes before he saw the SUV, black with windows tinted, no lights on, sitting as silently as a grave right in the center of the narrow throughway. Carver paused about fifty feet from it and, sticking close to the dark tree line, lowered himself to one knee and brought the SAW to his shoulder. He waited nearly another minute before he saw the silhouette of Denham step out of the orchard, and then Barrett from the other side.

Both men shook their heads to signal that they had found nothing.

Carver nodded and rose to his feet again. He dared to edge closer to the SUV. He couldn't see inside it, but he knew. *They're in there. They know we're here.*

"Come out," he ordered loudly and clearly. "Open the door slowly. Hands where we can see them."

The two Division mercs held pistols aloft, ready for anything. Almost anything. When nothing happened, they glanced over at Carver.

"There's no way out of this," he announced, loud enough for anyone inside the car to hear. "Just come out, and I promise you won't be harmed."

Still nothing happened. Carver swore under his breath. "All right. Denham, get the door. Rear passenger side. I'll cover."

Denham sidled close to the SUV, keeping the pistol in his right hand while reaching for the door handle with his left.He yanked the door open. The dome light inside the car clicked on with the opened latch, and Carver recoiled immediately.

"Good god," he breathed.

"Fuckers!" Denham said hoarsely. "They killed Reinhold."

With the light on, they could see inside the cab of the SUV, where four men were positioned in the seats, front and back. Two wore suits; two wore black with Division patches on their shoulders. But all four were dead.

"Son of a bitch!" Carver spat. He wrenched open the driver's side door. In the center console were two cell phones, one in a pink case and one in green. Zero's daughters' phones.

But the implants…

It took him only a cursory glance to find those as well. He might not have noticed the rice-sized tracking chips if they hadn't been sitting in a small drop of blood.

They cut them out. They killed four men. They ditched the SUV all the way out here. Rage bubbled up in Carver's throat, acidic as bile. Zero definitely had help—likely Johansson, if he had to guess—and while they had been chasing him down I-95, his cohort was ditching bodies in the middle of nowhere, fifty miles out of the way.

"He's going to pay for this," Barrett grunted angrily. "What the hell do we do now?"

Carver lowered the SAW in one hand, frustrated and suddenly feeling exhausted. "I'll call it in. We'll have a team get out here and sweep for prints, hair, anything that might tell us who's helping him. In the meantime, get their wallets, guns, phones, anything that might be incriminating if someone else comes along and finds them."

Carver leaned over the body in the driver's seat and reached for the glove compartment to get the SUV's registration. He paused with his hand on the latch and looked down quizzically. There was something on the floor, bathed in shadow between the dead passenger's feet.

"The hell?" he muttered as he reached for it.

Then he stopped. His breath caught in his throat as he realized what it was.

The block of C4 had two wire leads stuck into one end of it, trailing underneath the seat.

"Get clear!" Carver staggered back, nearly falling over, and scrambled away from the SUV as fast as he could. "Get cl—"

The explosion sent him sprawling forward onto his stomach in the dirt. The air was flattened from his lungs as the detonation, deep and powerful, sent a shockwave through his entire body.

When he could breathe again, he sucked in a ragged gulp and forced his limbs to move. His head pounded as he struggled to roll over. Black smoke roiled thickly from the blasted-out windows of the SUV, the cab and its contents engulfed in orange flames.

Another shape, smaller, burned in the dirt road near it. It was Denham. He'd been incinerated in the explosion.

"Barrett?" Carver croaked.

The Division merc sat up from the dirt ten feet from Carver, his face streaked with soot and bleeding from one ear. The reflection of the flames danced in his horrorstruck eyes.

"I'm here," Barrett managed, his voice raspy. He groaned and slowly pulled himself to his feet. "Denham," he murmured. "Bastards got Denham."

Barrett's head snapped to one side in the same instant a rifle shot cracked the air. He fell sideways in the dirt and didn't move.

Carver lurched for the SAW, lying in the dirt a few feet from him. He tried to stand, but staggered and fell to his knees, still disoriented from the jarring explosion. Whoever had detonated the bomb was still here—and by the angle Barrett had been shot, they were hiding between Carver and his car.

He brought the SAW to elbow level and fired a volley of bullets into the darkness, spraying left and right. He was certain he wouldn't hit his assailant, but he needed the cover fire; he was a sitting duck on the dirt road, illuminated by the burning SUV. Carver climbed to his feet again and lurched for the darkness of the orchard.

Another rifle shot cracked off, sending a plume of scattered dirt where his left foot had just been as he rushed toward the orchard. A second shot smacked into a tree and sent slivers of bark whipping his face. In the relative safety of the trees and the dark, Carver froze, gripping the SAW tightly and listening as intently as he could.

He heard nothing except the dull roar of the fire and the occasional crackling of its burning contents.

This isn't Zero, he reasoned. Whoever this was had plenty of opportunity to blow the bomb before Carver noticed it. They had felled Barrett with a headshot but missed Carver twice. This was someone who didn't seem to want him dead, but wounded enough to be out of the game.

He was pretty sure he knew who it was.

"You still out there, John?" he whispered to himself. Three more minutes passed in silence. If it was his former partner, he was smart enough not to approach the SUV or pursue Carver in the orchard. He would have run by now.

Still, Carver remained silent as possible as he picked his way carefully from tree to tree, his eyes adjusting to the darkness as he regained his balance and faculties. His head still pounded, but at least he could walk straight. He navigated the trees and traveled parallel to the dirt road, staying vigilant and doing his best to estimate the distance to where he'd left the black sports car.

It wasn't until he was about to peer out of the orchard that he realized his error.

Denham had the keys.

"The hits just keep on coming," he murmured. He could hotwire it, but that would require taking his attention off of the road long enough to do so. If his assailant was still here, Carver would be an easy target. Besides, he wasn't about to take the chance that they hadn't stuck a bomb in their car as well.

Instead he stayed in the orchard and kept on moving, another half mile before the trees ended and he came upon the main road. He glanced left and right; there were no cars in sight, no lights, not even streetlamps on this stretch.

He started walking, back the way he had come in the car with the two other men.

After about twenty minutes and a relative certainty that he wasn't being followed, he made the call.

"Well?" Riker answered curtly.

"Well," he repeated flatly. "I think we're going to have to reconsider our strategy. It seems that Zero isn't quite as predictable as we thought."

Chapter Nineteen

Sara caught a glimpse of a sign through the windshield that read "WELCOME TO SUMNER. POPULATION: 353." They really were in the middle of nowhere, it would seem. The small Nebraska town looked as if it hadn't changed a bit in a hundred years. And just as quickly as they'd entered it, they were out the other side again, two minutes flat down a single main road.

It wasn't fair. It wasn't fair that they'd barely been back to some sense of normalcy just to get uprooted again, sent away. She knew it was for their own protection, and of course she didn't want to get caught again in the type of situations they had found themselves in before—in fact, she tried not to think about what had happened to them in Slovakia, the harrowing experience of being taken by human traffickers.

Still. It wasn't fair.

The tiny plane that had brought them here had landed in the middle of the night. The three of them—Sara, Maya, and Mitch—got into a waiting pickup truck and then drove in silence along a road that felt like a corridor through the vast wilderness. The road took them up a winding mountain pass and down the other side. Sara was sharply aware that they had nothing, no bags and no phones, only the clothes on their backs, a thousand miles from home with their lives in the hands of a stranger while their father did what he could to save the world once again.

It was disorienting, alarming, and surreal all at the same time. It felt like a dream from which she wished she could wake up.

Is this what our lives are going to be like now? she wondered, though she didn't dare say it aloud.

Mitch had hardly said more than a few words for the whole trip. He was a quiet sort, Sara noticed, who tended to answer questions as shortly and as vaguely as possible.

"Where are we?" Maya asked as they drove. Her older sister sat by the window while Sara sat in the middle on the bench seat in the truck.

"Nebraska," Mitch said simply.

Maya rolled her eyes. "No kidding. Where exactly?"

"Better if you don't know."

Despite everything, Sara wasn't nervous or frightened. She was mostly just worried for her dad. And, if she was being honest, a little irritated at their sudden upheaval once again.

At the far end of town, Mitch slowed the truck and turned onto a rural road overlooking a wooded hill. The homes they passed were spaced far apart, nearly a football field's length between them. Finally he cut the headlights and eased the truck into the driveway of a house that looked like a handmade log cabin. It was cute, Sara thought, rustic and cozy-looking.

"Wait here." Mitch got out of the truck and did a slow walk around the perimeter of the house. Then he stepped up onto the wooden front porch and inspected the doors, the windows. The cabin was completely dark; it didn't appear anyone was home or had been in quite some time. At last the mechanic got down on one knee and fiddled with the doorknob.

"What's he doing?" Sara asked quietly.

"Looks like he's picking the lock," Maya replied.

Then the door was open, and Mitch vanished inside for a few minutes. When he appeared again, he waved at them from the porch to join him.

The cabin was bigger on the inside than it appeared from the outside, but it was apparent that no one had been there in years. The furniture was covered by white sheets and every horizontal surface was coated in a thick layer of dust. Spiders had made grand webs in the corners of each room. And much like the town of Sumner they'd passed through to get here, there was no evidence that they hadn't time-traveled back to the nineteenth century somehow. There was no radio, no television, no computers or Wi-Fi.

The kitchen didn't even have a microwave.

"What is this place?" Maya asked, wrinkling her nose to illustrate her disgust.

"Some years back, this used to be a halfway house for witness protection," Mitch told her. "They'd send people here for a few days, holed up with an agent or two, while they arranged a new identity and a place to live. Nowadays all that stuff is digital and happens a lot faster. Government owns this house, but it hasn't been used in a long time. Lucky for us…" He flicked a light switch, and the overhead kitchen light came on. "They kept the lights on and water running."

"Why?" Sara asked.

Mitch shrugged. "There are places like this all over the country. I bet by now the expense has gotten folded into some 'miscellaneous' category on an expense report somewhere. Anyone who knew about this place is likely retired or dead."

"Except you?" Maya mused.

"Including me," Mitch responded cryptically. He headed down a short hall and pulled open a narrow closet door. The hinges squealed in protest. "Ah! Good. Linens. They might be a bit musty, but they'll do. There are two bedrooms in the back; you can share, or you can each take one. I don't mind the couch. Go ahead and make yourselves up somewhere to sleep. In the morning I'll make a run for supplies."

Sara went to the linen closet and grabbed a stiff, folded bed sheet and a scratchy wool blanket. The two bedrooms in the back were tiny, almost identical, each containing only a twin bed on a rusting frame and a small wooden nightstand.

She spread the sheet out over the bed, and then the blanket, all the while knowing that it would be near impossible for her to sleep. She hadn't been sleeping much lately, even at home, and now she was there in a Nebraska safe house in the middle of nowhere with a man they didn't know at all.

Sara sat on the edge of the bed and rubbed her face with her hands. A couple of months ago, she might have burst into tears at the very thought of their situation, but she hardly cried anymore. It was as if a well inside her had run dry. The only time she shed tears was during the nightmares about what she had gone through at the hands of the traffickers.

"Hey." She looked up sharply at the sound of Mitch's gruff voice and her hands fell away from her face. He stood in the doorway and leaned casually against the jamb. "You okay? Need anything? Hungry, or thirsty, or …?"

She shook her head no.

Mitch stared at the floor for a long moment. "You're, what, fourteen now?"

"Yeah." Her voice sounded tiny, even in the small bedroom. From beyond the doorway, she heard a heavy snore; it seemed that Maya had fallen asleep immediately. *Lucky*, Sara thought.

Her expression must have been showing it, because Mitch smiled paternally. "Can't sleep, can you?"

She shook her head again.

"I know how that goes," Mitch admitted. He gestured toward the floor of the bedroom. "Can I …?"

Sara nodded, and he lowered himself with a groan to a seated position on the floor, facing her. "I knew your dad, back in the day. We used to work together."

"Were you an agent?" Sara asked.

Mitch nodded. "I was. But that has to be our secret, okay? You can't tell anyone. I'm sort of supposed to be dead."

Sara blinked. She very much wanted to ask why he was supposed to be dead, but she held back. "Okay."

"Anyway, your dad used to talk about you. Both of you. He called you a firecracker. Call your sister a smartass." Mitch chuckled lightly. "Those were like his codenames for the two of you, so he didn't have to use your real names in the field. 'Firecracker' and 'Smartass.'"

Sara couldn't help but grin a little. "Maya is still kind of a ... you know." She drew up her legs and lay on her side on the bed. "What was he like?"

Mitch shrugged a shoulder. "Not all that different than he is now."

"No, I mean ... what's he like? You know. When he's working."

Mitch nodded slowly. He seemed to understand what she was asking; she wanted to know more about the side of her dad that she had only recently discovered, the hidden side that was terrifying and thrilling at the same time.

"Confident," Mitch told her. "Decisive. Proud. Capable. He was always the smartest guy in the room, but he didn't make you feel like it. If he trusted you, he wanted to know how you were feeling, what you were thinking." Mitch chuckled slightly and added, "Unless he didn't like what you had to say. Then he could make you feel like an outright idiot."

Sara smiled. She could feel her eyelids growing heavy. "I think you're a good person, Mitch. I think we can trust you."

Mitch smiled, the corners of his beard tugged upward. "I'm glad to hear that. But cool it with that 'good person' stuff. I've got a reputation to uphold." With another groan he rose from the floor, but he lingered in the doorway as Sara felt herself drifting off. "I'll keep you safe, though," he promised quietly.

Sara's last thought before she fell asleep was how much she wanted to believe that, and how little she actually did.

Chapter Twenty

Zero maintained as brisk a pace as possible as he hiked to Indian Head Point, despite his aching limbs and the increasing pain in his broken hand. Attempts to distract himself by thinking proved generally fruitless; his thoughts kept coming back to the myriad unanswered questions that were swimming through his mind. How much time did he have, if any? Had he made any headway in convincing Pierson? Why had the CIA declared him dead? Did his girls safely arrive in Nebraska with Alan?

None of them were questions he could answer alone in the woods in the middle of the night.

At long last he reached the ridge and the small park that accompanied it. It took some searching, but he found the gray sedan, about a decade old, on a dirt pull-off at the head of a hiking trail. He didn't approach it right away; instead he carefully and quietly scouted the perimeter.

He wasn't worried that Carver or the Division was there. He was worried that Strickland had gone against his word and was waiting for Zero to arrive so that he could follow.

At last he approached the car. The doors were locked but the keys were hidden atop the tire in the passenger-side wheel well. He checked the truck first; there was a small canvas bag there, and inside it were some supplies, the most welcome of which were three one-liter bottles of water. He drank one down in its entirety. Also in the bag were a Glock 17, a Ruger LC9, a black nylon holster for each, a sonic ear, headphones, a first-aid kit, a change of clothes, a wad of cash held together with a rubber band, and a burner phone.

Zero stowed the bag in the passenger seat and turned the key in the ignition. The car rumbled to life; the engine was loud, but otherwise it seemed to be in good shape and there was a full tank of gas. He backed out to the road and drove about ten miles north, until he reached a twenty-four-hour diner, where he parked in the lot.

First he checked the burner phone, half expecting Strickland to have left a message there for him, but there were none. There were two numbers programmed into it, one under "Eliot" and the other under "Doyle."

Zero frowned for a moment as he searched his memory. *I don't know anyone named Eliot.* The only person named Eliot that he could recall ever hearing of was the poet, T.S. Eliot...

He almost laughed out loud. T.S.—Todd Strickland. And the other name, Doyle, must have been a contact number for Watson. Arthur Conan Doyle was the author of the Sherlock Holmes books.

"Didn't know Strickland was that well-read," he joked to himself as he opened the first-aid kit. Inside was an orange prescription bottle of Toradol, a non-narcotic painkiller. He took two tablets with water, and then carefully unwrapped the bandages from his hand. They'd gotten wet, and then dried, and then dirty after his plunge in the Potomac and subsequent hike.

He winced; the pain seemed to increase with the sight of his hand. It was horribly swollen, purple and bruised all over, the metal splints over the broken bones staying in place by virtue of how puffy and disfigured his fingers were. The doctors had warned him that even after a few surgeries, the hand might never be the same.

One of those surgeries was supposed to be that very day. *I don't think I'm going to make that appointment.*

He gently wiped his hand down with an alcohol swab, and then set about rewrapping his hand and splints in layers of gauze, careful not to make it too tight and sucking pained breaths through his teeth.

Once he'd tended to his hand, he changed into the clothes Strickland had provided. It was a difficult process, changing with only one hand while seated behind the wheel of a car, but he managed to pull on the jeans, an olive-green T-shirt, and a light jacket, black and made of breathable cotton, as apt for the early spring weather as it was for concealing guns beneath.

He stuck the phone and cash in the left pocket of his jeans, the Glock under his right armpit, and the Ruger in the left pocket of the jacket. Then he went into the diner and ordered a coffee to go. As he carried it back to the car, another thought struck him. He set the Styrofoam cup on top of the car and knelt beside the tire. He ran his hand around the curve of the wheel well, and then did the same for the other three. He found nothing.

Zero popped the hood and searched under there, and then checked the car's interior thoroughly, the floors and the glove box and under each seat.

I know it's here. If I was Todd, where would I put it? He glanced up at the dome light. *Aha.* It took a minute or so for him to pry the plastic dome off with his thumb, but once it was free he found what he was looking for—a tiny black box, about the size of a dime, one side magnetic and stuck to the car's metal ceiling.

It was a tracking device.

Shame on you, Todd. He knew that Strickland had the best of intentions, but Zero wouldn't let him follow. Not this time. He glanced around the parking lot and saw a pickup truck with New Jersey plates. Someone far from home. When he was sure nobody was looking, he stuck the magnetic tracker in the passenger-side wheel well of the truck.

Then he drove north.

Zero parked the car three-quarters of a block away and across the street from a stately row house in the Georgetown neighborhood of Washington, DC. It was still dark out; it wouldn't be dawn for another two hours. But he had a decent view of the front of the house and its red front door in his side mirror.

Even with his memories returned, Zero had been to Deputy Director Shawn Cartwright's home only once before, and that had been just the week prior when he and Maria showed up on his doorstep to try to convince him that the Brotherhood terrorists apprehended in Syria were not the real ones.

His eyelids grew heavy as he sat there, waiting. He dozed in ten- or fifteen-minute intervals, snapping awake quickly and stretching his sore limbs. The hike hadn't helped. He was exhausted, yet knew he couldn't sleep. Not yet.

It was about 6:30 in the morning, the sun just barely awake itself, before a car backed down the driveway. It wasn't Cartwright's car; it was a blue mid-sized SUV that must be his wife's, Zero reasoned, but then he caught a glimpse through the window and saw who was driving it.

Zero started the gray sedan and rounded the block, pulling back out onto the street three car lengths behind the SUV.

Cartwright drove for about eight minutes through light morning traffic, close to the university, and pulled onto a downtown street lined with boutiques, coffeehouses, and taverns. Then he pulled into a parking spot. Zero kept going for about a half a block and parked as well, watching in the rearview as Cartwright fed the meter.

Where's he going?

He watched as Cartwright disappeared into a coffee shop.

Zero grunted in disappointment. He didn't know if Maria had contacted Cartwright yet, or if they had established a meeting time or place; he only knew that she would get to him, and following Cartwright was the fastest route to get back to her and Sanders.

The deputy director emerged again two minutes later with a tall green and white cup in his hands. But he didn't return to his car; instead he took a seat at one of the small metal tables on the sidewalk just outside the coffee shop.

Zero understood right away what he was doing and grabbed quickly for the sonic ear that Strickland had provided. He pulled the headphones over his head, lowered the passenger-side window halfway, and directed the satellite dish–shaped end of the device toward the sidewalk table.

He hadn't even noticed them at first. But seated at another outdoor table right behind Cartwright were two women. The one with her back to him had blonde hair, pulled up under a black baseball cap with a bun sticking out the back. She wore yoga pants and a track jacket, as if she had just come from the gym. The woman opposite her also wore sporty apparel, with short brunette hair and large dark sunglasses on her face.

It was Maria and Sanders. They'd been sitting there in plain sight, even as he cruised right past them. They were well disguised, chatting idly and pulling apart scones.

Zero carefully tweaked the dial on the rear of the sonic ear, honing in on their conversation. In the mirror, he saw Cartwright bring a phone to his ear.

Then the conversation came through.

"Johansson," he heard Shawn Cartwright say. "Just what the hell is going on?" He didn't raise his voice; he kept his eyes ahead and the phone to his ear as if he was answering a call. Maria didn't turn either; she faced Sanders as if she was talking to her.

"Too much for me to lay out on the table right now," Maria admitted. "I'll have to give you the abridged version. Iran is a conspiracy. Pierson is a pawn. If we go to war, it'll mean that we take the strait, while Russia moves in on—"

A trio of high school–aged kids walked by Zero's car, laughing loudly and jostling each other. He cursed as they drowned out the conversation for a moment, and when they'd passed he dialed in again.

"…Sounds too crazy to be true," Maria was telling Cartwright quietly. "But that's the long and short of it. I need you to believe this."

Cartwright sighed heavily. "Jesus. I knew Riker was up to no good, but I thought she was just gunning for director. Not this."

Zero couldn't help but notice how oddly familiar this felt, him spying on those he was supposed to consider allies. It was the same tactic he'd employed two years earlier. He'd compiled data on everyone—not just those he thought might be involved in the plot, but people close to him as well. Maria and Watson and Morris and Reidigger.

"Is there any news on the Iran front?" Maria asked.

"Yeah, there is," Cartwright admitted glumly. "Shortly after you contacted me this morning, I got word that three IRGC ships have been destroyed in the Persian Gulf, not far from the strait. The official US Navy report claims that they were in pursuit of the *Constitution*, the ship that fired on theirs originally. An American battleship took all three out."

"So that's it then," Maria murmured, almost too quiet for Zero to hear with the sonic ear. "It's going to be war."

"Not yet," Cartwright countered. "Iran knows they don't stand a chance against the entire Fifth Fleet. Declaring war would make it open season on their ships. They'll force our hand. They're going to close the Strait of Hormuz."

"When?" Maria asked. "Is there any speculation?"

"There doesn't have to be," Cartwright told her. "They're already doing it, as we speak."

Zero shook his head. On the one hand, he had forewarned Pierson that this was precisely what would happen. With a little luck, the president would realize that he was right and act accordingly. On the other hand, closing off the strait to the US would only make tensions mount in the Persian Gulf.

"What do you need me to do?" Cartwright asked, jarring Zero from his thoughts.

In the mirror, he watched as Maria transferred a brown satchel from her lap to the ground beside her chair. "In this bag are documents that Kent had been gathering, transcripts of calls and other evidence on the conspirators involved. I need you to make copies. Keep one in a safe place. One needs to get into the hands of the UN. One needs to get to President Pierson. And fast."

"What am I supposed to do, waltz up to the White House and knock? How do you expect me to get these to the president?"

"Use whatever connections you can," Maria insisted. "You're a CIA director. You must have someone who can help. Besides, you can get a hell of a lot closer than me or Kent can."

Cartwright sighed. "Good ol' Zero. I suppose he never considered going digital."

"You and I both know the agency searched his computers," Maria countered. She was right; there was no way he would ever keep backup copies of something like that lying around to be found. The CIA employed some of the best hackers the world over.

"Speaking of," Cartwright said. "The CIA declared him dead."

Maria, in her surprise, almost turned around to face him. "They did? Jesus, you don't think—"

"No," Cartwright said quickly, "I don't. There was no body. They know just as well as you or me that he's still out there. Any idea why they would do that?"

Maria shook her head. She thought for a minute, and then said, "Actually... yeah. If Kent wants to put a definitive stop to this, he can't just assume Pierson will do the right thing. He'll try to get back to the president. Declaring him dead will make it easier for him to get around, possibly lull into a false sense of security."

"He's smarter than that," Cartwright scoffed.

You bet your ass I am, he thought with grim amusement. There was no way he could get back to Pierson, not now, nor could he put his faith in Cartwright to get those documents into the right hands. He needed to come up with a new plan as soon as he reconvened with Maria and Sanders.

"We have to go," Maria declared. "We're going to try to find him before any of that."

"How can I reach you?" Cartwright asked.

"I think it's better if you can't. You hold up your end; we'll get to Kent. And we'll go from there. If we need to contact you, we'll reach out." Maria stood, and Sanders with her. "Thanks, Cartwright. Good luck."

"You too," the deputy director murmured.

Without so much as a look over her shoulder, Maria and Sanders walked away, down the street in the opposite direction from Zero's position, looking as if they were chatting idly with each other. Cartwright lowered the phone from his ear and remained at the table.

Zero quickly tore the headphones from his head and stuffed the sonic ear back into his bag. He could drive around the block, tail them to a safe distance from the coffee shop, and then make his presence known.

His hand reached for the ignition, but he paused. In the side mirror, Cartwright sipped his coffee and then rose slowly from the table. He tossed his cup in a nearby trash bin, stuffed his phone in his pocket, and picked up the brown satchel that Maria had left behind, on the ground between their two chairs.

Zero sighed. The smart thing to do would be to rendezvous with Maria. Form a plan. Contact Strickland and see if he had found a way to contact the Fifth Fleet. But he already knew that he'd made up his mind.

He reached for the door handle instead. He had some questions for his former boss.

Chapter Twenty One

Zero fell in stride with Cartwright when he was only a few yards from his car.

"Keep walking," he said quickly.

Cartwright did a double-take, but he didn't break his stride. "Zero! Jesus. Does Johansson know you're here?"

"Not yet. I have questions for you. Just keep walking." The two of them continued past Cartwright's SUV and down the street at a casual pace. "You have my documents, everything I worked to build two years ago." He gestured to the brown bag over Cartwright's shoulder. "If those fall into the wrong hands, they'll know exactly what to bury so that none of this comes to light. I need to know I can trust you, and the only way to do that is with the truth."

"You should have come to me with this sooner," Cartwright told him. "We could have stopped this before it started."

"I didn't know it sooner," Zero said honestly. "It was hazy, disjointed. It's clearer now."

Cartwright stopped suddenly and stared at him. "Are you back? Like, fully back?"

"Keep walking." Zero pressed on, and Cartwright jogged a few paces to keep up with him. "An answer for an answer."

"That's fair."

"Yes," Zero told him. "I'm back. It happened yesterday, just all came flooding in on a trigger."

"That's great, but why—"

"An answer for an answer," Zero interrupted, and then he got straight to business. "Two years ago, did you order the hit on me? Did you send Reidigger and Morris to kill me?"

"Dammit." Cartwright sighed heavily. "Look, I could give you all the answers you want, but time is of the essence here—"

"Just answer the question," Zero demanded. "The faster we get this over with, the faster you can go do what needs to be done." It was important for him to know the parts of his past that had been left hanging when the memory suppressor was installed. And if there was even a chance that he was going to die trying to stop the war and the plot, he would die knowing the truth.

"I didn't give the order. The order came to me."

Zero scoffed. "That's a bureaucrat's answer."

"What do you want me to say? You were out of control. If you're back, then you remember."

He did remember. He could recall the sharp pain left in the wake of Kate's death—*her murder*—and the agency's insistence that she had died at the hands of an Amun assassin. He remembered his wild tear across Europe and the Middle East. Killing. Torturing. Refusing to come in. Looking for answers in all the wrong places.

And none of it would have happened if he hadn't been lied to in the first place.

"The order came down that you were to be eliminated," Cartwright explained. "Reidigger and Morris volunteered. They didn't want some assassin or Division merc capping you in the back. I'm sorry, Zero. I really am. I blindly followed an order. But I'm not the same person I was then. Neither are you."

They walked in silence for several seconds before Cartwright asked his question. "My turn. How can you be certain that President Pierson isn't in on this plot?"

"Simple," Zero said. "Because we're not at war yet. I saw the look in his eye when I tried to tell him what was happening. He's either an incredible actor, or had no idea. Pierson is a pawn in this game. They thought it would be easier to sway him, but by going to him first I've at least delayed their plan. But if Iran is closing the strait, Pierson will be easier to manipulate. The pressure will be on and the stakes will get high. That's why he needs to see those documents. He needs to know that I wasn't lying."

"My sources told me he's returning to the White House today," Cartwright said. "They think you're dead. Pierson thinks he's safe. You can't go within a mile of that place. You know that."

"I know. Turn left here. We'll loop back around to your car." They took the corner and walked a tree-lined avenue of Georgetown. "One more question, Cartwright. Who killed my wife?"

Again the deputy director stopped in his tracks, staring at Zero in bewilderment. "What?"

Zero stopped too, looking him in the eye. He wanted to gauge his reaction, watch his facial tics, determine whether or not he was telling the truth. "My wife," he repeated. "Kate Lawson. She was murdered. Her autopsy showed she had ingested tetrodotoxin, a powerful poison that causes respiratory paralysis." He felt a lump in his throat; it was the first time he had ever spoken the words aloud. But he pushed himself to continue. "Her diaphragm was paralyzed as she was walking to her car after work. She suffered respiratory failure and died on the sidewalk. And you..." Zero pointed a finger at Cartwright's chest, hovering an inch from his shirt. "You were the one that called me. I was overseas, on an op. And you called me to tell me what had happened. You told me it was—"

"The assassin," Cartwright finished. "The Amun assassin. The one that took your girls. The one you killed in Dubrovnik."

"That's right," Zero said evenly. "You told me that Rais did it, and I killed him for it. He was a psychopath who took pleasure in killing. With his dying breath, he told me about my wife's murder. But it wasn't to gloat. It was to tell me that he didn't get the chance to kill her. Because the CIA did it first."

Cartwright's mouth opened slightly, his lower lip hanging slack. Zero searched for some flicker of betrayal, of recognition, of guile.

But he saw none.

"Zero," he said in almost a whisper, "that's not—"

Distant gunshots cracked sharply, interrupting Cartwright. He crouched instinctively and looked around wildly. Zero perked up, listening as intently as he could as two more shots went off.

That's a Glock 17. About eight blocks away.

Maria.

"Were you followed?" he hissed.

"What? No!" Cartwright insisted, his eyes wide.

"*I* followed you!"

"Then you should know better than me!"

"Come on." Zero grabbed him by the shirt and pulled him along, running back down the avenue the way they came. "We'll get to your car and get out of here. You can drop me as soon as we're clear of—"

Tires screeched, and a black Jeep careened around the corner just ahead of them. Zero spun quickly and pushed through the nearest door. "Come on!"

Cartwright followed as the two of them dashed through an antiques shop, sidling around customers and shelves toward the rear. An elderly female clerk looked up in alarm at the sight of them, but didn't get a word in before they ran past her and into the back.

Zero shouldered open the back door and the two of them leapt out into a narrow alley between two rows of buildings. He looked left and right as Cartwright struggled to catch his breath. "Left. Let's hope they don't double back…"

No sooner had he said it than they heard the roar of the Jeep's engine approaching at the southern mouth of the alley. It zoomed past, and then brakes screeched. They were coming back around.

"Other side…" He started to run in that direction when a siren whooped. A black cruiser with a magnetic-mount dome light squealed to a stop, red and blue flashing, blocking the other end of the alley.

"Basement!" Zero dashed across the alley and down six concrete stairs to a subterranean door. He reared back and kicked it twice before it gave. Cartwright followed, clutching the brown satchel in both arms.

Zero pushed the door closed and glanced around quickly. The basement's floor and walls were smooth concrete, clean, lined on both sides with steel-cage storage units filled with all manner of belongings, each labeled with a number and a letter. They were in the basement of an apartment building.

"Upstairs," Zero ordered. "Come on—"

"Wait," Cartwright panted. "Just wait a second. That was a Division Jeep. They're here for you. Run. I'll stall them as long as I can."

Zero shook his head quickly. "I can get us out of this—"

"I'm a high-ranking CIA official. You're a rogue agent that threatened the president. If I'm found with you, I'll lose all credibility, and these documents will never get to where they need to go."

He couldn't argue with Cartwright's logic. Outside, he heard the shouts of men approaching rapidly.

"Listen to me." Cartwright put a hand on Zero's shoulder, but couldn't seem to make eye contact. "They didn't know the truth. They were following an order, just like I was. We've all been lied to."

"What…?" Zero blinked in confusion. Outside, they could hear boots stomping on cement as the Division men descended on the basement.

"Go!" Cartwright gave him a shove. "Go now!"

"Agent Zero!" called a deep-voiced male from the other side of the basement door. "Drop any weapons and put your hands up! You have to the count of three! One…"

Zero sprinted for the stairs that led up and out of this basement. They turned at the landing and led to a steel door and the first floor of the apartment building.

"Two!"

But he didn't go through the door just yet. Instead he crouched in the stairwell and drew his Glock.

"Three!" He heard the sound of the basement door flying open and smacking against the wall behind it. Heavy footfalls as more than one pair of boots rushed into the basement, and three voices overlapping, all shouting over each other: "Hands up! Hands where we can see them!"

"All right, all right!" Cartwright shouted back. "Jesus. It's me."

Zero cautiously lowered himself to the landing and dared to peer down as best he could without showing himself. All he could see was Cartwright's legs and shoes, and three pairs of black Division boots that surrounded him.

"Where is he?" demanded the voice.

"Where's who?" Cartwright said innocently.

"Agent Zero. Where is he?"

"I don't know," Cartwright insisted. "Isn't it your job to find him?"

The Division man scoffed. "Then what are you doing down here, Director Cartwright?"

"I heard gunshots. I sought safety."

"Uh-huh. And you just happened to be in the vicinity of a known terrorist?"

Cartwright frowned. "I'd hardly call Zero a terrorist."

"Not Zero," said the Division man. "Emilia Sanders. The CIA picked up facial recognition on a traffic cam a few blocks from here."

Zero shook his head, certain that it was a lie. No software was going to pick up facial recognition with the huge sunglasses that Sanders had on her face. They were tracking Cartwright, and they had set a trap. They'd let the meeting happen at the coffeehouse, and then followed Maria and Sanders.

Which meant they'd followed Cartwright and him as well.

He gripped the Glock tighter. *They know I'm here. They waited so they could trap me. But why are they waiting now?*

"What's in the bag, Director?" the Division man asked.

"Official CIA business. Certainly none of yours." Zero saw Cartwright's feet take a cautionary step backward. "Is Sanders in custody?"

"We got her," the man answered. "Along with another agent. One of yours."

Maria. He hoped she was alive. The only gunshots he'd heard were from a Glock, or so he believed. So he wanted to believe.

"And I'm guessing that whatever is in that bag is pretty important to them," the Division man said. "Isn't that true, Director?"

"Are you deaf?" Cartwright said angrily. "These are sensitive documents that require specific security clearance. And frankly, it's none of your damn concern. Now if you believe that Agent Zero is in the area, I suggest you stop wasting my time and get after him!"

"Wasting your time," the merc repeated quietly. "You know what I think? I think he's already gone. I think you're stalling for him."

Outside the basement, wheels screeched as at least two more vehicles arrived. *That's why they're waiting*, Zero realized. They were waiting for backup. They weren't going to risk pursuing Zero with only three men.

"But you're right," the Division man agreed. "We should get after him. Especially after what he's done here today."

"What? What has he done?"

"He killed Deputy Director Shawn Cartwright." A gun barked twice. The deputy director fell silently, his wide eyes staring up at the stairwell where Zero hid.

Chapter Twenty Two

Blind rage overtook him. It slowed his mind while his body reacted in the only way that made sense to him in the moment.

Zero leapt down the stairs, gun in hand, and landed hard on the concrete floor but ignoring the pain that shot up his leg. The Glock 17 was up in an instant, before the three Division men could even look his way.

They had expected him to run.

He shot the first one in the forehead at fourteen feet. He tracked right and fired twice, hitting the second man in the stomach and knee. His aim was slightly off with his left hand.

The third merc hit the deck and rolled, parallel to Cartwright's body. There was a bullet in the deputy director's chest and another in his forehead.

Zero was only vaguely aware of the shouts from outside. Then the broken door to the basement flew open again and, before either he or the merc could get another shot off, a smoke grenade rolled into the basement.

Go. The voice in his head prodding him to get the hell out of there sounded like Cartwright. *Go now.*

He took two steps forward, making a bid for the satchel, but the third Division merc fired blindly in his direction. Zero backpedaled quickly, narrowly missing having his right foot shot through. He sprinted back up the stairs, skidding across the landing and hurtling toward the door. He shouldered it open and found himself face to face with two black-clad Division men on their way to block the door.

Neither party had been expecting the other.

Zero didn't stop. He dropped the Glock and threw himself towards the closer of the two, bringing his hand up in a chopping motion across the merc's neck. Then he twisted around and used his right elbow to catch the second merc's arm before he could get a pistol up.

He dropped his weight, throwing the man off balance, and then brought his elbow to his ear—and with it, the arm. The man screamed as his shoulder twisted in a way it shouldn't.

Then he snapped up the Glock and pistol-whipped the first merc in the back of the head.

Can't just go out the front door. Can't go back. The only way to go was up. He sprinted across a lobby lined with mailboxes as another pair of men came through the glass front doors.

These two wore ties and blue windbreakers. He couldn't see their backs, but he was certain he'd find the letters "FBI" emblazoned across them.

"Freeze!" one of them shouted as they pushed through the door.

He would have rolled his eyes if he hadn't been in such a rush. Instead he dropped to his knees, sliding across the tile, and fired three shots. The FBI agents dove for cover. One of them cried out, but Zero didn't wait around to see where he'd been hit. He leapt to his feet and ran up another flight of stairs, taking them three at a time.

As he reached the first-floor landing he heard the voices shouting, boots stamping, magazines locking into weapons behind and below him. It sounded as if there could have been a dozen of them.

And he was trapped in this building. The Division would have it surrounded. They had already called in the Feds and could call in the police as well. They didn't have to tell anyone that it was Agent Zero, he realized; all they had to say was that an active shooter was in the building.

He kept going, aware of the aching protests of his legs but forcing himself onward, up the stairs to the second floor. The voices behind him grew further; they were likely forming a plan to trap him.

He slowed at the second-floor landing, leaning against the banister and catching his breath for a moment.

Cartwright is dead. The Division is going to pin it on me. They'll have the documents. Maria and Sanders were apprehended. Iran is closing the strait.

Everything had gone completely to hell inside of an hour.

But I'm not caught yet. And I'm not giving up.

He gritted his teeth and forced himself onward, up the stairs again to the third-floor landing. He glanced upward, trying to determine how many stories this building was. It looked like five total; two more would take him to the rooftop, but that wasn't a safe bet since they'd called in a helicopter the last time they'd chased him—

"Don't move," commanded a voice.

Zero turned and glanced down the third-floor corridor. He sighed in dismay. "You've gotta be kidding me."

In the hall was a young man, mid-twenties at best, in boxer shorts and a white T-shirt and with a service pistol in both hands, aimed right at Zero.

"MPD," the man announced. "Put the gun down, and show me your hands."

Of all the buildings I could have chosen, I picked one with an off-duty Metro cop. Zero hung his head for a moment. "Just wait a second," he told the young cop. "You don't know what's going on…"

"No?" His hands tightened around the gun. "Shots fired. Report of an active shooter over the scanner. At least three dead and three wounded so far. You want to tell me again that I don't know what's going on?"

Zero noticed a bead of sweat on the young man's forehead. He heard the voices coming up the stairs, the heavy boots stomping their way up toward him.

"You ever fire that at someone before?" Zero asked quickly. "You ever shot anyone?"

"First time for everything," he said back. But the bead of sweat rolled down his temple. His finger, Zero noted, trembled a bit on the trigger.

"Okay," Zero said. The Division was getting closer. He held up his gun. "Just don't do anything stupid." Zero frowned then, looking past the kid and down the hall behind him. His eyes widened in shock.

There was, of course, nothing there. But the young cop saw the rapid change of expression and couldn't help himself. He instinctively turned, just for a second, and checked his six.

Zero fired only once and hit the young cop in the leg. He yelped and flopped to the ground. Zero was on him in a second; he kicked the gun away, and then directed the young man's hands over the bullet wound. "Hold it there, tight. Help is coming."

Then he raised his Glock and fired down the hall at the oncoming Division mercs. A wave of them had reached the third floor. He fired until the clip was empty, and then snatched up the cop's service pistol—a semi-automatic M17—and fired off three more shots. The Division backtracked down the stairwell, shouting behind them.

They'll try to gas me, he knew. *Unless I do it first.* He glanced up and down the hall, and then scrambled for the fire extinguisher mounted in a small alcove. He tore it loose and, winding back like he was throwing a bowling ball, hurled it down the hall. It bounced twice in the time it took Zero to aim the M17. And then he fired.

The pressurized fire extinguisher exploded in a dense white cloud, completely obscuring the stairs, the landing, and the end of the hall. Zero heard the Division men coughing and cursing as they attempted to navigate the thick fog.

But it would only buy him a precious few seconds. One of these apartments was the young cop's door. He tried the nearest knob. It was locked. So was the next one down. He ran across the hall and the door opened easily.

Please be single and childless, Zero hoped as he closed the door behind him.

No such luck.

"Zach?" A young woman, pretty but looking frightened, dared to peek out of the bedroom. Zero had the gun up in an instant. She sucked in a terrified breath.

"Don't scream," he said quietly. "Don't move. Don't make a sound."

She took a step backward, her eyes instantly brimming and lip trembling. "Is he alive?" she asked.

"Yes." Zero hurried across the apartment to the window. "He's hurt, but not too badly. Open this window for me, I've only got one hand."

"No," the woman said. She didn't meet his gaze and tears fell down her cheeks, but still she refused his request.

"Seriously?" he blinked at her. "I'm trying to get out of your hair. Just open the window."

A fist pounded on the door. "Shot another cop, Zero?" came a jeering voice. "Drop the gun and open it up, or we're busting it down and opening fire."

"My wife is in there!" the voice of the injured young cop screamed.

"I have a hostage!" Zero shouted back. He popped the latch on the window and tried to push it up with only one hand, but it hardly budged. "For god's sake," he pleaded with the young woman, "would you *please* just open the window?"

The glass exploded inward and fire scorched through Zero's shoulder. He glanced up quickly to see a Division shooter on the adjacent rooftop, only slightly higher than eye level with him, reloading a bolt-action rifle.

Zero took aim as well, and squeezed off two shots in the one-point-five-second span that it took the shooter to reload. His head snapped back and he fell to the rooftop.

The bullet had barely grazed his shoulder, cutting open a gash that bled worse than it hurt. He turned back to the young woman to tell her to stay away from the windows.

Then the door to the apartment crashed open.

Zero shoved the woman backward, through the open bedroom door, and threw himself out the broken window. The skin of his thigh snagged on some broken glass as he rolled out to the fire escape and ducked, covering his head.

A fusillade of automatic gunfire thundered through the apartment, shattering windows and puncturing walls.

"The fire escape!" a gruff voice called.

Zero set down the M17, staying low behind the partial brick wall beneath the window, and waited. The instant he saw the barrel of an AR-15 come sticking out, he reached up, grabbed onto it firmly, and dropped his body weight. The Division merc came tumbling out after it. Zero dropped to his back and planted a foot on the man's chest. In one swift motion, he sent the man over the railing and falling twenty-something feet to the alley below—but not before securing the AR-15 in his own hands.

Then he spun and emptied the entire magazine into the apartment.

It was not just a random spray of bullets. Zero brought the rifle to his left shoulder, cradling the barrel under his injured right hand, and fired off precision bursts of three rounds at a time. His mind instantly told him there were five targets in the apartment. He started at the left, fired off three shots, neutralized the target. In his periphery he saw a barrel tracking toward him. He deemed it the next highest threat and quickly took him out. Then the next. And so on. The action was mechanical, so much so that it might have been alarming if his amygdala wasn't preoccupied with attention and memory.

It was a skill he didn't know he'd had and now knew all too well. Shooting ranges, moving targets, rubber bullets firing back at him. Later, the real-life experience of firefights and raids. It would have been frightening to him if he wasn't already aware, somehow, that he could do it and had done it before—which in a very bizarre way was even more frightening to him.

In seconds it was over. Five down. One man in the alley below him, screaming in agony at whatever had broken when he fell. In the hall, the downed cop groaning in pain. Down the hall, out of sight, more voices coming.

He tossed the AR-15 aside. *Now what?* They were just going to keep coming, and the longer he stayed here the more reinforcements they could call. There wasn't a helicopter yet, but there could be soon.

Zero leaned over the railing of the fire escape and saw two men in blue jackets running down the alley toward the building, each with a pistol in hand. *Were they really FBI, or Division posing as FBI agents?* He couldn't be sure, but he couldn't stop and ask.

There was movement behind him. More of the Division was getting into cover around the door to the apartment. An arm swung through the frame and flung something out at him.

"Grenade out!" the man shouted as the cylinder soared through the window and bounced at Zero's feet.

It wasn't a smoke grenade, as he'd expected.

It was an actual, live fragmentation grenade.

Zero kicked at it, sending it careening off the fire escape. It was halfway to the ground before it exploded. He dropped to the metal grating and covered his head. Below him, the men running down the alley were very suddenly running the opposite direction at the very notion of raining grenades.

He scrambled to his feet and ran for the metal stairs—not to go down, but to head up. His feet pounded the steps as he headed for the fourth floor of the building, past windows that he thought might explode with bullets at any moment.

Can't stay here, he reasoned. *Can't go back down. Have to find another way.*

At the fourth-story fire escape level, he glanced over the railing and saw the rooftop of the adjacent building, where the dead sniper lay. It was about twelve feet away and maybe a ten-foot drop.

I can make that.

Before he had time to rethink it, he climbed onto the iron railing of the fire escape, steadying himself carefully and lowering into a crouch. "Okay," he murmured. "Ready, and…"

Bullets pounded the fire escape from directly below him. Sparks flew as they bounced off of metal. Zero covered his head and swayed dangerously forward, threatening to lose his balance and fall out over nothing. He waved his arms backward and arched his back, struggling to regain stability.

There were two of them below him on the fire escape, firing directly upward.

He had no time to steady himself. He pushed off with both feet and launched himself out over the void between the two buildings.

And for the briefest of moments, it looked like he was going to make it.

Chapter Twenty Three

Zero hit the rooftop at his midsection, folding in half over it and then sliding backward. He clawed desperately at the roof's edge with his only good hand while pain shot up his injured right as it slapped uselessly against stucco.

Just as he was about to lose his grip and slide right over the side, his hand closed around a stubby vent pipe. It gave slightly but held, though his body hung uselessly over the side, fully exposed to the two Division members on the fire escape behind him.

He waited for the impact of bullets to smack into his back, the searing pain to tear into him. But when he heard the next thunderous crack, it didn't come from behind him.

It came from above him.

He squinted up at the figure, but the still-rising sun was practically blinding from this angle. Whoever it was on the rooftop with him had the dead sniper's rifle in his hands and had fired off a single shot. With a rapid *shink-click-clink*, he reloaded and aimed again. A second shot fired. A male voice cried out, and then fell silent.

Two hands wrapped around his arm then and pulled, heaving Zero up onto the rooftop. Pain roared through the shoulder that had been shot—grazed, really—as Zero flopped onto the horizontal rooftop, catching his breath and waiting for the pain to lessen.

He looked up.

Then he sprang to his feet, staggering only slightly, and pulled the Ruger LC9 from his pocket.

"Zero, wait—"

He aimed the gun at Agent Carver. "Give me one good reason I shouldn't shoot you right here."

"I'll give you three," Carver said quickly. "I'm unarmed—this gun is empty. I just helped you. And you're still being pursued. It's going to be seconds before they get into this building and up here."

Zero's finger twitched on the trigger. He very much just wanted to fire; Carver had turned on him, lied to him, and tried to kill him twice now.

But when he glanced over his shoulder he saw the two Division men dead on the fire escape. Carver had shot them both, helped Zero up onto the roof, and then dropped the rifle. At the moment the tall agent had both hands up, palms out and empty.

Why? Just what the hell is going on?

"They killed Cartwright," he said breathlessly.

"I know." Carver appeared remorseful. "He's not the only one. It's too much, Zero. I know what they're up to now, and I need your help. I could have killed you easily."

Zero clenched his teeth hard enough that they felt like they might break. If this was a trick, it didn't make much sense. Carver was right; he could have easily killed him just now. He could have shot him. He could have just stomped once on his hand and watched him fall.

"How do we get out of here?" Zero asked quickly.

"This way." Carver took off across the rooftop toward the far side. Bullets rang out behind them, blasting pieces of stucco around them. Zero weaved as he dashed across the roof in a serpentine pattern. At the other end, tied around a thick turbine vent, was a coil of black nylon rope. Carver kicked it over the side and it unfurled to ground level. He grabbed onto one of the two devices threaded through the top of the rope—a double-pulley rappelling device with a rubber-gripped handle.

"See you down there." Carver went first, as if proving to Zero that it was safe. He simply jumped over the side, the device slowing his descent as he zipped toward the ground.

Zero hesitated. *Do I follow? What if this is a ruse to get to me?* That didn't make sense either; Carver had just killed two Division members in cold blood. He knew about Cartwright. Maybe he finally realized that the Division had their own agenda, and what all of it ultimately meant for the world.

He didn't have time to wonder. Zero stuffed the LC9 back into his pocket, grabbed onto the thick handle, and leapt out after Carver. The rappel device slowed his fall to about ten feet per second; when he reached the ground he bent his knees with the impact to avoid injury.

Then he looked left and right for Carver, who seemed to have disappeared.

An engine roared from nearby, and a motorcycle fishtailed out from behind a dumpster. Carver tossed him a helmet. "Here. Get on."

Zero hesitated. He had no idea where Carver would take him if he got on the motorcycle.

Carver scoffed. "Fine. Take this." He reached into a black leather saddlebag and pulled out an MP5 machine pistol. "Make us a path."

Zero pushed the helmet over his head. He heard shouting voices, approaching quickly from the southern end of the alley. Two men rounded the corner, pistols in hand—not the Division, but uniformed police officers. He instinctively raised the MP5 and fired off a short burst, not directly at them, but just over their heads. They both threw themselves to the ground as bullets pelted the brick behind them.

He saved my life, and then he armed me. This would either have to be one hell of an elaborate ruse, or Carver was really trying to help him. *I hope I live long enough to regret this.* He jumped on the back of the bike and wrapped his right arm around Carver's waist.

The motorcycle spun, and then Carver shot up the alley to the north at an easy forty miles an hour. He barely slowed as he turned the corner.

Zero balked. There were no fewer than half a dozen police cars blocking the street outside the apartment building, plus three black Division Jeeps and at least two unmarked cars that he could see.

But that was all he saw, because an instant later Carver fishtailed out onto the avenue and then opened the throttle. Zero was almost bucked off the bike as it leapt forward, to seventy, and then eighty. Carver veered around cars and twice mounted the sidewalk, sending pedestrians leaping out of the way and screaming.

His heart jumped into his throat. He didn't like not being the driver, not being in control, but he had to remind himself that Carver was just as well trained as he was—*well, nearly so.* He let Carver focus on what was in front of them, and twisted around to glance behind them.

Sirens whooped as two cruisers and a black Jeep screamed after them. They were fast, but not nearly as maneuverable as the motorcycle. Just for good measure, Zero raised the MP5 and fired a few short bursts at the front grilles. Sparks flew and a tire blew out on one of the cruisers, sending its front bumper careening into the one beside it.

The motorcycle jerked to the left to avoid a slow-moving car and once again Zero nearly slipped off. He clenched his arm tighter around Carver's waist; his broken hand flared in fresh pain.

Carver took the next left too fast, leaning far too hard and almost laying the bike on its side. Zero gritted his teeth as he leaned in the opposite direction, throwing his weight to counterbalance the falling bike. The motorcycle righted itself, and they took off like a shot again. Zero dared to look over Carver's shoulder and saw the speedometer's needle reaching one hundred. They zoomed by morning commuters as if the cars were sitting still. A glance behind him told him they'd lost the Jeep.

Carver pulled another sharp turn onto a mostly empty street and opened the throttle again. Zero knew this road; it led to an industrial complex not far from the waterfront. Carver slowed to sixty, and then turned into the parking lot of a long warehouse-type building faced with several wide, rolling-door garage bays. He headed straight for one that was partially open, only about five feet from the ground.

As they rapidly approached it Zero realized that Carver wasn't slowing down. He ducked his head as the motorcycle eked under the door and into the empty bay. Then Carver decelerated quickly, whipping the rear tire around as he did. Zero jumped off the back and slammed the garage bay door closed, grunting as he pushed it with one hand. Carver cut the engine and tugged off his helmet.

The sudden silence was deafening after the roar of the motorcycle and the echo of gunshots. Neither of them spoke for a long moment, listening intently for the sounds of sirens or engines approaching but hearing only the blood rushing in their own ears.

"All right," said Carver at last. He kept his voice low, but still it echoed in the wide empty garage bay. "I think we're s—"

Zero pointed the MP5 at the renegade agent's nose. "Start talking."

Carver put both his hands up around his ears, but he didn't back down or shrink away. "I don't expect you to trust me, but I just saved your life, killed two men, and gave you a gun. You think I did all that just to get you alone?"

"You couldn't wait to get me alone before, back in the freight yard in France."

Carver looked away. "I know. It's no excuse, but I was following orders. I thought I was on the right side." He glanced up and his somber gaze met Zero's. "I was wrong."

They were following an order, just like I was. Cartwright's last words came back to him, uttered only a minute before the Division gunned him down. *We've all been lied to.*

Was Cartwright talking about Carver? Did he somehow know that the formerly rogue agent was coming to Zero's aid?

"Please, just let me say what I came here to say," Carver implored, "and then if you still want to shoot me, well... you're the one holding the gun."

"Tell me."

"They're going to pin Cartwright's murder on you," Carver told him. "They're going to say that they heard gunshots, and by the time they got there it was too late. They're making you out to be delusional. And then…" Carver slowly lowered his arms to his sides. "And then they're going to kill him."

"Him who?" Zero demanded.

"The president, Zero. They're going to assassinate the president, and they're going to make Iran the scapegoat."

Chapter Twenty Four

The barrel of the MP5 wavered shakily in his grip. His palm was sweating and his shoulder was already aching from the chase and the bullet that had grazed him. Zero slowly lowered the gun, trying to process what Carver had told him.

"Why? How?"

"You changed the game when you went to Pierson directly," Carver told him. "Despite everything they try to tell him about you and your intentions, you still planted a seed of doubt in his head. He refuses to openly declare war on Iran. Now they're closing the strait. It's a huge wrench in their plot. And this was a very expensive plot, Zero. They're not just going to give up on it."

"But... killing Pierson?" He shook his head. He couldn't conceive of a higher form of treason, of betrayal, of deceit. "Did you actually hear someone say that explicitly?"

"No." Carver shook his head. "Of course not. I would've gotten it on audio if I could. Riker only alluded to it, but the message was clear to me."

"When?" Zero asked, still shell-shocked.

"I don't know. But it's going to be soon. Pierson still thinks you're dead, so now he's back in DC. The attack just now wasn't only to take out Cartwright; it was to confirm that you were here too. Riker knew you would come." Carver looked away. "I was supposed to kill you."

Zero rubbed his forehead with the back of his bandaged hand. "Do you know how they'll do it? Anything more to go on at all?"

Carver shook his head ruefully. "No. I'm sorry. They're very careful about the intel they let out. As soon as I realized what they were going to do, I came to you. We've had our differences—"

"You tried to kill me," Zero corrected.

"I'm not denying it. But this is bigger than you or me. If they take out Pierson, then the VP will take office, and he's in their pocket. It'll be open season on the Middle East, and they'll have the full support of the American people."

And that's what they'll do with anyone who isn't in their corner, Zero realized. Not just Cartwright or Pierson, but any high-ranking official who might be able to pull the rug out from under them—chief among them, Maria's father on the National Security Council, who Zero already knew was not in on the plot. *At least he hadn't been two years ago.*

The gravity of the situation was finally beginning to sink in. Everything that Carver was telling him made morbid sense: Kill the president, blame Iran, and get their war. It was a necessary circumvention that they hadn't planned for but would still work to the same ends.

And there was no way in hell he was going to let it happen.

"I still don't trust you, Carver. But I believe that you're trying to do the right thing." He held up the MP5. "I'm keeping this." Then he gestured to the motorcycle. "And I'm taking that."

"Wait, where are you going?"

"To stop it." Zero strode over to the sports bike.

Carver scoffed behind him. "Jesus, you *are* predictable. Don't you realize they're counting on that? They know you're not dead! They *want* you to try to get to Pierson! I'm telling you this so you can get as far away from here as you can. Get your girls and disappear."

Zero spun on him. "And let Pierson die? Let them get their way? If they're successful, it wouldn't matter where I go. I'd be on the run forever. So would my daughters."

"You can't be Agent Zero. He's not this stupid—"

Zero spun on Carver angrily. "What was that?"

"I just risked my goddamn life to get you out of there and tell you this!" Carver practically shouted. "Not just so you can march in there and put yourself in the line of fire!"

"You don't need to worry about what I'm going to do." Zero stepped closer to him until their noses were only inches apart. "What are *you* going to do with this, Carver? Are you going to run and hide somewhere too, hope this all just passes and no one figures you out? Or are you going to help?"

Carver struggled to meet his gaze. "Help how?" he asked quietly.

"Do they know you've turned on them?"

"No. Not unless someone can identify me at the shootout. The only two that I know saw me are dead."

"Then go back to them," Zero said, "and try to figure out what their play is. How they're going to do it."

"I'll need a number to contact you."

Zero shook his head. "I still don't trust you, remember? You give me a way to contact you."

Carver nodded slowly. "All right, Zero. I will." He huffed a breath. "Never really thought I'd live all that long anyway." He reached into a pocket and pulled out a white card with a number printed on it and nothing else. "Reach me here. Don't check in too often."

Zero pushed the MP5 back into the leather saddlebag of the motorcycle and then mounted it, noting with irritation the pain in his legs and left knee. "One more thing. Johansson and Sanders were taken into custody by the Division. Try to find out where they are."

"Sure," Carver muttered. "No sweat." He strode over to the motorcycle and held out his left hand. "When all this is over, I hope we'll be square. I'm trying to do the right thing here."

Zero hesitated, but he shook Carver's hand, pumping it once in the air. "If you're telling the truth, then yeah. We'll be square." He pushed the helmet over his head and started up the bike while Carver hefted the garage door up enough for him to get out. The engine roared, and the motorcycle took off like a shot out into the industrial complex.

His mind raced just as fast as the pistons beneath him. *They won't try to kill Pierson in the White House,* he reasoned. *They'll do it in public, where they can make up an easier story about how Iranian terrorists might have gotten to him.*

He needed to know where the president was going to be, and fast.

Zero piloted the motorbike about three miles east, parallel to the waterfront and closer to DC, keeping an alert eye all around for cops and black Jeeps. Finally he slowed and parked in the small lot of a public park, leaving the helmet on the bike seat and walking among the trees as he made a call on the burner.

Strickland answered midway through the first ring.

"Either you're three hundred miles west," he said flatly, "or you found the tracker in the car."

"Sorry," Zero told him, "but I told you I didn't want to be followed, and you're predictable. I've got a situation. A dire one."

"Are you saying you need help?" To Strickland's credit, he kept the tone of amusement out of his voice.

"Yes. I need help. I need you and Watson to meet me at the Third Street Garage in Alexandria. I'll be waiting."

Carver closed the rolling garage door behind the motorcycle and waited until the high-pitched whine vanished in the distance. Alone in the cavernous bay, he pulled out his phone and made the call.

"Yes?" Deputy Director Riker answered the phone curtly.

"It's done."

"He bought it?"

"Seems that way," Carver told her. "He ran off to do something about it. Just like you said he would."

"Good. Does he trust you?"

Carver scoffed. "Of course not. But I promised him intel. I need something to give him when he calls. The two women that were caught, Johansson and the other one... He wants to know where they are."

"For now? They're at Langley Air Force Base at the moment, being put on a plane bound for H-6. But I don't suspect they'll be there for long."

"Why not?" Carver asked.

But Riker didn't answer. Instead she said, "I've got something for you to give him. Tell him who's going to do it. Tell him who's going to be the one to pull the trigger on the president."

Chapter Twenty Five

"Mmph." Maria groaned as she came around. Her senses were dulled, her vision fuzzy. She smelled diesel fuel and felt a rumbling beneath her. She was sitting on a hard bench seat, in a dimly lit corridor.

She tried to move her arms and metal bit into her wrists. Her hands were cuffed tightly behind her back.

"Welcome back," Sanders muttered from beside her. She was cuffed as well.

Maria winced at the pain in her cheek and jaw. She remembered walking away from the meeting with Cartwright. She remembered getting about two blocks away before the black Jeep screeched to a halt in front of them. The Division had found them. She had freed her Glock and fired off several shots while she and Sanders ran for it.

Then she had turned a corner, and the last thing she remembered was the butt of an automatic rifle speeding toward her head.

Now the two of them were seated in the back of a cargo plane, military by the looks of it, to a narrow bench seat bolted to the side of the hold. A thick-necked soldier in a drab green shirt and fatigue pants stood nearby, a rifle cradled in his arms as he kept watch over them. Three other soldiers tugged a supply pallet up the ramp of the plane on a jack.

She worked her jaw around in slow circles to make sure nothing was broken. "How's my face?" she asked. Her words were slightly slurred with the pain and the haze of recent unconsciousness.

"It's looked better," Sanders admitted. "Do you have any idea where they're taking us?"

"Yup," Maria murmured. "I sure do." She was certain they were going to Hell Six in Morocco, the CIA black site where the agency dumped people they wanted forgotten.

"Hey," the soldier growled. "No talking."

Maria shot him a glare as the other three soldiers parked the stacked pallet a few feet from them and then headed down the ramp for another. She didn't have to ask where they were; she knew they'd be at Langley Air Force Base in Hampton, Virginia. It wasn't uncommon for H-6 prisoners to be transported by cargo plane during supply runs to the black site.

She switched to Ukrainian as she asked, "How many outside?"

"Besides the four soldiers, there were two Division men in the Jeep that brought us here," Sanders answered in Ukrainian.

"That's all? Just two?" She frowned. The Division and CIA might not know who Sanders was, but Maria would have thought that she'd be a higher security risk than just two men.

"The others ran off while we were still in Georgetown, after something else."

Cartwright. Maria hoped he was all right. Their meeting had been a trap. They had been watching, letting it happen, and it was more than likely that they now had the documents in their possession.

"I thought I told you to shut up," the soldier snapped.

"Or what?" Maria challenged in English. She turned the uninjured side of her face toward him. "Are you going to make me symmetrical?"

The soldier curled a lip and hoisted his rifle in both hands, but didn't point it at her.

"Can you get out of those?" she murmured to Sanders in Ukrainian.

"I am working on it." Maria heard a slight pop as Sanders dislocated a thumb, all without the slightest grimace or wince. She couldn't help but be mildly impressed. "Can you slip yours?"

"Too tight," Maria told her. "But I'll manage."

Sanders scoffed. "Too tight? I thought you were a CIA super-spy."

"Shut up!" The soldier brought his rifle to his shoulder, his face growing red.

There was chatter on the plane as the three other soldiers pulled another pallet up the ramp, idly talking about a baseball game from the night before. One of them glanced over, noticed that the guard had his rifle aloft, and grinned.

"What's the matter, Burnside?" he taunted. "These ladies giving you grief?"

"They won't shut their damn mouths," he grunted.

"Don't go shooting up the plane now." The three soldiers chuckled as they headed back down the ramp. "Two more pallets and we'll be done."

The thick-necked guard lowered the rifle, but continued to scowl down at Maria. "Keep it up," he warned her. "Because I'm making this trip with you."

"That so?" Maria smiled up at him sweetly.

"Mm-hmm." He nodded, leaning over and sneering in her face. "And that means I'll be there to watch them pull your teeth out, one by one, with a pair of pliers—"

Sanders vaulted up from her seat in an instant and whipped the vacant handcuffs around Burnside's neck. She put both knees into the small of his back, looped her fingers in the closed cuffs, and bared her teeth as she leaned her body weight backward.

The big soldier's tongue lolled out of his mouth as he choked. The AR-15 fell from his grip and clattered to the floor of the plane as he fell backward. Sanders grunted as his weight fell upon her, but she kept the tension on the chain biting into his throat.

Maria wasted no time. She lifted her butt and quickly maneuvered the handcuff chain down past her thighs, her knees, and then her ankles. With her hands now in front of her, she snatched up the AR-15.

"Don't kill him," she hissed. Burnside's face was turning purple.

"What?" Sanders asked in bewilderment. "Why not?"

"He's just an Army grunt following orders. Don't kill him."

Sanders scoffed, but she released the pressure on the handcuff chain. The soldier sucked in a ragged gulp of air just before the Ukrainian spy dropped an elbow on his temple. Maria passed off the assault rifle to her—it would do her little good with her wrists cuffed together—and relieved the unconscious soldier of his sidearm.

"Yo, Burnside!" The three other soldiers were coming up the ramp again with the pallet jack. "Those ladies still giving you a hard time?"

Maria spun around the supply pallet with the pistol raised while Sanders went the opposite way with the assault rifle. "Hands on your head," Maria ordered.

"Jesus—" one of them started.

"Quiet," Maria ordered. "Hands on your head and get on your knees."

The three soldiers did as they were told. None of them were carrying weapons as they loaded the plane.

"Are those two Division guys still out there?" she asked quickly.

One of the soldiers gulped and nodded. "They said they'd stay until the plane took off."

"Stay here," Maria ordered, "just like this. You move, you die." She turned to Sanders and said in Ukrainian, "We'll have to move quickly. You shoot. I'll drive."

"Oh, so I can kill these two then?" Sanders asked.

"Fire away." Maria led the way quickly down the ramp with Sanders right on her six, the AR-15 against her shoulder.

The two Division members stood near the rear bumper of their black Jeep, chatting idly. One of them glanced up and saw the two women striding down the loading ramp. A lit cigarette fell from between his lips.

Sanders fired off a burst of three rounds and ended him. His buddy jumped, startled by the sudden gunfire. He was cut down before he even realized what was happening.

Maria scanned the runway. There were always military planes parked on the Langley AFB tarmac—fighter jets, Warthogs, cargo planes—but there didn't seem to be anyone in the vicinity.

Still, someone would have heard the shots, and the soldiers on the plane wouldn't stay still for long. Maria jumped into the driver's seat of the Jeep. The keys were dangling from the ignition. Sanders slid in beside her, and Maria gunned the accelerator.

A quick glance in the rearview mirror as they sped away showed her the three soldiers running out of the plane, waving their arms and shouting for help. They wouldn't be alone for long.

"Now what?" Sanders asked.

"Look around for my phone." Maria drove straight across open tarmac, the speedometer needle steadily approaching ninety.

Sanders checked the center console and then the glove box. "Got it."

Tires screeched as an olive-green Humvee skidded out behind them in pursuit. *Military police. Great.* She already had the pedal to the floor. "Find something to start a fire."

Sanders blinked at her. "Sorry?"

"That Division guy was a smoker. Find a lighter."

Sanders rifled through the center console again. "I think my talents would be better served shooting at our pursuers, don't you think?"

"We're not killing soldiers," she repeated.

"Ah! There we are." Sanders pressed the stubby black cigarette lighter into the dashboard socket. "Now what?"

"Hang on." Maria pulled the wheel to the left and the Jeep swerved around a parked F-22 Raptor. Then she slammed the gas again, heading straight for the gate, a twelve-foot chain-link fence topped in spirals of barbed wire.

Two men in white helmets sprinted for the gate. In their arms each of them held an M4 carbine, the lighter cousin of the M16 assault rifle.

"Shit," Maria muttered. "Duck!" She tucked her shoulders and neck down as low as she could behind the wheel. Sanders threw herself sideways, her head practically in Maria's lap.

The gas-powered carbines rattled as the two MPs fired at the oncoming Jeep. The windshield blew out; bullets smacked the grille.

A tire blew and the Jeep swerved dangerously. But Maria kept a firm grip on the wheel and her foot on the gas, keeping it as straight as she could without being able to see where she was going.

The machine guns stopped and the two men shouted as they leapt out of the way. The Jeep crashed through the gate with a jarring smash and kept going.

Maria dared to sit up. They were losing speed fast with the blown-out tire, and the engine light on the dash told her that something important had been hit.

"They're gaining on us," Sanders warned as she glanced behind them. They'd put some distance between them and the Humvee, but it was still on their tail and coming up fast. "We can't outrun them…"

"We're not." Maria jerked the wheel to the left and the Jeep fishtailed, rounding toward the front entrance of the main building. She pressed the pedal down and headed for the parking lot beyond. The Jeep bucked, struggling to shift gears and accelerate; the transmission was damaged. They were topping out just under sixty.

Just a little further, she pleaded mentally.

The Jeep entered the lot and flew down a long row of parked cars on either side. The Humvee was still on them and closing the gap, less than fifty yards between them.

Tock! The black cigarette adapter popped to let her know it was ready for use. *About time.* Maria tucked the gun in her pants, steering with one hand, and then yanked the cigarette lighter from the socket. She slowed as she reached the end of the row and jerked the wheel, spinning the Jeep in a tight about-face.

Then she pushed the pedal to the floor again. The Jeep bucked twice as it sped toward the oncoming Humvee.

"What are you doing?" Sanders shouted as the gap between them closed.

"Get ready to jump out." Maria stared straight ahead, playing chicken with the Humvee, which refused to slow.

"When?"

"Now!" Maria pushed open the driver's side door and rolled out. She didn't hesitate long enough to see if Sanders had done the same. With the black cigarette lighter smoldering, gripped between two knuckles, she hit the pavement and rolled twice. Pain shot through her body; she'd definitely be bruised all over, but it wasn't the first time she'd jumped out of a moving car.

The Jeep kept going, barely slowing the last fifteen yards between it and the Humvee. The green MP vehicle tried to slam its brakes and veer, but there was nowhere for it to go and not enough room to decelerate. The black Jeep smashed into the left front end of the Humvee; the Jeep's passenger-side wheels came off the ground and it rolled sideways onto two parked cars. The Humvee slammed through it, swerving, and collided into the opposite row of cars.

But Maria didn't wait around to watch. As soon as she stopped rolling, she clambered on her hands and knees between two cars and stole down the lane between them. A glance over her shoulder showed her that Sanders was not far behind her, wincing with each movement but seemingly okay. The AR-15 was slung over her back by a strap.

"That was a fine trick," Sanders said breathlessly, "but it won't buy us more than a minute or so. There are more of them on foot, and now neither of us are in condition to run."

"We're not running," Maria replied quietly. She tried each door handle they passed, staying low and out of sight. The sounds of shouting and footfalls were not far off.

After the seventh or eighth car she tried, one of the doors finally opened, left unlocked by its owner.

"We don't have time to hotwire a car," Sanders said in exasperation.

"Just shut up a second," Maria snapped. She pulled the latch to access the gas tank, and then tore off the left sleeve of her shirt with a grunt. Sanders brought the assault rifle around and held it in both hands, barrel aimed upward, as she waited for them to be discovered.

Maria twisted off the gas cap and stuffed the sleeve into the tank as far as she could, leaving only a few inches hanging out.

Then she held the Jeep's orange-tipped cigarette lighter under it.

"Come on," she coaxed quietly. The voices were getting closer. The fabric smoldered, but didn't ignite. "Come on, come on..."

A flame jumped as the sleeve caught. "Let's go!"

"One moment." Sanders stood, brought the gun to her shoulder, and fired off a burst. Men shouted and leapt for cover. Maria had already started running. Sanders followed, staying low and moving quickly as the sleeve burned.

The fire reached the gas tank and the car exploded in a cacophonous bellow. Maria didn't stop, didn't even glance back at the orange fireball that plumed into the sky or the black smoke that rolled thickly into the air. But she heard the shattering of adjacent car windows as they blew out from the explosion, and then a second resonant boom as a nearby car caught fire and its fuel tank combusted.

The two of them ran serpentine through the parking lot, staying low, until Maria paused beside a plain white sedan that looked like it was sufficiently old enough for their purposes. She winced instinctively with another thunderclap of a detonation in the tightly packed parking lot.

She glanced around to make sure no one was in their vicinity. The black smoke of the fires was a thick curtain between them and their pursuers. Then she smashed in the car window with an elbow, popped the lock, and pried the casing off the ignition column. It took her thirty-five seconds to hotwire the car; she needed a vehicle old enough for it to lack the transponder chip that many newer models contained that made stealing them at least slightly more difficult when in a rush.

"See anyone?" she asked Sanders as she touched the two ignition wires and the engine turned over.

"No." Sanders scanned left and right carefully, holding the AR-15. They could hear the voices, the panicked shouts and calls for aid behind the roar of the three-car fire, but it had given them the precious minute and a half they needed to get some distance and get to a car.

"Get in." Maria slammed the pedal down and they were out of the lot in seconds. She glanced in the rearview; it didn't look like anyone was chasing them, but that didn't mean no one had spotted them leaving. "Tell me you grabbed my phone."

Sanders pulled the burner from her pocket and passed it over. "That was good thinking back there," she noted.

"Yeah, thanks." She pressed a speed-dial button.

"Strickland," he answered before the second ring.

"It's Johansson. We need a quick pickup."

"Tell me where and when."

"Ten minutes. The grocery store just off of Cherry Street, southwest corner. White sedan, late nineties."

"I'll be there."

"Wait, Todd. Do you know where Kent is?"

"Not at the moment," he replied. "But I know where he'll be."

Chapter Twenty Six

President Pierson drummed his fingers against the tabletop of the Situation Room, irritable and anxious in equal measure. Three years of his term had gone more or less swimmingly, and now it felt as if the world was falling down around him.

He was quite proud of the fact that his hair hadn't grayed during his time in office, as it had with so many other commanders-in-chief. Now he feared that with less than a year to go, there was still plenty of time for the stress to permeate his roots.

He was glad to be out of Camp David and back in the White House; the retreat was a lovely property, but it felt isolated, and even though most of his news and reports came through his chief of staff, Peter Holmes, regardless of where he was, communicating only by phone or computer made him feel all the more detached from his duty. He thought he would feel stronger and more capable again once he returned, but here and now in the Situation Room, surrounded by the men and women who helped him lead this country, he still felt agitated, overwrought, strangled by the state of affairs that plagued his position.

"I gave a direct order." He did not have to speak loudly. The Situation Room was silent enough to hear a pin drop. "I commanded that the Fifth Fleet be pulled back. Why was that not done?"

"Sir, if I may." Secretary of Defense Rigby straightened in his chair. "The coordination of turning about that many ships from a direct course is not as simple as making a phone call. I understand that you don't have military experience, but—"

"My experience has nothing to do with this," Pierson snapped. "And now three more IRGC ships are destroyed."

"Mr. President," Peter Holmes intervened calmly. "The report from our navy clearly states that the USS *Constitution* was, in fact, backing off from the strait and Iran's blockade. The three Iranian ships in question pursued our destroyer. They recognized it as the ship that fired on theirs. There is no question about it; they were out for retribution. Had the USS *Pennsylvania* not been there to assist, the *Constitution* might have been destroyed. You can read all of this for yourself if you'd like. It's in Admiral Buchanan's report."

Assist, Pierson thought bitterly. *Is that what we call the wanton destruction of foreign vessels?* "Then it was an act of war," he said aloud.

"Tehran is still refusing to openly declare it," Rigby said. "They're content to make themselves appear the victim in the eyes of the global community. In fact, they believe it justifies their actions." Rigby leaned forward, his gaze meeting Pierson's somberly. "They're closing the Strait of Hormuz, Mr. President. And not just to American vessels, but to any country that allies with us. This is what we feared. It's happening now."

Pierson rubbed his temples. "The United Nations won't stand for that. There will be a military response—"

"The UN is in the process of launching an investigation into the events that have already occurred," said Roland Kemmerer, the secretary of state. "They're currently reviewing our naval reports, and will be sending a team to the Persian Gulf to make an assessment. Suffice it to say they're not necessarily in our corner." He paused for a moment before adding, "And frankly, sir, we don't have the luxury of waiting for a conclusion."

Pierson frowned. "If it comes down to a diplomatic resolution, we'll *make* the time, Roland."

Kemmerer glanced over at Rigby for help. The general, in response, slid a sheet of paper from the folder in front of him and passed it to the president.

"What is this?" Pierson asked, though as soon as he looked at it he knew right away. The sheet was a graph, bearing a red line that rose precipitously. He didn't need to look at the axis to know what it represented.

"A forecast," Rigby answered, "put together by our top economic analysts. Sir, more than thirty percent of the oil consumed in this country passes through the Strait of Hormuz. As you can see, within mere hours of a shutdown, oil and gasoline prices will spike. Within days, the price per barrel is expected to rise by more than one hundred dollars. For context, the current price is approximately seventy-nine dollars per. In less than two weeks, we could see gasoline prices surge as high as seven to eight dollars per gallon. We're talking about crisis levels—"

"Crisis levels." Pierson dropped the sheet to the table and scoffed. "We're talking about money, General. Money is not a reason to go to war." Even as he said it, he knew that history had set a much different precedent. Money, in one form or another, had always been a reason to go to war.

"It's not as simple as that," said Kemmerer gravely. "We have to consider the judgment of the people and how they're going to perceive this. In the wake of a major terrorist attack on our own soil, perpetrated by Muslims at the cost of hundreds of American lives, they're not only going to see the administration as kowtowing to a foreign Muslim power, but also paying dearly for it." He shook his head. "We need only to look at the post-9/11 zeitgeist and combine it with the oil crisis of the seventies. It would be a very volatile situation, sir."

"Satellite imaging and foreign intelligence suggests that Tehran is outfitting the IRGC with warheads," Rigby continued. "There are growing concerns about the Shiite militias in Iraq and Oman, from which Iran has already garnered support. I've seen war, Mr. President. I don't wish it on anyone, least of all our men and women that are on the frontlines in the Persian Gulf. But we have to acknowledge that the time for peaceful resolution has passed. Every hour that passes puts more of a stranglehold on the American economy. Every minute that ticks by gives Iran more of an opportunity to plan, to coordinate efforts with the militias and devise a way to combat the Fifth Fleet. We have to recognize that we are not infallible, and they've already found the chink in our armor. Money."

The president rubbed his temples. "You're right. You've seen war. You've also seen them avoided. So if that's your professional stance, General, then what do you suggest?"

Rigby's chest puffed out slightly, as if he'd been waiting for this moment. "First and foremost, sir, I believe we should declare the IRGC as a terrorist organization for their activities in the Persian Gulf."

"You can't be serious," Kemmerer interjected quickly. "They're a branch of Iran's armed forces—"

"Technically," said Rigby loudly over him, "the Islamic Revolutionary Guard Corps is a militia, and therefore we'd be well within our right. We do so in response to the closing of the strait and to pull focus from Iran in the eyes of our people. Secondly, we dispatch B-52 bombers to Bahrain. If Tehran really is outfitting their ships with warheads, we need to be prepared for a measured counterstrike. And lastly, sir, you're going to have to address the nation. They're going to have to hear all of this from you."

Kemmerer nodded his agreement. "He's right. Your approval rating is still strong; people will rally behind you. We have you explain that despite the immense pressure, you're doing everything you can to avoid war and the possible expenditure of American lives. And we do it today, as soon as possible, so they're not hearing it from CNN or the internet first."

Pierson nodded. He had not yet addressed the nation since the initial bombing of the first IRGC ships; America deserved answers, and they deserved them directly from him.

"I have an idea about that," said Chief of Staff Holmes, raising his pen in the air to punctuate his point. "There's a commemoration ceremony being held on the Queensboro Bridge this afternoon. New York is closing the upper lanes for one hour while the mayor gives an address for those who lost their lives in the Midtown Tunnel bombing."

Pierson stroked his chin, already certain he knew where Holmes was going with his train of thought.

"Every media outlet in the northeast is going to be present for it," the chief of staff continued. "We could organize an unexpected appearance from the president. I'm sure the mayor would give you fifteen minutes to say what needs to be said. Rather than give an address from the safety of the White House, we take people by surprise and show them that you're out there among them, grieving alongside them. I think that could really help your stance."

Pierson nodded slowly. A public appearance during a commemoration for lives lost would be very poignant. And on the Queensboro Bridge, no less, suspended over the same body of water in which the attack place. It would be a symbolic gesture.

"All right," he agreed finally. "Let's make it happen."

"A wise decision, sir." Holmes smiled broadly. "The people won't ever forget this."

Chapter Twenty Seven

Zero parked the motorcycle in front of a deli about a quarter mile from the Third Street Garage and walked briskly to the building. He didn't know if the plates had been identified during the brief chase from the cops and the Division and didn't want to take any more chances than he had to.

He made the short hike with his head low and both hands stuck in his jacket pockets, his left wrapped around the Ruger LC9 and his injured hand out of sight. It was too easy of an identifying mark, yet he had no way to obscure it other than sticking it in a pocket. It pained him terribly, but he'd left the rest of the painkillers that Strickland had provided in the glove box of the car, which was still parked in Georgetown near the coffeehouse. There was no going back for it now.

Third Street Garage was a squat building with three garage bays and a small attached office to the right. He'd been there once before, when his daughters had been taken by the assassin Rais. Mitch, née Reidegger, had hooked him up with a fast car and supplies for the road—among other things, one of which was distracting the police during a chase by sending an eighteen-wheeler careening sideways across three lanes of traffic.

He couldn't help but shake his head and smile a little at the thought that his old friend was not only still alive, but had been helping him from the shadows as he had. But the smile evaporated as he considered what sort of life Alan had been living for the past two years.

Probably the same kind of life that I'll be forced to live if I survive this, he thought glumly. He didn't know what he would do, or worse, what the girls would do. What sort of college prospects would they have being the daughters of someone identified by the federal government as a terrorist? And Maya, she had her heart set on becoming a CIA agent herself.

He secretly hoped that her desire might sour after this experience. That was not the life that he wanted for her.

As he neared the garage, he saw that the lights were off and the "closed" sign was displayed in the window. Still he approached the glass door to the office and gave the handle a tug. It opened easily.

No such thing as too cautious, he reminded himself as he pulled the LC9 from his pocket and swung into the dim space.

He lowered it almost immediately. "I figured it would be you," he said to the man sitting behind the steel desk.

"And you still pulled a gun," Watson mused.

"You never know. Are you alone?"

A thud sounded directly overhead in response. Zero crouched and instinctively pointed the gun toward the ceiling. "Someone's on the roof."

"I know." Watson was not a man who smiled often, but seeing Zero react as if he was going to shoot at someone through the ceiling made him smirk. "You made a request, remember? Go ahead. I'll wait for Strickland."

"We have a situation, Watson—"

"We always have a situation," Watson interrupted. "This is important. And it's the only thing you can do at the moment."

He was right; they had to wait for Strickland to arrive and then form a plan. He pushed open the back door of the office and found a steel security ladder bolted to the back of the building. As he reached the roof, he peered over the top of it and saw an older man, sweating a bit under the sun in a gray button-down. His hair was graying and he wore thick horn-rimmed glasses on his nose as he knelt beside a small satellite dish mounted on a tripod. Near him was a laptop computer set up atop a black footlocker, and beside that an open case that appeared to be some sort of advanced communication array.

The memories of their relationship flooded Zero's brain. They didn't appear suddenly as they had before, based on some visual or auditory trigger; they felt as if they had always been there, just now surfacing like a breaching whale. The eccentric CIA engineer, Bixby, had been with the agency longer than anyone he knew, even longer than Zero had been. On nearly every op it was Bixby who outfitted him with weapons and gear. They had more than a rapport; they had a friendship that Zero had been neglecting in the time before his memory had fully returned. Yet Bixby had never faltered.

They also had a customary greeting. So as Zero climbed up onto the roof behind the engineer, he said, "A guy walks into a psychiatrist's office wearing nothing but Saran wrap."

Bixby grinned without looking up. "And the doctor says, 'I can clearly see you're nuts.' Come on, Zero. You've told me that one before."

"I didn't exactly have time to come up with fresh material."

Bixby stood and wiped his hands on his trousers. "It's good to see you. It's been too long."

"I just saw you last week," Zero reminded him. Bixby said nothing in return, but there was a curious look in his eye that Zero couldn't quite read. *Can he tell? Does he know I'm back?* But if he did, he wasn't saying. "I don't want you mixed up in this."

"Too late," Bixby said with a shrug. "I already am. I helped you before, and I'll help you again."

"You don't know what we're up against—"

"And frankly, I don't want to know," Bixby admitted. "But I knew something was rotten when the Brotherhood had hold of CIA tech. Then Riker had me outfit those Division guys with weapons. I hear things too, you know. I know they went after you and your kids. I guess you can consider this atonement for my complicity."

"Well, first you're going to tell me what this is." Zero gestured toward the miniature satellite dish and the communication equipment.

"Agent Strickland said you needed a way to contact the Fifth Fleet. This is that."

Zero blinked in surprise. He hadn't forgotten about the request; he just didn't think it would be possible. "We can do that without anyone knowing?"

"Well… in a manner of speaking. There are far too many possibilities for communication to get intercepted, but what we can do with this is interrupt the satellite relay temporarily. I'm talking thirty seconds max. We can get a message to a single vessel, but it's not going to be a conversation. It's going to be a one-way transmission, and it has to stay brief."

"You're talking about a voicemail," Zero said plainly. "We're going to leave the Fifth Fleet a voicemail?"

"No, of course not. That's a gross oversimplification. We're going to temporarily disable a specific satellite from anyone's use but ours and the ship in question, and then we're going to send them an encoded message that will remit only to the chief communications officer aboard the…" He trailed off at Zero's flat expression. "Yeah, okay, we're sending them a voicemail. I'm sorry, Zero, but a two-way communication is way too high-risk."

"It's okay. This will have to do. Thanks, Bixby."

"Of course," said the engineer. "Let me finish setting up here while you think about what you need to say." He turned back to the communication array. "Who are we going to send this to? I need to nail down precise coordinates."

Zero knew exactly who they needed to speak to. "The USS *Constitution*."

While Bixby honed in on the ship's position in the Persian Gulf, the small satellite whirring with tiny mechanical adjustments, Zero paced the roof and thought of what he was going to tell them. Whatever it would be, it had to be convincing enough to believe—and moreover, persuasive enough that if he failed to stop the assassination attempt, the crew of the *Constitution* might heed his warning and avoid engaging further with the IRGC.

It seemed impossible. But he had to try.

"I think we're set here," Bixby announced after a minute or so. "Are you ready, Zero?"

"No," he admitted honestly. "But if you're ready, we have to do this. We're running out of time."

Chapter Twenty Eight

The mood on the deck of the USS *Constitution* was palpably grim, and had been ever since the destruction of the trio of IRGC ships at the hands of the battleship *Pennsylvania.* Lieutenant Cohen had been offered another four-hour reprieve from the radar, but he turned it down. He knew he wouldn't be able to sleep, nor would he be able to think about anything other than the blatant lie that Captain Warren had demanded of his officers.

They fired first. The United States was half a world away; the news they received from the Persian Gulf was the news that their Navy provided them. And while that was normally the truth, it was now shockingly apparent that it could be whatever the captain and those above him deemed it should be.

Beside him at the communications array, Lieutenant Davis was equally silent, his expression reading as if he too was thinking the same. Cohen wanted to say something, to talk about it, but he didn't dare. Although Captain Warren had spent much of the time since away from the bridge, the XO was never far. And even the suggestion that the captain had been less than honest could be considered treasonous.

Instead Cohen stared at the array and watched the blips that represented the IRGC blockade of the Strait of Hormuz. They had been maintaining their position for hours, waiting as more of the Fifth Fleet sailed in from further corners of the gulf and Bahrain. Even the partially assembled fleet was a formidable showing, dozens of destroyers, battleships, and aircraft carriers at the ready, organized in staggered rows on the sea. There was easily enough firepower among them to obliterate Iran's blockade—which was exactly what Cohen feared might come next.

He thought of his girlfriend back home in Pensacola, his would-be fiancée if he ever made it home. But every indication told him it was going to be war.

"Cohen." He perked up suddenly at the sound of his name. Lieutenant Davis had his thick headphones over his ears and a faraway look in his eye, as if he was listening to something intently. He glanced quickly around the bridge to make sure no one else was looking their way, and then waved him over.

Cohen scooted the short distance to him. "What is it?"

"Listen to this," Davis said quietly, passing him the headphones, "and tell me if it's as crazy as it sounds."

Puzzled, Cohen fit the headset over his ears as Davis leaned forward and pressed a playback button on the console in front of him. A message began playing; a man's voice came through, speaking rapidly but clearly, low but urgently.

"This message is for the chief communications officer aboard the USS *Constitution*," the message began. "My name is Agent Kent Steele with the Central Intelligence Agency. I have been disavowed, labeled a terrorist, and declared dead for uncovering a conspiracy that permeates the highest levels of the federal government. The plot is to instigate a war between Iran and the US in order for us to seize control of the Strait of Hormuz. I don't have time to go into the details of this plot; I am sending this message to you because you have already borne witness to the events that may very well lead to war. I am going to try to stop this. But if I fail, you will soon receive orders to advance on the strait and engage with the IRGC. I implore you: disobey. Rebel. Do whatever is necessary to avoid this conflict. The future of not only the country, but of the state of the world, may fall into your hands. Please—do the right thing."

The transmission ended as abruptly as it began. Cohen felt a shiver run down his spine, particularly at this alleged agent's insistence that they rebel. "Mutiny" was not a term that was ever uttered aboard a naval ship, not even in jest; the punishment for it would be a court-martial, but the inevitable result would most likely be a lifetime in the walls of a godforsaken military prison like Leavenworth.

He was still processing the eerie message when he realized that Davis was staring at him expectantly. "Well?" he asked quietly.

"I think…" Lieutenant Cohen sighed. "I think that if I heard this yesterday, I would have thought it was crazy. But today is a very different matter."

"My thoughts exactly." Apparently while Cohen had been dumbfounded, Davis had been thinking. "Look, we've all heard about this kind of thing from guys in Afghanistan and Iraq, right? Orders to fire on civilian populations, missiles launched on villages… Almost no one talks about it under threat of court-martial, and if they do the government squashes it fast. We've got an opportunity here to stop this before it starts, instead of trying to convince people after the fact."

"Davis," Cohen said quietly, "what you're talking about is—"

"I know," he said quickly. "But you were there last night. You saw it and heard it. I'm not going to stand by idly, so you're going to have to make a choice. Either report me for talking about it, or grow a pair of balls and help me."

Cohen hesitated. Davis, it seemed, had a stronger spine than he did, but he wasn't about to admit it. "What do you suggest?" he asked.

"I can encrypt this message and get it out to a few people we trust," Davis told him. "Kennedy on the *Pennsylvania.* Schriner on the *Intrepid.* Guzman on the *Lincoln.* They've all heard what we've heard, and some have even seen what we've seen. We disseminate this carefully, and…"

"And then what?" Cohen interjected. "Mutiny?"

"Sorry, Lieutenant Cohen." A deep voice startled them both. "Can you repeat that?" The XO stood only a few paces behind them. They had been so engulfed in the recording and their conversation that they hadn't noticed him approaching. Cohen felt a nauseating knot of panic bubble in his stomach. Executive Officer Nathan was second in command of the USS *Constitution* behind

Captain Warren. He was a career man, eighteen years in the Navy and most of those spent on the seas. He folded thick arms over a broad chest and glared down at the both of them. "I can't possibly have heard what I think I just heard. So by all means, Lieutenants, set me straight."

Cohen glanced over at Davis nervously. But he did not return his pleading gaze. Instead Davis set his headphones down on the console and stood, facing the XO as straight and tall as he could—which was at least four inches shorter than the commanding officer that towered over him. Still, he did not falter or shrink as he spoke.

"Sir, I have received an encoded transmission from a man claiming to be a CIA agent that briefly details a conspiracy to use the Fifth Fleet as pawns to instigate a war with Iran for control of the strait. In conjunction with what we witnessed yesterday, I believe that Captain Warren's command is compromised, and that this may go up the chain as far as Admiral Buchanan. I do not intend to take any part in this, and in fact plan to do whatever I can to stop it."

Cohen's heart felt as if it stopped at Davis's candor. The XO glared down, his eyes narrowing. "And this message," he said slowly. "It was sent only to you?"

"I believe so," Davis told him. "It was addressed to me."

Nathan nodded once, slowly. "As you were, then."

Davis blinked rapidly. Cohen didn't realize it, but his jaw dropped open slightly.

"Sir?" he said.

"I've suspected that Warren's command was in question," he told them, his voice low. "We all know what the strait represents to both the US and the world. It's been my unfortunate experience that people in power tend to believe they can do as they please because they are in power. It seems that this now applies to our captain. But this is *my* Navy, and I'll be damned if I'm going to lose a single soul so that some men on the Hill can stay in their seats. So you do what you intend to do, Davis—carefully, and quietly. I'll deal with Captain Warren."

"Yes sir," Davis breathed.

"And Cohen," the XO remarked. "Blink or something. You look guilty as hell." With that, he turned and strode off the bridge.

Cohen sucked in a long breath, as if he'd forgotten how to inhale for the last minute or so. "This is really happening," he said.

"It sure is." Davis took a seat at his console. "So are you going to help me, or what?"

Chapter Twenty Nine

Sara stood in the backyard of the rural Nebraska cabin, hugging her elbows. There was a chill in the morning air, but it was still better than being stuck inside. She was feeling a bit stir-crazy.

To call it a "backyard" was a tremendous understatement. Despite having houses within view on either side, it looked like the property stretched into the wilderness behind it, down a gently sloping hill dotted with trees that afforded her an admittedly pretty view.

She had only slept a few hours the night before. When she woke, Maya was still asleep and Mitch was gone. He'd left a note saying that he'd run out for supplies, food, and changes of clothes and toiletries. He promised he'd be back soon.

Sara meandered a short distance into the trees. The grass badly needed to be cut and the morning dew soaked the toes of her sneakers. She had tried to find something, anything, to do in the small cabin, but quickly grew bored and decided to venture outdoors. She didn't see the harm. No one "out there" knew where they were— "out there" being anywhere at all in the developed world beyond the small cabin and yard.

She stepped carefully through the grass, wondering if she should be concerned about ticks, when she saw a flash of light in her periphery. She glanced up quickly, just in time to see a shape jump behind a tree.

Sara froze. In that instant her brain convinced her that the flash of light was the sunlight glint from a rifle scope. *It's those men from the Division. Somehow they found us.*

Then she took a deep breath and reminded herself that no one knew they were here. No one followed them.

"Hey!" she said loudly, mustering what she thought was her most authoritative voice. "Who's there? I saw you. Come on out, slowly."

She held her breath as the figure stepped out from behind the tree, and then she released it in a sigh of relief to see that it was not the Division.

It was a boy.

He looked like he was around her age, with brown hair cut in a sweep across his forehead. He wore a gray hooded sweatshirt and jeans with a tear across one knee. He was tall, at least five inches taller than her, and in his right hand he held a smartphone.

"Who are you?" Sara demanded.

The boy jerked a thumb over his shoulder. "I live over there."

"Yeah?" She folded her arms defiantly. "Well, you're trespassing."

The boy frowned. "Nuh-uh. Your yard ended back there. Technically, *you're* trespassing."

Sara threw a glance behind her, her shoulders slumping. "Oh." Then she turned back and bristled again. "Did you just take a picture of me?"

"No."

"I saw a flash."

The boy hesitated. "What's your name?"

The question took her off guard. "Um... Sam. Samantha. But people call me Sam." She certainly couldn't give her real name, not when they were supposed to be hiding. "What's yours?"

"Ethan." He gestured toward the cabin. "Did your family just move in there?"

"Uh, yeah," Sara told him. "Me, my sister, and my dad."

"No one's lived there for years," Ethan said. "The place must be a dump."

"We won't be staying long."

Ethan kicked at a rock idly. "That's too bad."

Sara felt her face flush with heat. *Is he flirting with me?* "I should be getting back," she murmured.

"Yeah. Okay." Rather than turn back to the direction he claimed his house was in, Ethan continued down the gentle hill, picking his way around tall stands of wild grass. "See you around, Sam."

"Wait. Where are you going?" she asked.

"Oh. I'm meeting up with a couple of friends. We have this spot we like to hang out. We just, like, listen to music and talk and stuff." He thought for a moment. "You wanna, I don't know, come along?"

Sara bit her lower lip. She glanced back over her shoulder toward the cabin and saw no signs of movement. It would be at least an hour, maybe more, until Mitch got back. And Maya was sound asleep. They were in the middle of nowhere. Their trackers were gone. Their phones had been left behind.

"Yeah," she agreed. "I'll come. For a little bit."

Sara followed Ethan as he picked his way down the sloping hill and then back up another. They chatted idly, and Sara was surprised at how easy she found it to make up lies once she had started. Yes, of course she'd heard of Sonic Youth. Yeah, school sucked. And her family was boring too.

At the crest of the second hill he pointed toward a small ravine worn by what might have once been a river. "Down there," he told her as he led the way. Below, Sara could see two other kids, talking and laughing about something.

"Guys," Ethan announced as they reached the bottom, "this is Sam. She just moved here. Sam, this is Trudy and Mix."

"Hi," Sara said quietly. The girl, Trudy, had a round face and stout cheeks and way too much eye makeup. The boy was gawky and tall with spiky blond hair. "I'm sorry… did you say Mix?"

"He's Mike," Trudy corrected. "He thinks 'Mix' sounds cool."

"It does sound cool," the tall boy muttered.

"Anyway," Ethan interjected loudly, "Sam is going to hang out with us."

Sara looked around the narrow ravine. There were a few upended tree stumps, some candy bar wrappers, and a few crushed beer cans, the labels worn white with weather and time. "What do you guys do down here?"

"You know," said Trudy. "Get away from our folks. Hang out. Listen to music." She turned to Ethan. "Did you bring your Bluetooth speaker?"

He groaned. "Dammit. I forgot."

"Great," said Trudy as she sat heavily on a stump. "So no music."

"Hang on, I got something else." Mike, or Mix, or whatever his name was, unzipped a backpack at his feet and pulled out two aluminum cans. "Managed to sneak these from my dad's garage fridge."

"Two beers?" Trudy scoffed.

"It was all I could take without him noticing," said Mix defensively. "We can each have, like, half."

"Oh … uh, I don't …" Sara stammered. "I don't drink."

All three pairs of eyes were on her. Scrutinizing. Judging, she felt.

"That's okay," said Ethan. "But you gotta take at least one sip."

"Right, so that you can't rat on the rest of us." Mix popped the top on one of the cans. "Here, you go first. Just one sip. Then we we'll know you're not a narc."

Just go home. The voice in Sara's head told her to leave, to get out of there, to hike right back to the cabin and stay there. But their eyes were all on her again. *This isn't what kids normally do. Is it?* It felt like it had been a long time since she felt like a normal kid.

Before she knew what she was doing, she had the can in her hand. She put it to her lips. *Just take one sip. It won't hurt anything.* She tipped it back—

"Sara Jane!" The voice was shrill and commanding and so startling that Sara dropped the can in the dirt, beer pouring out onto the ground.

"Who the hell is that?" Mix exclaimed.

Sara already knew who it was. A knot of panic formed in her stomach as Maya marched angrily down into the ravine, her hair still a bedheaded mess and somehow making her look even more imposing than usual. "I'm her sister, that's who the hell I am." She bent over and plucked up the mostly empty beer can from the dirt. "What is this?"

"God, it's no big deal," said Trudy.

Maya shot her a murderous glare. "I wasn't talking to you. Go home, the three of you."

The tall boy, Mix, scoffed at her. "You think you can just come around here and tell us what to do?"

Maya spun on him in an instant. Even though he was taller than she was, Sara noticed that he wilted visibly under her gaze. "I will kick all three of your asses if you don't go home right now."

The two boys glanced at each other. Sara could read their expression clearly; they seemed to be considering whether or not they were willing to fight a girl, or more importantly, if they were willing to *lose* a fight to a girl.

"Fine," Ethan muttered. "Your sister's a loser anyway. Come on, guys." The three of them sulked off from the ravine, picking their way back up the shoe-treaded path without looking back.

Once they were gone, Maya turned her angry gaze on Sara, and she felt herself shrinking under it just as the tall boy had. "What the hell, Sara? What are you doing out here?"

"Nothing," Sara muttered, unable to meet her sister's glare. "I just..."

"Just what? We're supposed to be hiding out. Staying under the radar. And you're running off into the woods with shady boys? Drinking?" Maya shook the nearly empty can near Sara's face.

"No! I didn't..."

"But you were going to."

"I wasn't..."

"I saw you!"

"I'm sorry!" Sara shouted. She was surprised at the volume of her voice, as much so as her sister, evident by the small step that

Maya took back at her outburst. "I just wanted to remember what it felt like to be normal!"

"But we're not," Maya countered. "We're here hiding in these ridiculous backwoods because our lives *actually* depend on it."

"I didn't ask for this," Sara murmured. "I just want things to be the way they were."

"I know, Squeak." Maya corrected herself quickly. "Sara. I want that too. But we both need to face the fact that things are never going back to the way they were. They're just not."

Sara stared at the ground. Dead leaves and crushed beer cans. This was just one more time that she might have cried, in what felt like another life. But no tears came.

"Come on," Maya prodded. "Let's go back." She turned and led the way toward the sloping side of the ravine. But they hardly got more than a few paces before a voice called down to them.

"Excuse me, ladies." They both looked up sharply. The woman standing on the ravine's edge wore dark trousers and a beige collared shirt. A gold badge was clipped at her breast.

A cop, Sara realized grimly.

"Why don't you come on up here so we can talk," the female officer called down. She didn't sound friendly.

Maya seemed to realize then that she was still holding the beer can, dropping it quickly as it if was on fire. "Oh, dammit," she muttered.

Deputy Director Ashleigh Riker was seated at her desk, reviewing the documents that the Division had obtained from Cartwright, when her cell rang.

"Riker," she answered hastily, hoping that someone had gotten a lead on Johansson or the other renegades.

"It's Bradbury, ma'am." Bradbury was the new assistant director that Mullen had assigned to take her former position. He was two years her senior, but likeminded in his goal to move up the chain.

Once all was said and done, Mullen was set to retire, leaving Riker the reins as director of the CIA and Bradbury to fill her position as deputy director. "We've got a bead on Zero's kids."

Riker blinked. That was not at all the news she was expecting, but certainly no less welcome. "From where?"

"Some kid's social media account was flagged. A mobile phone in Nebraska posted a very recent photo of a teenage girl on it. Facial recognition against yearbooks is a ninety-seven percent match to Sara Lawson."

"Nebraska," Riker said thoughtfully. They couldn't have gotten that far without help; she very much doubted they were alone. "Who owns the phone?"

"Just some teenager living in the middle of nowhere," Bradbury told her. "But the kid posted the photo along with a caption about a 'new girl next door.' We're running a check on every address in the vicinity."

"Good," Riker said. "Dispatch a Division team and alert them as soon as you have a location."

Bradbury was silent for a moment. "With all due respect," he said at last, "don't you think we should just send an agent to pick them up and detain them? They're just a couple of kids—"

"Just a couple of kids?" Riker scoffed. "These are Agent Zero's kids, Bradbury. They may be minors, but they're connected with four murders in the past twenty-four hours alone. Possibly six. They should be considered armed and dangerous and are probably not alone. Tell the Division to use extreme caution and necessary force. One way or another those 'kids' are going to face the music—dead or alive."

"Yes ma'am," Bradbury relented quietly. "I'll keep you updated."

Riker ended the call and sat back, smiling. Soon she would be able to pull the thorn from her side that was the Lawson family—as well as all the other traitors who had aligned themselves with Agent Zero.

Chapter Thirty

Fifteen minutes after leaving a message for the USS *Constitution,* Zero stood in the Third Street Garage with five others. Strickland had arrived, and he wasn't alone; Maria and Sanders had managed to escape the clutches of the Division, though not entirely unscathed. Maria had an oblong purple bruise down the side of her face that she didn't seem keen to discuss. Along with Bixby and Watson, these five were the only people in the world that he felt he could trust with his secrets, his lies, and his life—outside of a trio holed up in rural Nebraska.

Zero explained as quickly as he could all he knew, from Pierson's refusal to go to war to the alleged attempt on the president's life that would occur in short order. Sanders immediately borrowed Bixby's laptop and logged into her email account. While undercover as a presidential aide, she had installed a back door that could access the White House network remotely. It was risky, since the network was undoubtedly being monitored, but she only needed to be in it long enough to find Pierson's schedule and see where he would be that day.

While Sanders worked, Zero gathered his fellow agents to deliver the grim news. "Cartwright is dead," he told them plainly.

Maria put one hand over her mouth. Strickland hung his head and sighed. Bixby groped behind him for the edge of the desk and sat upon it, a faraway look in his eye.

"The Division caught up with us in Georgetown," Zero continued. "They shot him in a basement and took the documents, which are no doubt in Riker's hands by now."

No one spoke for a long moment, either giving the deputy director a reverential moment of silence or perhaps not knowing quite what to say.

When someone finally did speak, it was Watson, still seated stoically behind the desk. "Where did you get the information about the assassination?"

Zero blinked. "Did you hear what I said? Cartwright—"

"I heard you. And there's nothing we can do about that right now. I'm more concerned about the reliability of your source."

"It's reliable," Zero said quickly. He did not want to tell them that the intel had come from Carver; they would immediately distrust it.

Luckily, he didn't have to.

"Got it," Sanders announced from behind the laptop. "A flight manifest to New York was just scheduled for Marine One, departing in less than an hour and bearing eight people."

Zero frowned. "What's in New York? A visit to the UN?"

"There's a commemoration today," Strickland said, "on the Queensboro Bridge for the people that died in the Midtown Tunnel bombing. You think Pierson is going to make a surprise visit?"

"I'd say it's a good bet," Zero agreed. "What time is it going down?"

"One p.m.," Sanders told him from behind the computer. "That's less than three hours."

"Less than three hours to get to New York," he muttered. "I'd need either a very fast car or a very inconspicuous helicopter." He turned to Watson. "I don't suppose our mutual friend left anything behind for me, did he?"

"He might have." Watson rounded the desk, pulled open a drawer, and then tossed Zero a key.

He caught it easily. The key was small and brass, attached to a keychain that bore an oblong orange float. "Is this a boat key?"

"It's a very fast boat key. I'll show you where to find it."

"Thanks." Zero turned to Strickland. "If anything happens to me I need someone to make sure the girls are safe. Right now they're in a Nebraska safe house with a man named Mitch. I trust him…" His gaze flitted quickly to Watson, but the passive agent was expressionless. If Watson knew that Zero had divined Alan's identity, he didn't show it. "But he's a stranger to the girls. They'll need someone they know."

"Yeah," Strickland murmured. "Of course, Zero." He handed over another set of keys. "Take my car. There's some gear in the trunk."

"Thank you."

"I'm coming with you," Maria declared. "It's not up for debate."

He smiled at her. "I thought you might say that." But the smile faded quickly. "Maria, you got into this mess for a reason. Your father is not a part of this. But if they're willing to kill a president, we have to assume they'll be willing to take out anyone who disagrees or gets in their way. You need to go to him, and get him somewhere safe."

Maria thought for a long moment, and then shook her head. "I won't trade one life for another, or many. I'm coming with you to stop this thing. If we pull it off, I won't worry about keeping him safe." Her slate-gray eyes met his. "I'm coming with you."

"What can I do?" Sanders asked.

Zero was a little surprised at the offer. But he knew that she had just as much to lose from the conspiracy as any of them. "I want you to make a couple of calls for me. Get in touch with Mossad Agent Talia Mendel and Interpol Agent Vicente Baraf." Talia Mendel had helped them stop the Brotherhood's attack on New York; Baraf was a department head at Interpol with whom Zero had worked on more than one occasion, going back to the attempted bombing at Davos. "I'll give you the numbers. Make them aware of what's going on in the Baltic and with Russia. Interpol needs to know. Mendel can alert the UN. You need to hold up your end of the bargain with the Ukrainians. Make this thing internationally known."

"I will," Sanders promised.

"Thank you." Zero glanced around the dim office at the faces that he might be seeing for the last time. "All right, everyone." *We don't say goodbye. Not ever.* That was what he and his team had established years earlier, before every op. It was never goodbye. "See you later."

He headed out the door toward the waiting car, with Watson and Maria behind him.

"Zero, hold up!" He paused as Bixby trotted out after him, carrying what appeared to be a small black backpack. "Take this."

Zero frowned. The pack was dense and weighed several pounds, but looked small enough to conceal under his light jacket. "What is it?"

"A prototype," Bixby said vaguely. "You're going to a bridge, right? If you need to make a quick getaway, pull this cord here right after you jump—"

"Jump?" Zero repeated blankly.

"Just in case."

Zero frowned. "Is it a parachute?"

"Um ... not quite. More like a sailcloth over an aluminum composite frame ..."

A hang glider? Zero took it, though he very much doubted—and very much hoped—that he wouldn't need it. "Thanks, Bixby."

"Of course. Take care, Zero. Good luck."

The three of them hurried to the car. Before he slid behind the wheel, Zero looked back to see that Strickland and Sanders had joined Bixby outside, watching them go.

He could only hope it wasn't the last time he'd see them.

Under Watson's instruction, Zero took 495 to Donovan's Pier, about thirty-five miles due east from Alexandria. He did his best to avoid scrutiny but still found himself pushing the car faster, doing about eighty-five on the highway while staying vigilant for state troopers.

Watson directed him to a small, private marina a little more than half a mile from the pier. Zero parked the car hastily, popped the trunk, and grabbed the bag that Strickland had told him would be there.

Watson and Maria were already making their way down toward the marina. Zero lingered behind the open trunk, deliberating. Then he pulled out his burner and called the number he'd been given.

"Carver."

"It's Zero," he replied. "I know where it's going to happen and I'm heading there now. You got anything for me?"

"Yeah, I think I do," Carver told him. "But only if you tell me where you're going."

Zero hesitated. "Why?"

"Listen." Carver sighed. "I can't believe I'm saying this, but if you need some backup, I'm overdue for a good deed. Just tell me where you're going and I'll get there. You shouldn't do this alone."

"I'm not alone." Still, he knew he could use the extra hands if need be. "Queensboro Bridge. Pierson is going to make an appearance there today, in just a couple of hours. We'll rendezvous at Roosevelt Island. Now, what do you have for me?"

"I have reason to believe the trigger man is going to be Secret Service," Carver said candidly.

Goose bumps rose on Zero's arms. He had been so busy investigating joint chiefs and upper administration that he hadn't gotten around to looking into the Secret Service. The very idea that the people behind the plot might have gotten to members of the highest law enforcement agency in the country—the world, even—was a harrowing notion.

"What makes you think that?" Zero asked, keeping his voice even.

"They have a man on the inside," Carver continued, "named Raulsen. He's a former SEAL and the special agent in charge of protective detail; basically the head of security for Pierson. He's the closest one to him, and I know they've gotten to him. Seems like the most obvious culprit. If they create some sort of distraction, it wouldn't be hard to make it look like Pierson went down while Raulsen was trying to protect him."

Zero thought back to his visit to the White House and the Secret Service members he'd observed there, recalling the man who seemed to be running the security show. "About six-three, maybe two-thirty, dark hair, clean-shaven?"

"That's him. Would you know him if you saw him again?"

Zero knew which boat they would be taking as soon as he saw it. It was twenty-eight feet long and only seven feet wide, with a deep gray planing hull that was made of carbon fiber, if he had to guess. The platform was long and narrow, the bow stretching into a sharp V.

It was a cigarette boat, or to those in the powerboat racing game, a "go-fast boat." He knew the design; two engines with a combined two thousand horsepower, capable of top speeds in excess of a hundred miles an hour on calm seas. These types of boats had been based on the rumrunners of yesteryear that had been created specifically to avoid interception by the Coast Guard. They were fast, they were agile, and they were difficult to pick up on radar.

And Zero had never ridden in one before. The tingle of excitement that crept up his spine was only slightly dulled by the fact that he wouldn't be the one driving it.

He tossed Maria the boat key and then tossed the bag of gear down into the small cockpit, barely large enough for the three of them.

"We should be able to get to New York in just over an hour," Watson said. And with the added benefit of no traffic lights, no speed limit, and no concern of cops, they would have nothing but open water between them and the city.

"And when we get there?" Maria asked.

"We've got just over an hour to figure that out," Zero told her. "You think you can drive this thing?"

Maria nodded emphatically. "Oh yeah. But you'll probably want to hang on to something." She started up the engines; they roared powerfully, the entire length of the boat rumbling. They left the dock slowly and made their way into open water, a few hundred meters out from the marina.

Then Maria pushed the throttle forward.

The whine of the twin engines screamed in Zero's ears as the boat lurched ahead with enough momentum to send him scrambling to grab hold of the railing to keep himself from tumbling right off the stern. The wind tore at his jacket as the powerboat cut a swath through the Atlantic Ocean as easily as a razorblade across paper.

They were on their way. But Carver's troubling prediction weighed heavily on his mind. Even if he managed to stop the assassination attempt, even if they were able to ascertain and apprehend the loftiest perpetrators of the plot, how many others would still be out there? How deep did this hole really go? How would Pierson ever be able to trust anyone close to him again?

One thing at a time, he told himself. *Because if you can't keep him—or yourself—from getting killed, you won't have to worry about all that anyway.*

Chapter Thirty One

"What?" Zero shouted over the roar of the speedboat's dual engines. Maria, at the helm, had yelled something over her shoulder, but he hadn't heard a word.

He maneuvered closer to her—they'd been on the water for about thirty minutes, and he was finally getting used to the inertia of the rocketing boat—and put his ear close to her mouth.

"I said, we're not going to get within a mile of the bridge on this thing!" she shouted in his ear. "There's going to be Coast Guard, police, probably helicopters. So what's the plan?"

"We're going to head up the East River to the southern tip of Roosevelt Island," he yelled back. "That's probably the closest we're going to be able to get. There's a tram that runs every eight minutes to the Manhattan side of the bridge."

"And from there?"

"We get on the bridge and save the president." Zero shook his head in exasperation. "You do realize I'm making this up as I go, right?"

Maria grinned. "That's why you try to do all this alone, isn't it? So no one notices that you have no plan?"

"There's no such thing as a mistake if you're improvising." He knelt in the small cockpit, now that he was seaworthy enough to no longer require the railing as a handhold, and unzipped the black bag from Strickland's trunk. There was a lot of gear in there; it looked as if either Strickland or Bixby had stuffed a bag with whatever was in the vicinity. He found three pistols, spare magazines, fragmentation grenades, flash-bangs, tiny disc-shaped EMP grenades, binoculars, a skullcap and a ball cap in the same shade of black, and a first-aid kit, among other things. It was much more than he needed and certainly more than he could carry.

We'll need to be inconspicuous. I won't be able to carry a bag of weapons onto the bridge. They would have to be picky about what they took with them; only smaller items that could be easily concealed and ditched if necessary.

Zero looked down at his injured right hand and had an idea. He took the Ruger LC9 out of his jacket pocket and compared it to the thick gauze wrapping. It was small enough to fit… And though four of his fingers were immobilized and splinted, his ring finger was unbroken and could bend, even though it would be painful.

As Maria continued racing forward with an open throttle, Zero set about unwrapping his hand.

They slowed on their approach to Roosevelt Island, the narrow islet on the East River with Manhattan to its west and Queens to the east. The Queensboro Bridge stretched over the island's center, due north of them.

Zero had rewrapped his hand, stowed a few pieces of gear in his pockets, and just for good measure had even put on the black pack that Bixby had given him, concealed beneath his jacket. *Better to have it and not need it than need it and not have it,* he thought wryly.

As they made their way up the rocky shore, Zero found himself glancing left and right, looking for any sign of Carver. He had told him to meet on Roosevelt Island, but he hadn't specified a precise point.

"All right, here's the plan," Zero said quickly. "Maria and I will go up to the bridge level. Watson, I want you to stay down here on the island. If things go south, someone needs to know the truth and carry on. Get a good vantage point atop one of those buildings. Record it if you can." He passed him the bag that held the remaining gear.

For a moment, he wondered if he should mention Carver. He was, after all, Watson's former partner. But he decided against it. He needed Watson to stay focused on the task at hand.

"Got it." Watson clapped Zero once on the shoulder. "Godspeed, both of you. And in case you don't make it out of this…"

"We don't say goodbye, John."

"I know," Watson told him. "I'm not. Just be careful, Reid." Watson hefted the bag and headed north on the two-mile-long island at a trot.

"Let's go," Maria prodded, and the two of them set off at a brisk pace toward the tram that would take them up a series of lengthy cables to the Manhattan side of the Queensboro Bridge.

"Hey," he said as they walked. "For what it's worth, I'm sorry."

"For what?"

"For not telling you sooner that I got my memory back. For accusing you of lying to me about us being together."

"It's okay," Maria murmured. "And I'm sorry too. For everything. I'm sorry that you had to send your girls away again. I'm sorry about what happened to Kate." She paused meaningfully before adding, "I'm not going to lie to you. When this is over and you've got some time to process all these newfound memories, there's probably going to be some unpleasantness. Some things you wish you didn't know."

Zero didn't slow his pace, but he frowned deeply. *What does that mean? Why did she feel the need to mention Kate?*

Cartwright's final words flitted through his mind again. *They didn't know the truth. They were following an order, just like I was. We've all been lied to.*

Those words came only moments after Zero had demanded to know about his wife's murderer. And while he hadn't considered it before, Zero was suddenly keenly aware that he had said "they," rather than he or she.

Was he trying to tell me something about Kate's death?

"Hey. Wait a second." Zero grabbed Maria's elbow and gently pulled her to a stop. "Why did you mention Kate just now?"

Maria's brow furrowed, her gaze searching his. "Because ... because it was a terrible thing, Kent. She didn't deserve it. You and your family didn't deserve it. And I'm sorry that it happened." She turned and continued on rapidly toward the tram.

Zero trotted after her, but now his mind was racing. It was the last thing he wanted to think about, but once it was in his head he couldn't seem to get it out.

Does Maria know the truth about what happened to Kate?

Did she have something to do with it?

Chapter Thirty Two

"Let's go over this one more time." The female police officer looked exasperated, sighing heavily and pinching the bridge of her nose frequently.

Maya and Sara sat in uncomfortable plastic chairs on the other side of the desk in the precinct of Sumner, Nebraska. It was a small place, just an expanse of tiled floor with a handful of desks, a few closed office doors, and a corridor in the rear that Sara could only imagine led to jail cells.

Luckily, despite Maya having been caught with a beer can in her hand by the female officer and refusing to answer her questions, they weren't in one of those cells, nor were they handcuffed.

"You can't tell me where you live," the officer said. The name tag over her left pocket said Pettit.

"No," Maya said coolly.

"And you can't tell me your names."

"No."

Sara's foot bounced anxiously on the tiled floor.

"You can't?" Officer Pettit challenged. "Or you won't?"

"Pick one," Maya retorted. Sara had no idea how her sister was able to keep such a cool head in the face of being arrested. Her own heart was practically pounding out of her chest. She had to imagine that anger and sarcasm was Maya's natural reaction to the situation—much like her own had been to run off into the woods with Ethan.

"Look, you seem like nice girls," Pettit said. "But you need to tell me who you are and where you live. This is a small town. I don't know you, and I know everyone. I'm not going to just let you walk the streets. I'll ask you again: is there someone we can call?"

Sara gulped. Pettit had already asked them that at least twice now. But neither of them knew the number to reach Mitch. They couldn't give their real names, and they couldn't just tell the officer about the cabin. It seemed like there was nothing they could do but sit there and deny.

"Fine," Pettit sighed. "Then you're just going to sit here until someone comes to claim you." The phone on her desk rang. "Excuse me. Sumner Police, Officer Pettit speaking." As Sara watched, the officer's gaze rose from her desk to the two of them. "That's right." Pettit's brow furrowed deeply. "Yes. I have them right here, sitting across from me."

Mitch? Sara thought. *Is he looking for us?*

"I will. Thank you." Pettit replaced the phone on the cradle and folded her hands on the desk before speaking. "I'm going to give you girls one more opportunity to tell me who you are, and what you've done," she said somberly.

Maya frowned. "What we've done? What are you talking about?"

"That was the FBI," Pettit told them. "Looking for two teenage girls, a blonde and a brunette, ages fourteen and sixteen. They'll be here in about five minutes."

Sara's breath caught in her throat. *The FBI? Why? How did they find us?*

But Maya's mind was already two steps ahead. "Listen to me, please," she said quickly as she leaned forward. "That was not the FBI. It was a group called the Division. They're mercenaries that are looking for us. They already came to our house and pretended to be agents. You can't let them take us."

Pettit stared at Maya for a long time. "Do you think I'm stupid? I know we might be a small town and a small precinct here, and I sure as hell haven't ever gotten a call from the FBI before, but I wasn't born yesterday."

"I'm not trying to trick you!" Maya pleaded. She glanced over at her sister and saw Sara's panicked expression. "Fine," she conceded to the officer. "I can't tell you our names because we're in hiding. Our father is a CIA agent who is trying to stop a war from breaking out in Iran, and..." Maya trailed off. She must have realized how ludicrous the story must sound to the cop.

Pettit rubbed her temples with her fingertips. "This was so much easier when I thought you were just drinking in the woods."

Sara cleared her throat and spoke for the first time since entering the precinct. "If you let them take us," she said quietly, "we're dead. No one will ever see us again."

Pettit stared at Sara. It wasn't a hard stare; there was some compassion behind her eyes. It seemed that Sara's words had made her think twice. Pettit shook her head. "I don't know what to do here. The chief of police is off today, but I'm going to give him a call and get his take. You two sit right there and don't move." The officer took out a cell phone, rose from her desk, and made a call. "Chief? It's Pettit. Look, we've got a bizarre situation on our hands here..."

As Pettit meandered away from the desk, Maya shook her head in dismay. "How? How did they find us? We don't have phones. We didn't use our real names."

But Sara already knew. There was only one way, one possible way the Division could have discovered their location. "That boy," she admitted in a whisper. "Ethan. He took a picture of me. He must have posted it somewhere."

Maya sighed in disappointment. "Sara." She squeezed her sister's arm, and then glanced over her shoulder. Pettit was across the room, speaking in low tones, her back to them. "We're going to make a run for it. Get outside and don't stop. Follow me and keep running. Ready?"

Sara's legs felt like jelly, but still she nodded. "Yeah. Ready."

"Go!" Maya jumped from her seat and hurtled toward the exit. Sara followed, almost stumbling off the mark.

"Hey!" Pettit shouted after them. "Hey, stop!"

Maya reached the door first. Her hands were on it when it swung open from the other side. A man in a beige uniform filled the doorway, looking just as surprised to see Maya as she was to see him there. She couldn't stop herself in time and bounced into him. The officer stumbled back a step, but Maya tripped over her own feet and sprawled to the floor.

Sara stopped in her tracks.

"Don't let them leave!" Pettit shouted.

The male cop, still bewildered, at least seemed to understand that much. He put out his arms and blocked the door.

Sara didn't try to get past him. Instead she helped Maya up from the floor. "You okay?"

"Yeah," Maya muttered, rubbing her elbow.

Pettit stepped in front of them, her cheeks flushed with anger. "Innocent people don't tend to run," she said. "Now you two are going to sit in those chairs, and you're not going to move a muscle until the FBI gets here!"

"FBI?" the male cop asked, puzzled. "Pettit, what's going on here?"

"A headache, Reynolds. A big headache."

Sara glanced over at her older sister. She knew that expression; Maya was thinking quickly. Before Sara knew what was happening, Maya balled one fist and swung it out in a wide, fast arc.

The blow connected with Pettit's cheek and sent her stumbling right into the arms of the male cop, Reynolds.

For a moment, there was only silence. Pettit stared in stunned fury. Reynolds looked absolutely bewildered. Sara stopped breathing.

"Okay," said Pettit. "Okay then." She grabbed Maya by one elbow and yanked it upward at an angle, high enough to make her wince. With her other hand she grabbed onto Sara's left arm. The female cop was stronger than she looked; her grip was tight and painful.

"Let's go," Pettit growled. She half-dragged the girls along as she marched to the back of the station and down the corridor, where three small holding cells awaited. Without another word, Pettit shoved them both through the door and yanked it close.

The jail cell locked with an echoing clank.

"That was your plan?!" Sara shouted at her sister. "To get us locked up?"

"We're safer in here than we are out there!" Maya argued.

"And now they know exactly where to find us!"

"Hey, none of this would have happened if you hadn't run off with that kid!" Maya paced the small cell, her hands on her head. "Just shut up a second, let me think."

Sara sat heavily on the small cot. Any moment now the man who had claimed to be from the FBI would be there to get them. *Where will he take us? Will he be alone? What if we told Officer Pettit our real names?*

Her last thought stuck in her mind. If they told Pettit who they were, she could make some calls, verify it... but what good would that do? No one would openly confirm that their father was an agent with the CIA.

"Watson!" Sara said suddenly. "We could call Watson. He'll know what to do. He'll tell her the truth. He'll—"

"Shh!" Maya hissed. She craned her neck at the bars as a new voice echoed down the corridor.

"Officer Pettit? I'm Agent Hargreaves, FBI. We spoke on the phone." He sounded cordial, almost friendly, but an icy shiver still ran down Sara's spine at the sound of his voice. "Do you still have the girls in custody?"

"I do. They're in a holding cell back here," said Pettit. "They tried to run, and then one of them took a swing at me."

"Oh my," said the agent. The voices grew louder, accompanied by footfalls as they approached the cell. "I'm sorry for any trouble they gave you."

Pettit appeared first, scowling through the bars, followed by a man in a gray suit with a trimmed black beard. He smirked slightly at the sight of them.

"Is this them?" Pettit asked. "The girls you're looking for?"

The man who called himself Hargreaves nodded once. "It's them." He reached into a pocket of his suit jacket and took out a pair of handcuffs. "We'll cuff them together so they can't make another escape attempt."

That was the same way that the assassin, the man called Rais, had transported them—by cuffing them together so escape would be difficult. The memory of that nightmare whirled through Sara's head and made her knees weak.

"Put your hands on the rear wall," Pettit instructed.

But neither of them moved. "If you let him take us," Maya said quickly, "he's going to kill us."

"Put your hands on the rear wall!" Pettit demanded.

"Do you have kids?" Sara asked the question impulsively, her face close to the bars. It was a desperate bid, but the only one she had. "Do you? I bet you can tell when they're lying. But look at us. We're not lying. That man is not who he says he is."

Hargreaves sighed. "This is ridiculous. You two aren't getting away from what you've done."

"What *have* they done?" Pettit asked. Apparently Sara's question had given her pause. "You must have something, a warrant for their arrest or a record?"

"I'm afraid it's a matter of national security, ma'am."

"Two teenage girls?" Pettit asked blankly. "I think I'm going to have to get your badge number. At least give me a moment to call this in and verify your identity."

"Of course, Officer." Hargreaves smiled as he took out a leather bi-fold ID holder and handed it to her. "Do what you think is best."

As Pettit inspected the agent's identification, Sara noticed his hand moving into his suit jacket.

"Look out!" she shrieked.

Pettit barely had time to glance up before a black pistol, its barrel long with a suppressor, was pointed in her direction. She tried to twist out of the way, but not fast enough. Hargreaves fired two shots into her chest.

Chapter Thirty Three

Officer Pettit gasped as she fell flat on her back. Sara shrieked.

"Pettit?!" called another voice. The male officer, Reynolds. "Pettit, what's going—"

Hargreaves raised the gun again, this time aiming down the corridor at an angle that neither girl could see. Not that they wanted to. He fired twice more. Reynolds grunted, and there was another dull thud of a body hitting the floor.

Tears were already streaming down Sara's cheeks as the agent turned to them, the barrel of his pistol slightly smoking. "Shame," he said quietly. He knelt beside Pettit and yanked a ring of keys from her belt.

Maya stepped in front of Sara, pushing her younger sister behind her as Hargreaves tried one key in the lock, and then another. He cursed each time he got the wrong key.

"Listen to me," Maya whispered in her ear. "As soon as that door is open, I'm going to rush him. You run. Get out and don't stop."

"Maya, no…" Sara shook her head rapidly. She couldn't leave her sister behind.

"Do it!"

A key turned and the lock clicked.

"There we are," said Hargreaves as he reached to pull the door aside.

A hiss of radio static distracted all three of them, their heads turning toward the corridor and the unseen angle. Reynolds's voice, pained and almost unintelligible, floated to them. "Active shooter," he grunted, "Sumner station. Active shooter…"

"Son of a bitch," Hargreaves spat. He strode out of sight and his gun barked once more. Sara winced at the suppressed report. The agent stalked back to the cell, his gaze furious and his gait like a predator beyond the bars. "You see how much trouble you two have caused? You think I wanted to do that?" He reached for the door once more.

Sara jumped, her breath catching in her throat as a fusillade of automatic gunfire thundered in the corridor, impossibly loud. The bullets tore into Hargreaves, his limbs jerking as he collapsed in a heap.

A burly man appeared on the other side of the bars, from the rear of the station, a trucker's cap on his head and a stout submachine gun in one hand.

"Mitch!" Maya exclaimed breathlessly. "How did you find us?"

"Same way they did, I imagine. Police scanner." He yanked the cell door open. "Come on. Hurry up."

They clambered out of the cell, stepping over Hargreaves's body. Sara didn't dare to look down at it. Mitch held the gun aloft and led the way back down the corridor.

Pettit gasped once, a rasping attempt at breath that made Sara jump again.

"She's alive!" Sara knelt beside the female officer, who stared back at her wide-eyed and fearful. "Wait, we have to help her!"

"Sara." Mitch glanced toward the door and then back down at Pettit. "We have to go. We'll call it in when we're clear, but we can't wait around. I know how these guys operate. There's never just one. They'll send a team."

"We can't just leave her!" Sara insisted. It was their fault that Pettit was shot. It didn't look good; the woman would be dead in minutes.

Mitch turned suddenly toward the rear of the station, his eyes narrowed. "We can't leave at all," he muttered. "They're here. Hold this." He passed the machine gun to Maya and knelt beside Pettit. "Sorry about this, ma'am."

Pettit cried out sharply as Mitch reached under her shoulders and dragged her down the corridor and into the main floor of the station. He positioned her beneath a desk as best he could, and then took the gun back from Maya.

In her periphery, Sara saw a shadow steal quickly past one of the windows. "Mitch?"

The burly mechanic grabbed the edge of another desk and flipped it over, crouching behind it for cover and ushering the girls beside him.

"Listen closely. They've found us. Pretty sure it's the Division, which means they'll try a basic flank maneuver, a few in the front and a few in the back, depending on how many are out there. Right now they're waiting for us to make a move, but they won't wait long. If I can cut a path, you two can make a run for it—"

"No," Sara said defiantly. "We're not just going to leave you."

A salvo of automatic gunfire rang out. A window shattered and glass rained down over the floor. Sara let out a small shriek and covered her head again. Maya squeezed her eyes shut until it stopped.

"This isn't up for debate!" Mitch growled. He pulled a set of keys from his pocket and passed them to Maya. "Here. The truck is parked outside. You get to it and you get out of here fast."

"I-I don't drive," Maya stammered.

"Learn fast."

From outside came an odd sound—a hollow *thunk*—and a small object sailed over their heads. The fist-sized canister bounced off Pettit's desk and skittered across the floor, pouring white smoke from a fissure in one end.

Sara reacted without thinking. She leapt up and kicked the canister down the hall as it trailed smoke. It spun across the tile and out of sight beyond the cell they had just been in.

"They're trying to smoke us out," Mitch hissed. "We're out of time. We have to make a move."

"Where do we go?" Sara asked frantically. "We have no idea where we are—"

Another canister rattled across the floor behind her, white smoke billowing rapidly into the station. Mitch scrambled over to Pettit and pulled her service pistol from her belt. He passed it to

Maya. "Here. Use it if you have to. Go into one of those offices and get out a window. I'll distract them. Don't wait for me."

"But what if…" Maya started to say, but her words were cut off as she coughed violently in the swirling white smoke. It was getting difficult to see; Mitch was little more than a silhouette.

Suddenly his body jerked, his right shoulder twisting. At the same time thunder split the air. Sara felt it, the deep and resonant boom of it deep within her stomach. It wasn't thunder; it was the crack of a gunshot. Blood plumed from Mitch's shoulder and he grunted as his right shoulder jerked with the impact. "Go!" he bellowed.

The sight of blood and his guttural shout spurred her to action. Coughing, Sara crawled on her hands and knees across the floor toward one of the closed doors of the offices. She hoped that Maya was right behind her.

Another shot rang out, and wood splintered just inches over her head. A shriek filled her ears; she wasn't aware that it was her own.

She fought tears as she reached for the doorknob and pushed it open, practically falling into the small office. At least she could breathe better in there. Maya crawled in after her and shut the door.

Then they heard the gunfire, rolling and devastatingly loud, sounding as if it was coming from right outside the office as Mitch fired on the Division men assaulting the station. More gunshots came from outside, along with unintelligible shouts and commands.

"Come on," Maya whispered, her voice tremulous. She pointed upward at a narrow window of frosted glass. It looked barely large enough for them to get through. They dared to stand and peer through it. The office faced the east side of the station and a side street. There was no sign of movement. Not at first, anyway.

Two men came around the corner from the rear with automatic rifles to their shoulders, though they hardly looked like men at all. They were entirely black-clad, with tactical vests and thick boots and gas masks over their faces, giving them the faceless appearance of some assailing aliens bent on eradicating them without mercy.

Sara ducked down as the two men passed by the window and headed toward the front of the police station. In between bursts of gunfire, she heard the vague shouts of more men coming from behind the building.

"He's going to die if we don't do something," Sara whispered urgently.

Maya looked down at the silver pistol in her hand. "We have to do what he said." She sounded as if she doubted her own words. "We have to go." She looked through the window once more, and then carefully pushed it up. The pane slid soundlessly. "I'll go first, and then I'll cover you."

Sara gulped but nodded. Her sister tucked the gun into her jeans, pulled herself up to the window's ledge, and wriggled through the small opening. It was tight, and Sara held her breath the entire time, knowing that at any moment a member of the Division might come around the corner and catch her halfway through and unable to defend herself.

Finally Maya popped free and fell to the sidewalk below. Sara looked out and saw no one else. Her sister gestured for her to follow. It wasn't as difficult for her to get through, and once her torso was out Maya held onto her and pulled her the rest of the way until her feet were firmly on the cement.

Maya had the gun out again in an instant. They stuck close to the building as they sidled along its façade toward the front. Sara saw muzzle flashes through the broken windows, thick white smoke billowing out. She winced with each rattle of shots.

As long as they're still shooting, Mitch is still alive. She was vaguely aware of sirens behind the cracking bursts of gunfire. *More police are coming. They'll help us.*

"There's the truck," Maya said, gesturing toward the vehicle parked at the curb. "Run to it. Are you ready?"

Sara nodded. Maya checked around the corner and then grabbed onto her sister's hand. "Let's go." They rounded the edge of the building and ran to the pickup, staying low. Maya pulled her around to the driver's side, facing the road, and yanked open the door. "Get in. Stay down and out of sight. Don't make a sound."

"Wait!" Sara cried. "What are you doing? Mitch told us—"

"I know what Mitch told us!" she snapped. Maya's glance flitted from her sister's horrorstruck face to the front doors of the police station. Sara knew what she was thinking. She wanted to help Mitch.

Before she could act, sirens whooped loudly and she heard a screech of tires. A police cruiser skidded to a halt less than twenty-five yards from them, the door emblazoned with the words "Sumner Police Department." Two officers in beige uniforms leapt out, their service weapons already in hand, and took cover behind their car.

Maya and Sara ducked down quickly behind the open door of the truck as a booming voice, amplified through a bullhorn, declared: "This is the police! Cease fire, and come out with your hands above your head!"

The gunfire inside the station seemed to cease, at least for the moment. Sara deliberated making herself known, standing and waving to the police, running to them. But she didn't move. Instead she peered around the edge of the truck and watched the dark front doors, white smoke eking out into the afternoon like it was the mouth of hell.

A figure stepped out. He wore all black and a bug-eyed gas mask over his face, an automatic gun in his hands.

"Drop your weapon!" one of the officers shouted.

The mercenary snapped the rifle to his shoulder and fired at the police car. The windows shattered and bullets thunked against the side of the car. One of the officers cried out as several rounds struck him in the chest, through the broken windows.

Sara didn't know if the second officer had been hit or not. She kept her eyes on the Division man as he reached for something small and round clipped to his belt.

"No!" she blurted out as he lobbed the grenade and it rolled beneath the police cruiser.

She dropped to her elbows in the street and covered her ears as the car exploded. If the second officer hadn't already been hit, he was certainly incinerated. Tears stung her eyes as she looked around, her vision blurry. She felt disoriented. She spotted a vague shape on the ground in front of her. Maya had dropped Pettit's gun, holding one arm over her own head and shielding her sister with the other.

Sara reached for it.

She got to her knees. The Division man stood a short distance from them, his rifle held limp in both hands. He cocked his head slightly, as if deliberating, and then the muzzle tracked toward her.

Sara didn't think twice. She raised Pettit's gun and squeezed the trigger. The gun jumped in her hands, bucking harder than she thought it would. Her eyes closed instinctively as she shot.

When she dared to open them again, the faceless Division man was staggering backward. Blood spurted from a hole in his throat, and he fell onto his back.

The gun shook violently in her hands as her eyes brimmed with the threat of fresh tears.

Maya was on her feet in an instant. She hugged her sister to her. "It's okay," she said quickly. "It's okay. You did the right thing." She wiped Sara's face with her own hands. "It's okay. You stay here. Keep that. Don't move."

"Maya..." Sara struggled to form words. Her entire body shook.

"It's okay," she said again. "It's going to be okay." Maya frowned then, and looked up toward the police station.

"What...?" Sara started to ask. But then she realized it too. There were sirens, loud and screaming and approaching quickly, but that wasn't what had Maya distracted.

The shooting had stopped.

As they watched, a shape appeared in the broken doorway of the police station. A burly man, limping badly, staggered out of the white mist. He had one of Pettit's arms slung over his shoulders and his own arm around her waist.

The front of his flannel shirt was torn in a few places and soaked in blood.

He's been shot, Sara realized dully. Her mind was working too slowly in the wake of shooting the Division man.

Maya was on her feet in an instant, running to them. Sara wanted to follow, but her legs were still shaking too badly to move. She could only watch as her sister ran to help. Before Maya could reach them, Mitch fell forward to his knees. Pettit fell too with a pained grunt.

Sara was barely aware as two more police cars arrived, these cruisers marked with as Nebraska state troopers. Behind them a fire truck screamed into view, screeching to a halt at a safe distance from the still-burning cop car.

She forced her legs to move, toward Maya and Mitch and the fallen officer, even as the state cops shouted at them behind her. Maya sat on her knees next to them, tears streaming down her cheeks as Sara dropped beside her.

"Mitch?" His eyes were closed and he didn't look like he was breathing. "Mitch! Wake up!" She shook him. "Don't die. Don't die. Help us!" She shook him again. "Mitch!"

"Alan." He coughed once, his lips barely moving. His eyes didn't open, but she had definitely heard him speak. "It's Alan. My name is Alan." Then a single groan escaped his lips, and his head lolled to the side.

Chapter Thirty Four

"Act natural," Zero murmured to Maria as they strode their way onto the Manhattan side of the Queensboro Bridge.

"You don't say," she replied flatly.

It was a strange sight, walking in the center of the bridge, following along with several other pedestrians who were heading toward the commemoration ceremony at the same time. The four lanes of the upper level had been closed off for one hour in order to hold the ceremony; the lower four lanes remained open out of necessity, since the bridge was now the primary thoroughfare between Queens and Manhattan in the wake of the Midtown Tunnel's collapse, but the NYPD had established a checkpoint on the lower level with K-9 units. As a result, the traffic jam was immense for anyone trying to head one way or the other. Zero could hear horns blaring and drivers shouting from beneath them.

About a hundred yards ahead, just as the bridge began to stretch over the East River, he could see a small crowd had gathered, perhaps forty or fifty people. As they drew nearer he could hear them clamoring angrily. Beyond them were four police officers and a barricade of tall orange pylons and yellow caution tape.

A pedestrian checkpoint. The officers held metal-detecting wands and waved them in the air as they tried to assuage the crowd. Zero knew they would not be able to simply waltz through; on his person he had two EMP grenades, a pistol, and a knife. No way would he get past the cops with all of that.

"We need to ditch the gear," he told Maria quietly as he adjusted the black ball cap on his head.

"We can't go in empty-handed," she replied. "Just follow my lead."

"What are you going to do?"

She shrugged. "I'll improvise. Just get through as soon as you're able."

They reached the back of the crowd and Maria began to shoulder her way through them, pushing toward the front as angry people shouted at the cops.

"People, please!" one of the officers shouted. "The event is at capacity and has already begun. We are not letting anyone else through. Let's all back it up!"

"Excuse me!" Maria said loudly as she shoved her way up to the officer. "This is unacceptable! We have every right to be there!"

"Ma'am, I just told you we're not letting anyone else through, all right? If you leave now, you can see the event on TV—"

Maria scoffed. "I'll have you know that my brother was killed in that attack! And you're going to tell me you can't let me through?"

"I'm very sorry for your loss," the officer told her, "but I cannot let you—"

"My husband was down there!" another woman in the crowd shouted.

"My cousin!" someone else yelled.

"This is outrageous!" Maria shouted in the cop's face. Zero stood at a short distance from her, bewildered at what she was trying to pull.

The officer put one hand up, to indicate that she should stay back, while his other hand reached for the shoulder-mounted radio. "This is Booker, we're going to need some riot control up on the bridge—"

"Riot control?!" Maria poked him in the chest. "Is that what you want, a riot?"

"Ma'am, you need to keep your hands to yourself, or you will be arrested!" the officer shouted in her face.

"Go ahead then! Arrest me! I'll sue your ass, your whole department, and then I'll… I'll…" She took a step back and staggered, frowning deeply.

Zero was so caught up in the act that he reached out instinctively and grabbed her elbow. "Are you okay?"

"Ma'am?" said the cop, taking a step forward.

"Just a little dizzy..." Maria's legs suddenly gave out from under her and she collapsed onto the bridge. Several onlookers in the crowd gasped and jumped back as she fell. A woman shrieked.

"Give her space!" the officer shouted, waving the people back. "Move back, people! Move!"

Zero's throat ran dry as Maria's entire body began quivering. Her eyes rolled back until only the whites showed, and a small amount of spittle bubbled from her lips.

It was so convincing that for a moment Zero forgot himself and his mission as Maria went into a full-on mock seizure.

"This is Booker! I need EMS up here, now!"

"Someone help her!" Zero shouted, taking two quick steps back.

The cop waved the other officers over and shouted orders. "Get something between her teeth! Elevate her legs! You, call EMS again!"

As the assembled security detail crowded around Maria, Zero understood what she was doing. She knew that they both wouldn't make it onto the bridge; she had created a diversion for him, much like he had done for her and Sanders on the banks of the Potomac.

He edged his way sideways between the orange pylons as the tight crowd of spectators closed in around the officers. Then he turned and strode purposefully down the bridge toward the commemoration. He didn't bother looking back for fear of looking suspicious.

A few members of the crowd saw him slip through and followed suit, nearly a dozen people in all. He blended in with them as they hurried along down the bridge.

Thanks, Maria.

With the clamor of the crowd behind him, Zero could hear the amplified commencement coming from up ahead. About a hundred and fifty yards further up the bridge was a sizeable crowd, between eight hundred and a thousand people by his best estimate.

He walked briskly past a black SWAT van that did not appear to have anyone in the cab, and a stalwart but similarly empty NYFD truck.

Security was noticeably lax. *By design, I imagine.*

Beyond the crowd was a small elevated stage, likely on wheels and brought in by flatbed, spanning one of the two lanes on the right side of the bridge's concrete center barrier. Upon the stage was a podium, and behind it was the mayor of New York, Richard Feinerman. He was a short man in person, mostly bald but with sharp eyes and a strong speaking voice, made all the stronger by the microphone and his trademark hand gestures, which he used to punctuate each statement.

"New York does not just survive," the mayor's voice boomed over the crowd, "we thrive. We do not just endure; we persevere. Once again we find ourselves at the heart of conflict, and while we may forgive, we will *never* forget."

It sounded as if the mayor was nearing the end of his address. His words became background noise as Zero maneuvered his way through the crowd, daring to edge closer to the front. There was a ton of media present, a wide semicircle of news cameras and photographers surrounding the temporary stage in a semicircle that cordoned the spectators from getting too close.

Zero pulled the brim of his black ball cap lower over his eyes as he drew ever nearer. To the left of the stage were a half-dozen men in black suits—Secret Service, he knew. He looked from one face to another but did not see the man he had mentally identified as Raulsen.

To the right of the stage were a handful of NYPD officers, a few firefighters, some EMS. The first-responders to the Midtown Tunnel disaster, no doubt. And several yards behind the mayor and the podium was a black town car, its windows tinted dark and two small American flags fluttering from the roof.

He noticed a few White House staffers lingering behind the Secret Service agents, but he did not see any of the major players—even the chief of staff, Holmes, and the press secretary, Christine

Cleary, were absent. *Because they know what's going to happen. They're staying out of the line of fire.*

Zero held his position about ten yards back from the front of crowd and waited, his injured right hand obscured in his jacket pocket. It ached terribly, but he didn't let his expression show it. Under the gauze and bandages was the LC9, carefully wrapped with his ring finger secured inside the trigger guard.

How is this going to go down? he wondered. He glanced upward briefly at the tall tower saddles overhead, the high points from which the suspensions and trellises were built. *There can't be a shooter up there; there wouldn't be a clear vantage point. Too much in the way.* And the NYPD was thoroughly sweeping cars on the lower level. It would have to be done by someone there on the upper level.

Suddenly Carver's suggestion of the Secret Service did not seem so farfetched. All they would need is a single person with a gun to fire off a round or two and all hell would break loose.

Zero was jarred from his thoughts as the crowd around him broke into applause for the mayor's address. "Thank you." The mayor paused a moment, waiting for the noise to die down, before continuing. "And now it is my genuine pleasure to introduce a very esteemed guest to our city today. Ladies and gentlemen, President of the United States Eli Pierson."

The crowd downright erupted at the announcement. Though many of the spectators might have already guessed it by the car and the presence of the Secret Service, the appearance of the president resulted in raucous cheers and thunderous applause.

A Secret Service agent opened the back door of the town car behind the stage and Pierson stepped out. He made his way around the side of the stage and the three steps that led up its side, waving to the crowd as he did. He shook the mayor's hand heartily, and then stepped up to the podium.

Pierson stood there for what felt like a long moment, smiling as he scanned the faces before him and waiting for the attention of those cheering for him.

"My fellow Americans," he began. "It was with a heavy heart that we once again saw New York bear the brunt of a brutal attack on its people."

Zero scanned the stage and the surrounding area quickly, left and right and back again, growing more desperate by the second. He was running out of time; the president's address would not last long, and he had little doubt that the staged assassination attempt would happen during it, on the world's stage in front of thirty news cameras.

But who? From where? How could they avoid being seen or filmed?

He couldn't very well just stand there and wait for someone to make a move. By the time they did, it might be too late for him to act.

"Yet I refuse to use the term 'victim' in reference to this attack on our nation," Pierson continued. "For me, to say 'victim' implies a level of helplessness, but this city, and this country, are far from helpless."

Zero saw movement behind the president. One of the Secret Service agents lifted a finger to his ear, and then murmured a few silent words into the nearly transparent earpiece. It was a seemingly innocuous motion for an agent, but to him it could have very well been a signal.

"This attack was about more than just a loss of life; it was an attempt to break our spirit. It was an attempt by a small group of terrorists to assert that our way of life is an affront to them. But I stand here today and say, no. Our way of life is a *threat* to them. And they should feel threatened."

He had to make a move. He took a step forward, trying to push his way further into the crowd, when a voice spoke firmly and quietly from behind him.

"Hello, Zero."

He froze, his heartbeat quickening.

"We will not back down to their whims," Pierson said forcefully, his voice rising an octave. A cheer went up from the crowd. "We will not be intimidated."

Someone stepped forward to stand beside Zero. He wore a flat gray suit and stood about three inches taller. His shoulders were thick and his hands clasped in front of him.

"Raulsen," Zero noted dourly.

"Hands out of your pockets," the Secret Service agent ordered, just loud enough for him to hear.

"We will not be goaded into confrontation," Pierson boomed to more applause. "The United States will show the world that we can rise above it."

Zero slowly pulled his injured right hand from his jacket pocket, and then his left, doing his best to hide the disc-shaped object in his palm. "You've been watching me. You saw me coming, didn't you?"

Raulsen nodded once. "Try something." He unclasped his thick hands and turned his left over, giving Zero just a brief glimpse of what he had there. The device was as oblong and black, as small as a Bic lighter, with a single trigger on one end.

But he had seen a device like it before. It was a remote detonator.

There's a bomb, he realized in horror.

Chapter Thirty Five

"Now we find ourselves facing yet another threat to our freedoms," Pierson said into the microphone as his gaze swept over the crowd. "But we will not bend to their will. We will not be threatened. We will rise above it..."

Zero's head swam, barely hearing the president's words as he realized the gravity of the situation. They had planted a bomb somewhere. Under the platform, perhaps, or in the podium. Maybe even inside the president's car. Before the event, the Secret Service would have insisted on doing their own protective sweep even after the NYPD. It would have been easy to plant.

But what is he waiting for? As much as Zero didn't want to see the president incinerated on international television, he couldn't help but wonder why Raulsen didn't press the button.

"Move forward slowly," Raulsen commanded, his voice low and close to Zero's ear. "We want you front row for this. Refuse, and I'll blow it. Make a wrong move, and I'll blow it."

An epiphany struck Zero as hard as a punch to the gut.

They're not pinning this on Iranians. They're going to pin it on me.

Raulsen had a finger on the trigger, the president on the podium, and a scapegoat right there beside him. This had all been planned. They knew he would come. They knew he would try to stop it. Not only would he be discredited, but so would his family and anyone affiliated with him. They would be arrested swiftly, and no one would ever believe what they knew to be true.

Zero took an even breath and a small step forward. His left hand palmed the EMP grenade, a small round device of Bixby's design about the size of a double-wide poker chip. To activate it, he needed to twist the two halves and wait five seconds.

But he couldn't do that with only one hand.

He needed a distraction, but one that wouldn't prompt Raulsen to detonate prematurely. He took another step forward, the Secret Service agent on his heels as he shouldered through the crowd.

"You're really going to do this, Raulsen?" he murmured behind him. "You're really going to betray him like this? What are they paying you?"

"Shut up," Raulsen hissed. "Keep moving."

"I've seen some of the account statements." Zero edged between two people, getting closer to the semicircle of media surrounding the platform. "I know what those oil execs paid Holmes for his participation. What was your payday, Raulsen? Roland Kemmerer got eight million, and that was just a down pay—*oomph!*"

Zero's foot caught on someone's ankle—rather, he caught his foot on someone's ankle—and he sprawled forward, putting his elbows out. He knocked into several people as he fell. *Don't blow it. Don't blow it…* As his elbows hit the concrete surface of the bridge, he stuck the EMP grenade between his teeth and twisted with his left hand.

One… Two…

Raulsen's strong grip wrapped around Zero's arm and hauled him to his feet. As he did, Zero tossed the EMP disc in a gentle arc over his head. It vanished just beyond the sea of cameramen.

The Secret Service agent's jaw went slack. "You dumb son of a bitch."

Then he pressed the trigger button.

Zero held his breath.

"Now more than ever," Pierson was saying into the microphone, we must stand together as Americans—" His voice cut out suddenly, though his mouth kept moving. The president frowned and tapped a finger twice against the mic.

Cameramen looked down at their equipment, puzzled. Phone screens in the air, recording the president's address, suddenly went black.

The EMP grenade hadn't made a sound, but it had knocked out everything electronic in a twenty-five-yard radius. Every phone, radio, camera, microphone, and remote-detonated bomb lost power in a blink.

Raulsen, confused, pressed the trigger twice more, but to no avail. Murmurs began to rise from the crowd, people looking at each other in bewilderment. Secret Service agents pressed their fingers to their ears, trying to get someone on the line and failing with their inert radios.

"It seems like we're having some technical difficulties," Pierson said loudly without the aid of the microphone. "Please just bear with us a moment, everyone…"

Zero breathed a small sigh of relief. But it was short-lived.

Raulsen dropped the useless detonator as he glared at Zero. "You think that was it? You think you've won?" He reached for the shoulder holster in his suit jacket as he bellowed, "It's Zero! Zero is here!"

Zero didn't wait around to see the Sig Sauer, let alone let it be pointed his way. He plunged into the crowd, shoving people aside and elbowing past.

"Gun!" someone in the crowd shouted frantically. The cry was carried out like a ripple of a lake, from the front to the rear, as people began hurrying in every direction, or trying to. There was nowhere for the front of the crowd to go. Spectators shoved each other violently, trying to push backward, toppling some and trampling over others.

I have to get to Pierson. The crowd was moments from anarchy; there was still opportunity for the assassination to happen. He doubled back, fighting against the current of the throng to make his way back to the stage. A man bumped roughly into his injured hand and he sucked in a pained breath.

In the half-second he took to wince, the air was driven from his lungs as a shoulder rammed powerfully into his midsection. Raulsen tackled him like a linebacker, driving Zero's feet right off the ground and taking at least four others down with them. His back and head hit concrete with two hundred and thirty pounds of Secret Service atop him and he saw stars for a moment.

A thick fist came flying at his face. Zero twisted his head and shoulders as quickly as he could, feeling his spine pop with the sudden movement. Raulsen struck concrete and screamed out.

Now we've both got broken hands. Zero struck him in the throat with two knuckles and bucked his hips, throwing the agent aside. The ball cap had fallen from his head, but he left it where it lay as he scrambled to his feet. He was halfway up when a fleeing spectator knocked into him full-force, driving him back down.

Raulsen rolled over, holding his broken hand close to his body and reaching for the gun he'd dropped. Zero clambered on his hands and knees and kicked him in the face. Then he snatched up the gun.

He glanced quickly up at the platform, and between the people rushing around him, he locked eyes with President Pierson. Two Secret Service agents had him flanked, guns drawn, while a third tugged on the president's arm, imploring him to move.

But Pierson stared back at Zero, and he could only imagine how it looked: fighting off his head of security, holding a gun.

Then the Secret Service pulled him away, down the steps of the podium while they stood in front of him as human shields. Zero needed to get there. He couldn't assume that Raulsen was the only one who had been compromised.

But first I need to clear this area. He held the Sig Sauer straight up in the air and fired off two crisp, deafening shots.

The response was immediate chaos. Screams echoed throughout the surging crowd as they doubled their efforts to get off the bridge. Any NYPD or backup that was coming would have a hell of a time getting through, he realized.

Raulsen rose slowly to his feet, staggering as a cameraman shoved his way past.

Zero leveled the gun at him. "Don't..."

The Secret Service agent let out a roar and charged at him. Zero fired once, striking him in the shoulder, but Raulsen barely slowed.

He swung his good hand wildly, blow after blow. Zero ducked and dodged as best he could.

He didn't want to kill Raulsen in clear view of the president and the Secret Service. As soon as the crowd dissipated, he'd be gunned down immediately. *Though that's probably already going to happen.*

He put up both forearms to block a hook and Raulsen swiftly drove a knee into his stomach. Zero grunted and staggered backward. But Raulsen didn't let up; he brought one foot up and, while Zero was off balance, he kicked him in the chest. Zero's hip hit a railing and he tumbled head over heels, landing painfully on the pedestrian footbridge.

Raulsen vaulted over the railing and kicked the Sig Sauer from Zero's hand before he could get it up in front of him. The gun skittered down the concrete walkway, several yards away. The Secret Service swung downward and landed a teeth-rattling crack across his jaw. Stars swam in Zero's vision as he felt himself kicked again, turning him over. A thick arm snaked around his neck. He tried to tuck his chin in time, but Raulsen grabbed his hair and yanked his head back.

Zero choked as his airway was cut off. He heard shouting behind him, the few Secret Service agents and NYPD officers that had remained behind to protect Pierson, but he had no idea where the president was. He tried to pry Raulsen from his neck, but he had only one good hand and felt the strength draining from it.

Raulsen responded by squeezing harder. "I was supposed to let you live," he hissed in Zero's ear. "To keep you alive so you could take the fall. But then again, that bomb was supposed to go off, so I guess plans are out the window."

Zero struggled for breath as the edges of his vision darkened. It felt as if time slowed down as Raulsen choked the life from him. He heard the steady thrum of a helicopter's rotors as an NYPD chopper flew toward the bridge from Manhattan. The screams of sirens as emergency vehicles fought the crowds to get to the president.

I'm going to die here, he knew, but all he needed was another minute or two. Their plan had been thwarted. The bomb had not gone off. The cameras had caught nothing. And in moments, when

SWAT and NYPD arrived, there would be too many witnesses to stage the assassination.

He looked out over the East River, sparkling blue as the sun danced across its crests. There were worse views to die from. An orange and white Coast Guard skiff cut a swath through the river toward the bridge, sailing parallel to Roosevelt Island. Help was on the way.

His daughters would be safe with Alan. Others would take up his cause. Keep fighting. Make sure that this was ended. And he, Zero, wasn't going to die a presidential assassin.

He heard a sharp hissing sound, almost a whistling, and before he could wonder if it was just in his head he saw an orange streak soaring skyward, trailing white smoke.

The streak struck the side of the NYPD helicopter as it turned its nose toward the bridge. The chopper exploded in a fiery ball that somehow lit the afternoon brighter than the sun itself.

"What the hell…" Raulsen breathed in his ear. His grip on Zero's throat slackened, only slightly, as they both stared in abject bewilderment at the falling debris of the burning chopper.

An RPG. A rocket-propelled grenade.

Where did it come from?

Zero sucked in a ragged breath, his throat and lungs burning horribly. "Raulsen," he tried to say, but it came out as a choked gasp.

He understood now. The RPG had been fired from the deck of the Coast Guard boat. The bomb in the podium—if there was even a bomb in the podium—wasn't the plan at all. Raulsen was as much a pawn as Zero was.

And as the thick arm around his neck fell slack, it seemed that the Secret Service agent was beginning to realize that as well.

"Sons of bitches," he murmured.

Zero tried to raise his right arm, but it felt heavy, too heavy. *The Ruger.* His failsafe.

With some effort, he lifted his catcher's mitt–sized hand, broken and throbbing and wrapped in layers of steel and gauze, and he rested it on his right shoulder.

His ring finger twitched, feeling the curve of the trigger of the LC9 he had concealed inside the dressing.

Then he pulled it.

The shot was startlingly loud in his ear, loud enough to send a rattling report through his own body. His hand burned in pain instantly, every broken bone and severed tendon screaming. The end of the wrapping blew outward, sending white bits of gauze into the air like confetti.

Raulsen's arm fell away from around his neck, and his body slumped to the concrete.

Zero caught his breath, panting as he glanced over his shoulder. The bullet had caught Raulsen just beneath the right eye and out the other side.

"Get up," he muttered to himself. There was still a threat.

A hail of gunfire split the air from behind him, jarring Zero into action. He pulled himself behind a thick metal trellis as sparks flew from the impact of bullets. The handful of NYPD officers and Secret Service agents fired on him from the opposite side of the bridge, hidden behind the concrete barricade.

He couldn't stay there. They'd flank him and take him out in seconds. But if he moved, they'd fire. Zero hazarded the briefest of glances around the railing, and then ducked back again as a shot bounced off the metal mere inches from his face.

The black presidential car was still there and not going anywhere fast. The EMP grenade would have knocked it out. Pierson was likely inside it.

He looked out over the river and saw, a hundred and thirty feet below, the hijacked Coast Guard skiff had slowed. From bridge height he could see figures on the deck, reloading the long shoulder-fired surface-to-air weapon with another missile.

"Get off the bridge!" he tried to shout, but the intermittent gunfire drowned him out.

The figure on the small boat lifted the RPG, aiming it upward at a sharp angle.

Aiming it at him.

Zero launched himself from his position. The choice between bullets and a warhead was not a choice at all. He heard the telltale hissing of the rocket approaching as he sprinted, or tried to sprint, down the pedestrian walkway.

He didn't get far. The RPG struck the Queensboro Bridge with a detonation that forced every muscle in his body to go lax. He felt the heat on his back as the force of the explosion threw him forward.

Chapter Thirty Six

Zero caught the concrete with both elbows and a shoulder. He rolled twice, end over end, as rubble rained down on him.

Slowly he managed to roll himself over. Everything hurt. One by one he wiggled each limb to make sure that nothing was broken, beyond the nine bones that had been previously. He groaned as he pulled himself to a seated position on the pedestrian walkway. His vision swirled; he was woozy, disoriented.

White smoke drifted in his periphery. He heard sounds, but they seemed distant. People shouting in both pain and fear. Horns blaring. A deep, resonant creaking that he felt in his bowel.

Pierson. Zero climbed to his feet and staggered forward into the smoky haze. His foot caught on something and he stumbled, nearly falling again. It was a Secret Service agent, or half of one. His eyes stared up at Zero unblinking.

He felt dizzy again and pressed the back of his hand to his forehead. It came away slick with blood. He was concussed, to say the least. Possible skull fracture. He'd deal with that later. He stumbled forward again, and then stopped just as suddenly as he saw the extent of the damage.

"Jesus," he murmured. The RPG had struck the upper level at an angle and blown away two and a half lanes. The enormous hole was like a gaping mouth in the Queensboro Bridge with exposed rebar teeth. He could see clear down to the lower level, where great chunks of concrete had fallen and crushed cars. There were people down there, screaming, running, struggling to free themselves from the snarled mess of traffic and destroyed vehicles.

He had seen this sort of devastation before, in what felt like a lifetime ago. Another bridge, much smaller, spanning a narrow river in Kuwait. An RPG had destroyed the entire bridge with a single shot, killing more than two dozen who had been trying to cross it.

A Koronet anti-tank missile, he knew. One of the strongest RPGs available, capable of penetrating the armor of an Abrams tank.

The bridge groaned, and Zero took two quick steps back as a section of unstable concrete fell away and caved in the roof of a car. The windows exploded outward. Zero looked away, hoping desperately that the car was empty.

The car. He glanced left and right, and then spotted it: the black presidential town car was to his right, teetering precipitously on the edge of the chasm. It had been overturned in the explosion, resting on its roof.

He rushed over to it and yanked on the rear door handle. It refused to open. "Help!" he shouted. But the emergency vehicles had stopped in their tracks; the bridge was unstable.

He yanked on the door handle again. *Where are the jets?!* he thought furiously. Protocol for a situation like this one would be to immediately deploy fighter jets to eliminate the Coast Guard ship. It would take them no more than three or four minutes to arrive—but he had the feeling that whoever was responsible for calling in the air strike was purposely delaying it.

Zero was on his own.

He put one foot against the side of the car and wrenched on the door handle as hard as he could with one hand, teeth gritted and pain screaming through his limbs. Finally it popped free, sending Zero to the ground once again.

He peered into the cab. A body was lying on the floor—the roof, in this case—and facing away from him.

"Mr. President," he panted. The body didn't move. "Pierson." He reached in and grabbed the man by the shoulder.

"Oh." Pierson groaned as he rolled over. His eyes immediately grew wide at the sight of his would-be rescuer. "Zero. How are you alive?"

I ask myself the same thing pretty often. But instead he said, "We have to move. Now."

"You're trying to kill me," Pierson murmured.

"No, sir. I'm the only one trying to save you right now. We don't have time; we have to go—"

Another cacophonous explosion rocked the bridge, sending Zero sprawling onto his back. He winced, waiting for fire to consume, or for the bridge to fall apart beneath him. When it didn't, he dared to get to his feet.

A wave of nausea roiled over him. The second RPG had struck the lower level, blasting a wide hole between bridge and water. Zero had seen some truly awful things in his life, but the sight of cars careening over the edge, falling away over one hundred and thirty feet of nothing and smacking the water, innocent people still inside them, made fury and disgust bubble up inside him.

They're not going to stop. The bridge groaned again; Pierson's car shifted slightly as the concrete beneath it threatened to fall away.

"I'm sorry," Zero said urgently, "but we have to go." He reached into the cab, took hold of the president's collar, and hauled him out of the car. Pierson cried out, cradling his arm over his midsection.

"I think my wrist is broken." Pierson rolled over and got to his knees. He looked up at Zero, his gaze desperate and confused. "Why? Why is this happening?"

Because of me. If he hadn't gone to Pierson first, if he had just worked from the shadows and stopped this himself, this wouldn't be happening.

No. He refused to blame himself for the deaths of innocent people, of police, or for the attempted murder of the president. These people were going to do whatever they needed to do to enact their plan, one way or another. He wasn't going to die on this bridge, and he wasn't going to let the president die either.

"Come on." Zero hauled Pierson to his feet. "Look. Look down there." He pointed down the length of the bridge, toward the Queens side. A little less than a half mile away was an armada of emergency vehicles, spanning the bridge's width but not daring to go further while rockets were flying. "That's your rescue, okay? That's where we're going. Run. Don't stop. Don't turn around. Got it?"

Pierson nodded frantically, soot streaking his terrified face.

"Good. Let's go." He grabbed Pierson's sleeve and pulled him along at a jogging pace. The president limped, favoring his right leg and holding his broken wrist against his body.

Zero knew that any moment, another RPG would hit the bridge. *They can't see us from below. They don't know where we are. They don't know if the president is still alive or not.*

Those thoughts were hardly comforting, particularly the last one; if the assailants didn't know if they'd successfully taken Pierson out, they wouldn't stop their assault until help arrived.

"Don't stop," he prodded in a puffing breath. "Keep going. Eyes forward…"

He heard the hiss of another rocket and yanked on Pierson's sleeve, pulling the president closer. As the explosion thundered behind them, Zero covered Pierson's head with both arms. The RPG struck a tower support less than twenty yards behind them, throwing metal shrapnel in every direction and sending both men flat to the ground again.

Suspension cables snapped as the bridge groaned in protest. The tower twisted slowly, leaning over their heads.

They're going to bring the whole bridge down. "Back!" Zero ordered, tugging Pierson to his feet. "Go back!" He pulled the president as the tower leaned dangerously and toppled, smashing concrete with tons of steel and cracking straight through the upper level.

Zero stared, slack-jawed, as their only exit was demolished. The path between them and Queens was gone.

He felt a hand clutch desperately at his arm. "What do we do, Zero? What are we going to do?"

There was only one thing they could do, only one way out from there. It was the very last thing that he wanted to do, but they were left with no choice.

"We have to jump."

Pierson's face drained of color as he shook his head. "No. No, Zero, no, we can't. The fall will kill us."

The president was only half-wrong. A trained cliff diver or a Navy SEAL could make the jump from that height. Even Zero had made similar leaps on more than one occasion. But for someone untrained like Pierson, leaping into water from a hundred and thirty feet would be the equivalent of jumping from fifty feet onto cement.

Wait. Zero had nearly forgotten about the backpack that Bixby had given him. He muttered a thanks to the prophetic inventor as he tore off his jacket and tossed it aside. "See this?" he said quickly as he clipped the straps together over his chest. "It's a… it's a parachute."

Pierson blinked several times. "You brought a parachute?"

"Yes," Zero lied. He wasn't about to tell the president that he was hinging their survival on the efficacy of a prototype hang glider small enough to fit in a backpack. "So we're going to jump, together, and we're going to be okay. But you need to hang onto me."

Pierson shook his head again. "Zero, I can't jump. I can't…"

"Just listen!" he snapped. "If you fall, make sure you fall feet first and keep your back as straight as possible. Breathe out. Clench *everything*. Do you understand?"

"Zero, I can't do it. I can't." The president was rambling, his head twitching back and forth, his gaze terror-stricken. "I can't. I'll die."

Zero grabbed Pierson by the lapels and shook him. "You'll die here!" he hissed. "Is that what you want?"

"No!" Pierson yelped.

"Then come on." He pulled Pierson back toward the blown-out tower support, a jagged hole on the side of the bridge exposed to the East River below. "When we reach the water, we'll swim to Roosevelt Island. It's only a couple hundred yards." He looked down, and suddenly doubted his plan.

One hundred and thirty feet was a long drop.

A bitter realization struck him: *If this glider doesn't work, maybe I will be responsible for killing the president after all.*

He couldn't think like that now, nor could he afford to wait and consider their options any further. It was now or never.

"God help us," Pierson murmured. He reached out and gripped Zero's arm.

"We jump on three," Zero told him. "One … two …"

The hissing of the rocket drowned out the finale of his countdown. An RPG struck the lower level of the bridge not thirty yards from their location, startling them both and shaking the ground they stood on.

Time felt as if it slowed down as Pierson's legs quaked and buckled. The president lurched forward, his arms flailing but finding nothing on which to gain purchase.

"No!" Zero bent his knees as Pierson tumbled out over nothing. Then he catapulted himself from the bridge as hard as he could, reaching out with both hands. His arms wrapped around Pierson as they fell together, rolling in midair over and over as the wind tore at them.

Zero had no choice but to let go with one hand. He ripped at the cord by his right shoulder. He heard the glider unfurl behind him, saw in his periphery a sky-blue sailcloth expand on either side of them.

The glider caught the breeze, yanking hard on both of Zero's shoulders. He grunted and held as tightly as he could onto Pierson as their descent slowed, gliding on a forty-five-degree angle downward.

"Don't let me go!" Pierson shouted.

Zero gritted his teeth, struggling to maintain a hold and steer the device at the same time. Then he heard a sound that immediately caused his stomach to turn. The aluminum frame groaned.

This isn't designed for two adult men.

As soon as he thought it, the frame buckled. The glider folded inward, the sailcloth flapping wildly. Pierson cried out again as they half-fell, half-glided in a tight spiral down to the East River.

But the glider, at least, had bought them time; it had slowed their descent a lot, so now, as he looked down, Zero saw that they only had about twenty feet before impact. It would hurt, and it would be freezing, but it wouldn't kill them.

They plunged into the water with an impact that was as jarring as it was freezing. Pierson slipped away from his grip as Zero tumbled twice in the river, struggling to free himself from the glider that was now keeping him from reaching the surface again. He clawed at it, his limbs screaming against the knife-like sting of the frigid water.

Somehow he managed to tear himself loose from the backpack. He swam for the surface, hoping against hope that the president hadn't succumbed to shock in the icy river.

Chapter Thirty Seven

Commander Ali Mahasi stood upon the bow of the *Jamar*, an Iranian Moudge-class frigate and lead ship of the blockade facing the Persian Gulf. He scratched at his dark beard idly; it was a tic he had developed years earlier, scratching at his chin whenever he was in a particularly pensive position—as he found himself currently.

The *Jamar* was a ninety-five-meter-long ship, among the larger vessels in the Islamic Revolutionary Guard Corps, outfitted with anti-submarine torpedoes, surface-to-air missiles, and anti-ship box launchers.

Yet the threat that they faced currently was hardly one they were prepared to deal with.

Ship from the United States' Fifth Fleet had come from seemingly every direction, less than a mile between them and the Strait of Hormuz, where the Iranian blockade waited. If they wanted to destroy the IRGC vessels, they could do so in mere minutes. Yet they seem to have stalled their approach, and Mahasi could do nothing but watch and wait.

President Sarif had ordered the blockade and nothing more. They were not to go on the offensive, and while the commander thought that it was a foolhardy decision given what the Americans had already done, there were rumors circulating that Sarif held out hope that he could reach a diplomatic solution. The decision to close the strait had been one of necessity, but the president would not openly declare war against the US. Commander Mahasi had heard directly from the IRGC commodore that attempts to reach the American president had thus far proved fruitless.

We are waiting here to die, Mahasi thought bitterly. If it was up to him, the entirety of the Iranian fleet would fire everything they had, in concert, and destroy as many as they could at once. He doubted the Americans would stand long for the strait's closure. It would not be long before…

"Sir." Behind Mahasi, his communications officer cleared his throat.

"Yes, Mahmoud?"

"One of the American ships is hailing us, Commander."

"What do they want?"

Mahmoud hesitated. "They won't say. They… asked to speak to you specifically."

Mahasi's nostrils flared. *They want to make their demands,* he thought. *They will order the IRGC to stand down, or be destroyed.* The moment was up. And he, it seemed, was the one who would speak on behalf of Iran.

Mahasi briskly followed Mahmoud to the bridge and fit a headset over his ears. "This is Commander Mahasi of the *Jamar,*" he said crisply. "Identify yourself."

"My name is Lieutenant Davis of the USS *Constitution.*" The US naval officer spoke almost flawless Farsi. "Commander, I am contacting you not on behalf of the United States, or the Fifth Fleet, but that of the men and women who serve upon our vessels. It is vital that we negotiate a cease-fire between us. No more lives lost, Commander."

What? A cease-fire? Mahasi furrowed his brow in confusion. "And you speak for your captain and admiral?"

"I do not, sir. The commanding officers of the Fifth Fleet have been compromised and deemed no longer fit for leadership."

The Iranian commander could hardly believe what he was hearing. "Is this a deceit?"

"No, Commander Mahasi," said the American lieutenant. "This is mutiny."

Chapter Thirty Eight

Zero coughed up a mouthful of river water as he gripped a dark, craggy rock on the northwestern shore of Roosevelt Island. His right arm was bent around Pierson's shoulder, dragging him along as they reached shallow water.

The president's face was pale, his eyes closed and lips blue. Zero knew he had to get him out of the water, administer CPR, and hope to any higher power that was listening that he was still alive.

Above and just north of them, pieces of the Queensboro Bridge continued to collapse and fall, splashing down into the water below. It seemed that the lower level had been evacuated, save for the unfortunate souls who had been within the immediate blast zone of the RPGs.

Zero winced as a trio of screaming F-16 jets soared overhead. As he watched, a single Sidewinder missile fired forward and obliterated the hijacked Coast Guard skiff in an instant fireball. The jets pulled up, over the bridge, and banked around the island of Manhattan.

It seemed that the day had been won, by most accounts, but Zero had no strength left in his body. He was completely and utterly exhausted; even pulling himself further up on the rocks seemed insurmountable, let alone providing any aid to Pierson.

"Help," he tried to call out, but his voice was hoarse and rasping, barely more than a harsh whisper. "Someone." There was no one around; it looked as if Roosevelt Island had been evacuated as well, but there couldn't possibly have been enough time for that. The entire ordeal had unfolded in mere minutes.

"Please." He clutched at Pierson, struggling to get him turned on his side in case he had swallowed too much water. Even if Zero had strength left, chest compressions with a broken hand would have been difficult. "Anyone?"

"Zero!" A voice. A male voice. Zero looked up the sloping, rocky shore, squinting against the bright afternoon sun as a silhouette picked his way carefully down toward them. "Looks like you need some help."

He knew that voice.

Carver knelt beside him, looking him over in a mixture of amusement and disbelief. "Told you I'd be here." He chuckled lightly. "I saw you two jump off the bridge. Goddamn, Zero. You don't half-ass anything, do you?"

"Help him," Zero panted. But something in Carver's expression made him very much doubt that help had arrived.

"What, is he still alive?" Carver scoffed and leaned over Zero to feel Pierson's pulse. "I'll be damned. Well, that won't do."

A cold shudder ran up Zero's spine.

Carver had never intended on helping him. He had led Zero here, into the midst of all of this.

"Help!" he tried to shout again.

"No one's going to hear you," Carver told him. "We sent everyone on the island down to the southern tip, away from the bridge. Ferries are coming to get them. There's no one out here but me and you."

Zero heard the steady thrum of helicopters, and for a moment he had hope that help was on the way. He craned his neck as best he could, his muscles aching in protest.

But the red and white rescue choppers were not headed toward the island; they were going to the bridge.

"Is it…" Zero coughed violently. "Is it worth it?"

"Yeah," Carver nodded. "It is." He stood, lifted one boot, and put it gently against Zero's throat, easing downward as if pushing a pedal, cutting off Zero's airway. He sputtered and clutched at the boot with his left hand, but he couldn't move it. It might as well have been a car on top of him for all he could do about it.

His arm shaking, Zero lifted his bandaged right hand and pointed it at Carver. He pulled the trigger of the LC9.

But nothing happened. The gun was waterlogged and useless.

"Goodbye, Zero. I'll put in a good word, see what I can do about making you a hero."

His vision blurred. His lungs burned for air, his mouth opening with gulps of nothing, like a fish out of water.

Carver leaned over him. "We're still going to have to kill your friends, though. Your kids, too. Sorry."

His vision darkened as images of Sara and Maya flickered across his mind. *Alan will keep them safe.* He had to tell himself that; if this was going to be his last moment, he had to believe that.

Suddenly Carver yelped. The boot lifted from Zero's throat and he sucked in a liberal gulp of air as Carver fell forward across the rocks.

"That's enough, Jason." A deep voice, familiar, flat and almost emotionless.

Watson.

Zero pushed himself to his elbow with a heavy groan as Carver rolled over, a thin knife stuck just above his right kidney. Agent Watson stood on the rocks, pistol in hand, but there was no one behind him. It seemed he'd come alone.

"Oh, you son of a bitch," Carver gasped. "In the back, John?" He yanked the knife out with a small yelp as Watson hovered over him and pointed the Glock. "You shoot me," Carver huffed, "and NYPD will be here in seconds. SWAT. FBI. How are you going to explain that you shot a CIA agent that was trying to save the president from a criminal?"

"I'm not going to shoot you," Watson said passively. He put out a hand and Zero took it, pulling himself to a seated position. Then he flipped the Glock around in his palm and held it, handle out.

Zero took it. "Thanks," he murmured. "Maria. Is she okay?"

Watson nodded as he knelt beside Pierson. "She helped evac the lower level of the bridge." He gently lifted the president's neck and started chest compressions.

Zero saw Carver reaching for his hip and quickly turned the pistol on him. "Stop. I don't want to kill you." That wasn't really the case; he would've very much liked to shoot Carver on the spot. "I want to bring you in. Make you talk. Force you to give up all your intel, all your contacts in this plot."

Carver grinned, even as he winced in pain. "All right, Zero. I'll give you intel. Let's start with this little tidbit. You know, me and John were partners for a long time. I knew all his dirty secrets."

Watson paused briefly, glancing up at his former partner, but said nothing. He pinched off Pierson's nasal passage and leaned over, performing ventilation.

"You know what he did to you?" Carver asked. "To your family?"

"What are you talking about?" Zero asked quietly. His hand shook; he hardly had the strength to keep the Glock aloft.

"He never told you?" Carver said snidely. "Of course he didn't."

They didn't mean it. They didn't know the truth.

"Our pal John here isn't just handy with knives and guns. Sometimes... well, sometimes he's downright poison."

Zero's hand trembled even as Watson continued to administer CPR.

They were following an order, just like I was. We were all lied to.

With his last ounce of strength, Zero forced the gun upward and fired two shots.

The first hit Carver in the clavicle. The second, just to the left of his nose. The renegade agent's head snapped back and he fell against the rocks.

Both of Zero's arms fell limply at his sides as Watson performed CPR on the president. Finally Pierson coughed, expelling river water from his lungs as he came around.

"Lie still, Mr. President," Watson told him. "Don't try to move."

The president sputtered between them, lying on his back with his head tilted to one side. Zero's vision blurred again, this time from the threat of tears.

But they weren't tears of sorrow or misery. They were tears of anger.

Watson leaned back slowly and sat against a rock as sirens wailed somewhere on Roosevelt Island, the sound of the police responding to the shots fired.

"I want to hear it from you," Zero murmured.

"I suppose you deserve that." Watson sighed through his nose. "I went into the museum where she was working under the pretense of delivering a package. I dosed her tea with TTX. I didn't know who she was or why the agency wanted her dead. I found out the truth afterward, when I saw the obituary and learned your real name. But that doesn't matter now." His gaze met Zero's, and he could see the genuine sorrow that Watson was so good at hiding. "I killed your wife, Kent. I would tell you I'm sorry, but that's hardly going to matter either."

Zero looked down at the Glock in his fist. He understood now why Watson had given it to him. It wasn't just to kill Carver. It was to make a choice. And he deserved that too.

His hands shook. This man had saved his life, had helped him when he needed it most, had even saved the lives of both of his daughters on more than one occasion. Zero had questioned it in the past, but now he knew the truth.

It wasn't help. It was penance.

"You do what you feel you need to do," Watson said. "The cops will be here soon."

Pierson wheezed, lying on his back with his eyes shut. In his half-drowned state, Zero doubted the president would recall much of what occurred right there on the island's shore.

So he made his decision. His grip shaky and his arm weak, Zero lifted the Glock once more with what felt like his last ounce of strength.

And he hurled it into the East River.

"Go." His voice sounded like little more than a hissed whisper. "Disappear. Don't ever come back. If I see you again, I swear to God I'll kill you."

Watson nodded once. He rose to his feet and made his way along the shore, stepping carefully over the rocks away from them.

The sirens blared closer as Zero sat there in the afternoon sun. It was a beautiful day. But he just felt cold.

Chapter Thirty Nine

Secretary of Defense Quentin Rigby jogged down the hall of the Pentagon toward his office. He felt the spike of a migraine coming on like an ice pick at the front of his skull.

Everything had gone upside-down. Pierson was alive. He'd been found on the shore of Roosevelt Island with three complex fractures and multiple contusions, but very much alive—and in the company of one Agent Zero.

There was only one way out of this that Rigby could think of, only one way to even begin to right what had been wronged: swift and irreversible action in the Fifth Fleet. Complete devastation of IRGC forces. The UN be damned; their plan could not fail now. They'd come too far and spent too much.

Rigby hurried into his office, pausing only to slam the door behind him and twist the lock before snatching up the red telephone on his desk. "This is General Rigby," he said quickly, before dispatch could ask him for identity. "Connect me to Captain Warren on the USS *Constitution* immediately!"

He waited for the satellite connection, pacing back and forth in front of the desk as far as the telephone's cord would stretch. His cell phone rang from his pocket; he pulled it out to see the name "Holmes" on the screen.

He ignored it. The chief of staff would have to wait. This was more important.

⚜ ⚜ ⚜

Lieutenant Cohen watched from behind the radar array as Captain Warren plucked up the red phone on the bridge of the USS *Constitution.* "This is Captain Warren. Mm-hmm. Yes, sir." The captain lowered the phone and turned briskly to XO Nathan, who stood nearby at attention with both hands clasped behind his back.

"Nathan, give the order to fire missiles," Warren stated firmly. "Target any IRGC ships within range."

Cohen's throat felt tight. This was it, the moment that would define whether they would start a war or rebel against their own authority.

"No, sir." Nathan stared Warren down. "We will not fire upon those ships without provocation."

Warren's eyes narrowed dangerously. "What did you just say?"

From the communications array beside him, Cohen saw Davis stir. He rose to his feet, as did Cohen. XO Nathan unclasped his hands from behind his back.

One of them held a black pistol.

Nathan did not point the gun at the captain, but held it in front of him in an almost casual manner. "Captain Warren, we are relieving you of duty. We're going to escort you to the brig now. I'll leave it up to you to decide whether you'd like to come quietly, or by force."

Warren dropped the red phone. The cord went taut and the receiver clattered against the steel wall. "This is mutiny," he hissed.

"Yes, sir. Mutiny in the interest of saving lives." Nathan nodded to Davis. "Lieutenant, if you would."

Davis reached for his belt, where he had stowed a pair of handcuffs for the occasion. Warren's gaze flitted toward the door to the bridge, the nearest exit, but Nathan stepped into his path. "Please, sir. Let's not make this any more difficult than—"

Captain Warren bolted forward and put up both hands in an effort to shove the XO away. But Nathan was taller, built solidly, and Warren bounced from him like a rubber ball against concrete. Davis was on him in a second, forcing one arm behind the captain's back and cuffing him even as Warren squirmed and shouted in protest.

"You'll all be court-martialed for this!" he bellowed. "You'll spend the rest of your lives in prison!"

"Maybe," the XO said as he hauled the cuffed Warren to his feet. "But at least we won't have any more deaths on our conscience." He and Davis escorted Warren off the bridge, heading down to the brig.

Cohen rose from his seat slowly, half in disbelief. They'd done it. But the red phone was still swinging from its cord. He picked it up, about to replace it on its cradle, but then thought better of it and put it to his ear.

"This is Lieutenant Cohen," he said into the phone. "Who am I speaking with?"

The voice was male, definitely older, and outright furious. "This is General Quentin Rigby," the man growled, sounding as if his teeth were gritted. "The secretary of defense. What the hell just happened?"

"Captain Warren was discovered to be unfit for command," Cohen said as clearly as he could muster. "XO Nathan and Lieutenant Davis are escorting him to the brig as we speak."

"That is treason!" Rigby shouted into the phone. "Admiral Buchanan will—"

"I'm sorry, General, but I think you'll find that the admiral will be similarly relieved of duty," Cohen told him, "if he hasn't already."

"On whose authority?!" Rigby bellowed.

"The United States Constitution," the lieutenant told him, and this time he was not referring to the ship. "Combined Task Force 152 is heading back to Bahrain, sir. The rest of the Fifth Fleet will be behind us. We have already communicated with the IRGC and made them aware that we are standing down."

"You will be charged for treason!" Rigby spat.

"Actually, sir, I think we might find that it will be the other way around." Cohen set the red phone down upon the cradle, feeling extremely satisfied.

"Hello? Hello?!" Rigby slammed down the receiver furiously.

It was gone. Everything they had worked for was gone. *How? How in the hell did they get to the Fifth Fleet?*

His cell phone rang again with Peter Holmes's name displayed. He snatched it up quickly. "What?" he nearly shouted.

"Get out, Quentin." Holmes's voice was hushed and panicked. "They're coming. Get out now…" There was a clamor in the background, and suddenly a dozen voices shouting all at once. "What are you doing? Get your hands off of me!" Holmes shouted through the phone. "On what charges? I demand to speak to the pres—"

The call ended. Rigby dropped the phone and rubbed his temples.

Outside his office, he heard the foreshadowing sound of a dozen pairs of boots marching closer.

"So this is it," he murmured to himself. He had only ever wanted what he thought was best for this country and its people. To not have to rely on unstable foreign powers. To flourish and thrive. But it had all gotten so, so far out of hand, and now he had no time to reflect on where things had gone wrong.

A fist pounded heavily on his office door. "General Rigby? US Marshals Service. Open the door, sir."

Rigby rounded his desk and pulled open the top drawer. He took out the .38 revolver there and checked the cylinder to make sure it was loaded, even though he knew it was.

The fist pounded again. "Open the door, sir, or we'll break it down."

"One moment," Rigby called back flatly. He cocked the hammer. "God forgive me," he murmured, as he stuck the barrel under his chin.

Chapter Forty

Ashleigh Riker pulled the old car into the parking lot of a gas station just off of I-70. She put it in park and briefly consulted the map on the passenger seat. She was about thirty miles outside of Columbus, Ohio, and headed west.

She checked her look in the rearview mirror. The hasty black dye job she'd done looked atrocious, a boxed drug-store color she'd done in the bathroom of a truck-stop diner. But she had a yellow scarf tied over her head, knotted under her chin, and large dark sunglasses on her face. She barely recognized herself.

For a moment she sat there in the car, adjacent to a gas pump, and just stared at the cracked vinyl of the steering wheel. It had all gone downhill so quickly.

Riker hadn't assumed this would happen, but she was smart enough to plan for the contingency. Her bug-out bag had been prepped for three weeks, bearing her photo on identification for a Charlotte Gardner of Virginia. She had a few thousand in cash, and the keys to an old sedan that she had bought at a police auction for next to nothing, the title and VIN both registered under Ms. Gardner's name.

She had also taken the precaution of tapping both Rigby's and Holmes's phones, so she knew they would be coming for her. Director Mullen was undoubtedly in custody. Cole, Poe, Cleary, Kemmerer…the dominoes had fallen. The higher-ups would attempt to take deals by narcing on those below them, their moles in the NSA and CIA and FBI, all of those they had so carefully brought into the fold over the course of the last two years.

It was all undone now. It was finished, but she wasn't. As soon as she received the alert that Holmes had been arrested, she calmly strode straight to her car and drove home. She heard the sirens wailing as she was pulling out of the parking deck, but no one had noticed her. Riker had gone to her apartment only long enough to grab her bug-out bag and open a can of food for her cat. She couldn't bring him; the cat was microchipped.

Then she was gone.

She'd headed west so far, and would continue to do so until Minnesota. Then she would cross the border into Canada at Manitoba, using Charlotte Gardner's fake passport. Riker had an aunt just outside of Winnipeg who would harbor her for a short while until she could secure passage to a non-extradition country, perhaps the UAE or Brunei.

This isn't how you go down, she kept telling herself. Despite having no field experience, she was surprised at how remarkably calm she was during the ordeal. She now understood the appeal of being an agent, like those she'd formerly supervised; it was almost thrilling, being on the lam, being incognito.

As long as she didn't remind herself that she'd just lost everything.

At length she finally got out of the car and headed into the service station, pushing twenty-five dollars in cash across the counter and muttering, "Pump three. Thanks."

Then she headed back out across the small lot. Her scalp itched terribly; the cheap dye was drying out her roots. She could use a shower, but a hotel room was out of the question. She needed to be conservative with the meager cash she had. She desperately wished she had made off with some intel; the names and identities of undercover field agents, perhaps, or some other national secrets that she could have sold to a foreign power for a tidy sum…

She was so lost in her thoughts that she didn't notice the woman until she was nearly back to the gas pump. Riker stopped dead in her tracks, rooted to the spot, the sunglasses falling slightly down the bridge of her nose.

The blonde woman leaning against the old car had her hair pulled up in a bun, as if intentionally displaying the long purple bruise down one side of her face.

"Ms. Riker." She nodded, her arms folded over her chest.

Riker's shoulders drooped as she deflated with a heavy sigh. "How did you find me?"

Maria Johansson picked casually at a fingernail. "Some friends of mine were keeping an eye on you. Funny thing, I was going to break ties with them. Even tried to a couple of times. But I'm glad I didn't. They turned out to be very helpful. See, they knew about this car." Johansson leaned deeply and stuck one hand under the passenger-side wheel well. She tugged something loose and showed it to Riker. It was a small magnetic cube.

A tracking device, Riker realized. "And it took you this long to get to me?"

Maria shrugged. "There were a lot of you to get to. I volunteered for this personally."

Riker's gaze darted left and right behind her sunglasses. It looked as if Johansson had come alone. There was a Beretta in her bag, but that was tucked behind the driver's seat. She would never get to it in time. And she knew she couldn't outrun Johansson.

"Don't try," Maria said, as if reading her mind. "Just accept it."

But Riker couldn't do that. She had come too far to simply relent. She sidestepped slowly around the gas pump, closer to the car, nodding as if she agreed with Johansson. The Beretta was her only choice. If she could get around the car and grab it, maybe she could get out—

Johansson moved suddenly, much faster than Riker thought she could. In two quick strides she was in the former deputy director's face, and then a fist flew at the bridge of her nose.

Riker's head snapped back. She saw stars and felt sharp, instant pain as her nose flattened under Johansson's blow. She fell on her rear in the parking lot, her broken sunglasses falling from her face as tears welled in her eyes.

One hand flew over her nose to stanch the blood running liberally down her face as she moaned in pain. "You ... you broke my nose!"

Johansson knelt beside her. "That was for Cartwright. I would just as soon put a bullet in your head, but I'd prefer that you get to see where you'll be staying from now on."

"No." Riker scooted backward, pushing against gravel with her feet. "No, you can't send me there. You can't!" She knew exactly what Johansson was talking about: the Moroccan black site, Hell Six.

She spun suddenly at the screech of tires as three police cruisers tore into the parking lot, followed immediately by two unmarked black cars. A coterie of armed men leapt out, guns pointed, cars surrounding her and filling the small lot.

Maria Johansson grabbed Riker by the elbow and hauled her to her feet. "Ashleigh Riker," she declared, "it is my genuine pleasure to tell you that you are under arrest."

Chapter Forty One

Zero stood under the shade of a thin tree with his hands clasped in front of him. It was a pleasant day; warm, only a few wispy feathers of cirrus clouds hanging in the spring sky. He wore a simple black shirt and black trousers, appropriate cemetery attire, with his head bowed slightly and his gaze directed at a grave marker about twenty-five yards away.

Shawn Cartwright's funeral had been hours ago, earlier that morning, but he hadn't attended. None of them had; they weren't supposed to have any public affiliation with him. So they held a small ceremony of their own, him and Strickland and Maria and Bixby. Emilia Sanders was there too, but only because Todd was taking her to the airport directly afterward.

"He was a good man," Bixby murmured solemnly.

Maria scoffed lightly. "Like hell."

"Jesus, Maria, have some respect," Strickland scolded.

She shook her head. "If he was here with us right now, he would have laughed at us for even suggesting that. Cartwright wasn't a good man, and he knew it. He was responsible for some truly shady shit over the years. He did as he was told, and most often didn't question it. He rose up through the ranks just like everyone else did, by stepping on the backs of others." She fell silent for a moment before adding, "But he tried to do the right thing in the end, and it cost him his life. More than that, he was a friend."

Zero bit his tongue. Cartwright's death was indirectly his fault. He might have even been able to prevent it. But Cartwright had known all along that Watson had murdered his wife, and had said nothing. Cartwright had called the hit on him two years ago and sent two of Zero's friends to do it. Cartwright had suspected for some time that something was amiss between the likes of Riker and Mullen and Carver, and he had done little to intervene.

Maria was right. He wasn't a good man. But it didn't mean he deserved to be gunned down in a basement.

"So," said Strickland after a long moment of silence. "Where do we go from here?"

It was a valid question, though none of them had an answer.

The three days since the attempt on President Pierson's life had been an absolute whirlwind of chaos, of conflict and arrests and media.

After Roosevelt Island, Pierson and Zero had been rushed to the hospital, where doctors confirmed that the president had suffered a concussion, multiple contusions, and a shocking amount of liquid in his lungs. Despite all of that, Pierson demanded two things. The first was that he was going to continue to lead the country out of this mess, even if it was from a hospital bed.

The second was that he refused to let Agent Zero leave his side. As far as Pierson was concerned, Zero was the only man he could trust. And that suited Zero just fine.

For three days he sat by the president's side and bore witness to the myriad concerns that required addressing. The first thing that Pierson did was order the arrests of the highest levels of his administration. He needed people he could trust, so he called in state troopers and US marshals to bring the perpetrators into custody.

Quentin Rigby took the coward's way out and shot himself in his office with marshals outside his door. Ashleigh Riker had attempted to flee, but was picked up seven hours later by Johansson. The others—Peter Holmes, Christine Cleary, Roland Kemmerer, John Hillis, James Mullen, Christopher Poe, and even Vice President Cole—were detained without incident. They begged and they pleaded, and they gave excuses, but ultimately it was names they gave up.

Zero's documents were rediscovered in Riker's office, and the USB stick with the audio files was found in a footlocker in Agent Raulsen's home. The evidence that Zero had gathered was enough to try the conspirators in court even if they denied knowledge of the plot.

He lost count of how many arrests were made over those three days, but it numbered in the forties.

Pierson's second act was to have the long overdue conversation with President Sarif of Iran. Zero was present for that as well; it took place via video conference in the president's hospital room. Pierson was transparent and honest. He told Sarif that his administration had been corrupted and that the attacks on the IRGC ships were orchestrated in order to spark a war. He promised court-martial and imprisonment for those involved, and offered the olive branch to Iran.

Sarif accepted, though hesitantly. Iran/US relations were still quite tense, and it seemed to Zero that it would take some time and effort to properly avoid further conflict. But Iran reopened the Strait of Hormuz to American vessels, and in return Pierson ensured that the entire Fifth Fleet returned to Bahrain. The president lauded the actions of Combined Task Force 152 and the USS *Constitution* for defying Admiral Buchanan and Captain Warren, and extended an invitation to the White House for the lieutenants who had first discovered the corruption in rank.

Zero stayed quiet on the part he had played in that. Those men and women deserved their honor, and he had no intention of detracting from it.

Talia Mendel and Vicente Baraf had done their part as well, bringing Russia's operations into the UN's spotlight. The president further assisted by publicly condemning those actions and promising swift and immediate military assistance to Ukraine should Russia make a single threatening move.

And finally, in a move that surprised even Zero, President Pierson made a public address. He had cameras brought right into the hospital room and he spoke to the nation. Just like with the Iranian president, Pierson was candid about what had transpired. The media went absolutely mad with the story of corruption at every level of government. Some called for Pierson's resignation. Others labeled him a liar, or accused him of complacency. But most, it seemed, appreciated his honesty and were glad to avoid war.

Though it seemed like the actions taken in the wake of the assassination attempt were beneficial, Zero knew the truth. The administration was in absolute shambles. The hierarchy was disrupted. Every single person, from National Security Council down to White House cleaning staff, needed to be vetted all over again.

The United States was weakened. But Pierson had shown his strength, and it gave Zero a glimmer of hope that things would once again be right.

Eventually.

"Where do we go from here?" Strickland asked.

"Vacation would be nice," Maria mused. "But I don't see that happening anytime soon."

"Back to the lab for me, I suppose," said Bixby with a shrug.

Zero said nothing. He knew that Maria's father, David Barren, was being appointed as the interim Director of National Intelligence, and was likely the best man for the permanent job. But a new CIA director had not yet been established.

He did not tell his friends that Pierson had offered him the position of deputy director over Special Activities Division—Shawn Cartwright's former duty. He neglected to mention it because, much like the NSC position before it, Zero had turned it down.

He had seen, firsthand and far too often, what the illusion of power did to people.

"I'm going to get my girls," Zero said in response to Strickland's question. "I'll see all of you around." And then he headed to his car.

His daughters were coming home today, and he couldn't wait to see them. It had been a rough three days for them as well.

"Hey." He paused as Maria caught up to him. "That's it? Just 'see you around'?"

"I'm tired," he admitted. "My body aches from head to toe. And I have *no* idea what comes next." He hardly had any desire to face the challenges that returning to his life would bring; it felt as if his existence was a sheet of paper that had been shredded and then taped back together. It seemed intact, but it would never be the same again. "What about you?"

Maria smirked lightly. "Well, my dad is going to be the new DNI, at least for a little while, so it looks like I'll be working for him."

"How is he? After learning about all this?"

"Oh, he's channeling it into a warpath for the people involved. He's making it a mission to take down the oil execs who first put the plan in motion. And we're supposed to have dinner tonight. So all in all, I think we're okay."

Zero couldn't help but chuckle a little too. *What strange lives we lead.*

"You should come by sometime," he told her. "In the next couple of days. I'm sure the girls would like that."

She nodded. "Yeah. I think I will. But don't let me hold you up. Go get them. I'm sure they're dying to see you." Maria leaned in and kissed him briefly. "See you around, Kent." She started away, back toward the tree and Strickland and the others. "Oh, wait," she called over her shoulder. "Have you heard from Watson at all? Seems he's gone dark. None of us can raise him."

Zero shook his head. "Nope. Haven't heard from him in three days."

And hopefully I never will.

CHAPTER FORTY TWO

Despite the protesting aches in his body, Zero ran to his daughters as they disembarked from a plane and came up the gate at Dulles International Airport. He caught them in each arm and hugged them both tightly, as if they had been apart for months and not only four and a half days.

"I'm so glad you're safe," he told them.

"You too, Dad," Sara said. She looked up at him somberly. "Are you okay?"

He almost laughed aloud. "I'm supposed to be the one that asks you that." He released them finally and looked them both over.

"We're okay," Maya told him, but there was a look in her eye, something grave and sobering and beyond her years that hadn't been there before. Or if it had, he hadn't noticed it.

He had already been informed about what happened to Alan. They had medevacked him to a hospital in Lincoln. He had been shot four times while defending Maya and Sara against the assailing mercenaries.

Zero rose to his feet as the burly, bearded man hobbled down the gate, leaning heavily on a cane. "Sorry," he grunted, "I'm a little slower than usual these days."

Zero smiled broadly and hugged Alan tightly, eliciting a small groan of pain from his friend. "Oh. Sorry."

"It's okay." The doctors had done everything they could for him, which ultimately meant removing a portion of his stomach and putting two screws in his hip. The fact that he was already mobile, however limited he might be, was nothing short of a miracle.

"You shouldn't have traveled," Zero said sternly. "Not with those injuries."

Alan shrugged. "No way was I going to let these two out of my sight."

"Thank you." Zero rubbed his eyes and blinked away the threat of tears. "Come on. All of you. Let's go home."

As the four of them headed slowly down the concourse and toward the airport's exit, Zero could not help but realize that it was no small relief that Alan had survived and was back in his life. He had lost so much. They all had lost so much. Now they had lost Watson too. Over the last month or so, Maya and Sara had built more than just a rapport with Agent Watson; he had sometimes driven them to school, and even occasionally checked in just to make sure they were doing well.

What Zero knew now would no doubt crush them.

What if they never knew? He was a little ashamed of himself for even thinking it, but as soon as the thought occurred it refused to leave again. *Everyone else who knew is now dead or gone. It's only me.* Would it be so bad if he took the secret to his grave? Wouldn't it be better for his daughters if they only ever believed what they had already been told, and avoided the heartache and misery of the truth?

"Dad," Sara said suddenly. "Are you listening?"

"Yeah." He shook himself from his thoughts as they headed out into the afternoon sunlight. "Sorry, honey. What were you saying?"

"I said, we slept in a jail cell."

"You *what?*" Zero balked. He knew that they had been under the protection of Nebraska state troopers for the last three days, but had no idea they'd been put behind bars.

"It was my idea," Maya told him. "Just in case any more of those Division guys came looking for us."

Sara shrugged. "It wasn't all that bad."

"Kind of cozy," Maya added, "as long as you knew you weren't stuck there forever."

"Whoa now. No daughters of mine are getting used to the inside of a jail cell."

Alan chuckled as they reached the car. Zero helped him into the front seat while the girls got in the back. He reached for the ignition, but then paused.

"Dad? What's wrong?" Maya asked.

"I, uh…" Zero sighed. He already knew, before leaving the airport, that their house on Spruce Street would not be a welcome sight. "I don't want to go home."

Too many people had died in that house. His daughters had been kidnapped from that house. Despite every security measure, intruders had made them feel unsafe in that house.

"Me neither," Sara admitted quietly.

"You're all welcome at my place," Alan offered. "Though it's not much. And it smells a little like motor oil."

"I've got a better idea," Zero said. "Let's go to The Plaza."

"The hotel?" Sara asked.

Maya frowned behind him. "Can we afford it?"

"Don't worry about that. Let's stay there tonight. Maybe tomorrow night too. At least until we can figure out what we're going to do next."

"Yeah," Maya agreed. "Okay."

"Will you come, Alan?" Sara asked.

Zero blinked in surprise. "They're calling you Alan?"

He shrugged. "I might have told them my real name when I thought I was going to die."

"I see. In that case…" Zero started the car and backed out of the parking spot. "Girls, this is Alan Reidigger. He used to be an agent too, and he was—is—my best friend. He's saved my life more times than I could ever repay."

"You can say that again." Reidigger smirked.

"I *knew* you weren't just a mechanic," Maya said.

"Can you tell us about it?" Sara perked up. "When you worked together?"

"I…probably shouldn't," Zero admitted. Despite what the girls knew about him and his work in the CIA, he hadn't really discussed it openly with them.

"Well, if you won't, I will." Alan twisted halfway around in his seat to face them. "So this one time, me and your dad were in Paris, tracking an arms smuggler who was trying to sell a warhead to the North Koreans. Maya, I think you were around eleven… no, you were just turning twelve, actually."

Maya scoffed loudly. "Is *that* why you missed my birthday, Dad?"

Zero bit his lip to keep from grinning as Alan told his daughters about pursuing terrorists through Europe. It was almost surreal. He had lost so much—but he had gained a lot too. He had his memory back. He had Alan back. His daughters were safe.

He wasn't sure what the future would hold, or where they would even end up tomorrow. But for now, that was okay. Everything in that car with him, he realized, was everything he needed.

Now Available!

RECALL ZERO
(An Agent Zero Spy Thriller—Book #6)

"You will not sleep until you are finished with AGENT ZERO. A superb job creating a set of characters who are fully developed and very much enjoyable. The description of the action scenes transport us into a reality that is almost like sitting in a movie theater with surround sound and 3D (it would make an incredible Hollywood movie). I can hardly wait for the sequel."
–Roberto Mattos, Books and Movie Reviews

In RECALL ZERO (Book #6), the President's translator is the only one privy to a secret conversation that can change the world. She is targeted for assassination and hunted down, and

Agent Zero, called back into the line of duty, may just be the only one who can save her.

Agent Zero, trying to get his life back in order and to win back the trust of his girls, vows not to return to service. But when he is needed to save the life of this defenseless translator, he can't say no. Yet the translator, he realizes, is as intriguing as the secrets she keeps, and Zero, on the run with her, just might be falling for her.

What secret is she keeping? Why are the most powerful organizations in the world trying to kill her for it? And will Zero be able to save her in time?

RECALL ZERO (Book #6) is an un-putdownable espionage thriller that will keep you turning pages late into the night. Book #7 in the AGENT ZERO series will be available soon.

"Thriller writing at its best."
—Midwest Book Review (re Any Means Necessary)

"One of the best thrillers I have read this year."
—Books and Movie Reviews (re Any Means Necessary)

Also available is Jack Mars' #1 bestselling LUKE STONE THRILLER series (7 books), which begins with Any Means Necessary (Book #1), a free download with over 800 five star reviews!

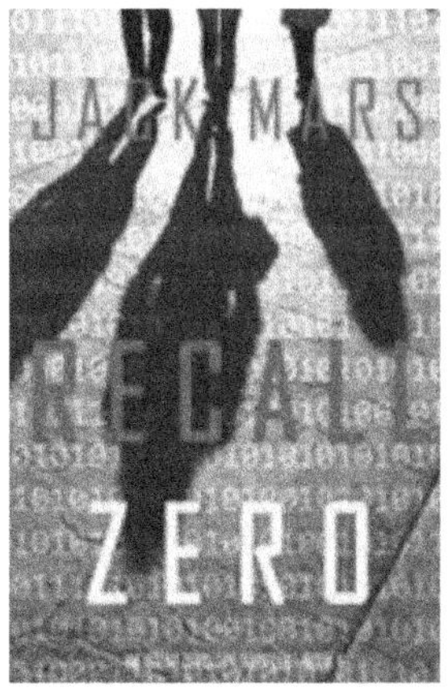

RECALL ZERO
(An Agent Zero Spy Thriller—Book #6)

CPSIA information can be obtained
at www.ICGtesting.com
Printed in the USA
LVHW040620180620
658399LV00005B/1250